MURDER NEW YORK STYLE
FRESH SLICES

An Anthology by 22 Authors of
Greater New York

Edited by Terrie Farley Moran

D1457057

L & L Dreamspell
London, Texas

Cover and Interior Design by L & L Dreamspell

This is a work of fiction, and is produced from the authors' imaginations. People, places and things mentioned in this anthology are used in a fictional manner.

ISBN: 978-1-60318-423-6

Visit us on the web at www.lldreamspell.com

Published by L & L Dreamspell
Printed in the United States of America

Contents

Foreword

When the New York/Tri-State chapter of Sisters in Crime began discussing a second Murder New York Style anthology, we were drawn to the idea of gathering crime stories from less-sung locales in the five boroughs, emphasizing settings beyond or behind the tourist-eye view. We were also enthusiastic about mixing genres and tones with the same kind of lively variety represented within our membership. According to the submission guidelines, that was exactly what we ordered, but as usual, our members delivered so much more.

These stories are slices of life from the most ethnically diverse, most densely populated city in America. They're not only written by crime fiction authors you know, but by chapter members making their debuts. By turns funny, tough, and somber, these tales reveal the desperate secrets of old-timers and the dangerous hungers of new arrivals. But these motley characters also reflect the city's most infectious, most unifying principle: that combination of adaptability and assertiveness recognized worldwide as New York attitude.

We thank our membership-at-large for supporting this collaboration as a chapter project. We recognize the dedication of our Board, story editor Terrie Farley Moran, and many generous submitters and volunteers who lent their talents before and after publication. We'd also like to offer special appreciation to Laura K. Curtis, and Leigh Neely, and to Joan Tuohy, for speedy proofing, above and beyond the call. We hope you'll enjoy every flavor of this city and its crime.

Clare Toohey, Anthology Chair

Tear Down
by Anita Page

The porch was gone and the windows had been removed from their frames. Lumber was piled in the small side yard. To Delilah, in the back seat of a taxi parked across the street, the house looked exposed, like a woman caught with her buttons undone.

The blue-haired receptionist at the physical therapy place was right. Margaret something. Delilah had known her for years from bingo. "Looks like they're ready to tear down your old house, honey." In that chirpy voice, like she was talking to a three-year-old.

Delilah, fighting off panic, had wanted to see for herself. That took awhile, because after the damn knee surgery, even hobbling to the bathroom was a production. Today, finally able to get around, she'd called the taxi service and stepped out into a chilly spring rain.

Well, she'd had her look, and now the panic was gripping her so bad she could hardly breathe. As she struggled to get out of the cab, she thought if she dropped dead that minute, she'd know who to blame—her nephew, that son-of-a-bitch, pasty-faced lawyer.

The driver jumped out of the cab to help her, but she waved him off and managed the few steps to where the street butted up against the narrow strip of beach. Leaning on her cane, she looked out at the water and breathed in the smells of the channel and honeysuckle and salt-tinged air. How many hours had her kids spent playing on that beach, like it was their own backyard?

When the flutter in her chest eased, she got back in the cab and gave the driver directions. He took her straight up Gerritsen

Avenue, past the laundromat and the bagel place and the library. Then he made an illegal U-turn and stopped in front of the white brick building across from the ball field. She told him to wait.

Her nephew was at his desk when she teetered into his office, swinging her cane to ward off the little blonde secretary with the perky behind, and then slamming the cane down on the desktop, leaving a nice scar on the mahogany.

Clyde yelled to the secretary, "Shut the door, why don't you! And bring her a glass of water before she passes out on me." Then, to Delilah, "How'd you get here?"

"I took a cab. How do you think I got here when you sold the car out from under me?" She sank into a chair, short of breath now.

"Which car is that, Aunt Dee? The one you almost drove into Shell Bank Creek?" Clyde, in his jokey way, pretending nothing she could do or say would make him mad. "The whole of Gerritsen Beach, the whole of *Brooklyn*, is on its knees every night giving thanks you're not behind the wheel."

Delilah waved away the glass of water the secretary held under her nose and gripped the cane with both hands. "I want to know how those people come to tear down my house when you were *told* to put in the contract that they could *not* do that, not if they owned the place for a hundred years."

"I did put it in the contract, but you hit the nail on the head." Then, very slowly, like he was talking to a dummy, he said, "They don't own it anymore. They sold the place six months ago. It's the new owners that are tearing it down. I hear they're going after that whole street to put up condos."

She sat back, taking that in. She'd sold the house only three years ago. That's how it was these days, buy and sell, buy and sell, everyone getting rich except the working people who could hardly afford to pay their taxes. She'd lived in that house for more than sixty years, and never thought of selling until Clyde started nagging at her. The stairs were too much for her, the roof was going, the boiler was making sounds like an old man taking his last breath. Still, Clyde should have realized what could happen.

She scowled at him. "Why didn't you put in the contract

that no one could ever tear it down? You know how to say that in lawyer talk."

Clyde was tapping a pencil on his teeth, the way he did. It drove her crazy.

"I didn't put it in the contract," he said, "because no one in his right mind would have bought the house that way. So now someone's tearing it down before it falls down, and it's no concern of yours."

No concern of hers. If he only knew.

Clyde was going on about her beautiful apartment, no stairs to worry about with an elevator to take her right up to her floor, a chance to make new friends.

"Bullshit." Delilah pushed herself to her feet, leaning on the cane. "How'd you like to live in some damn senior housing with nothing but a bunch of old people?"

"Aunt Dee, you're eighty-four years old."

"Screw you, Junior. I know exactly how old I am. And *you* better know that eighty-four isn't too old to call the State Bar, and tell them to take your license away because you are nothing but a piece-of-shit lawyer."

When the driver helped her into the cab, she shut her eyes and pressed her hand to her chest, as if she could stop her heart from bumping. Telling herself not to get worked up, that she still had one stop to make, one last hope. She directed the driver to one of the narrow streets that ran down to Shell Bank Creek, just a few blocks from where she'd grown up. Small houses, the neighbors so close they could hear each other spit. It was hard keeping a secret in a place like this, but she'd managed until now.

Walter's house had a tidy side yard and a bright blue door with shutters to match. Between her cane and the wrought iron railing, she made it up the steps. The rain had stopped but she felt the chill in her bones. She pushed the doorbell, waited, and then rapped on the door with her cane.

"Hold your horses!" she heard from inside the house. Then the door opened.

Surprised wasn't the word for the look on Walter's face. Struck dumb was more like it. They'd seen each other around town over the years—you couldn't help running into people in Gerritsen Beach—so she knew he recognized her old-lady face. And she'd know him anywhere, once she got past the white hair and the skin hanging under his chin like a rooster's wattle. The blue eyes and shaggy brows were the same. The same thin lips.

"Delilah." A smile crept into his voice.

"We got a problem," she said. Before she could go on, a high-pitched whine came from inside the house demanding to know who was at the door.

Delilah threw Walter a long hard look. Some things didn't change. "If your keeper will let you out, I need you to come over to my place. My new place." She told him the address.

"Give me a half hour," he said.

Delilah sat at the kitchen table listening for Walter's knock. Her new place, a pile of yellow bricks, the apartment so dark she may as well be underground. Now he'd see how she'd come down in the world. Her old house hadn't been fancy, but at least it got the daylight, just two steps to the beach. *We're going to the ocean*, her kids used to say, trotting across the street to the channel with their tin buckets. It wasn't the ocean, but close enough. And now here she was stuck in a hole on Knapp Street. Jail for old people was what it was.

The knock came and she let Walter in. He followed her to the living room, settling in the gray armchair she'd brought with her from the old house. Seeing him there, with his long legs stretched out, it was hard to think how many years had passed. "If you want a drink, there's a bottle of Jameson in the cupboard next to the sink," she said.

"A little early in the day."

"Never knew you to be a clock watcher, Walter. How about some coffee, then?"

He stood before she could get up. "You stay where you are. I'll take care of it." Then, with a smile, "I don't suppose you still keep those ginger snaps in the house."

"The things you remember," she called after him as he went out to the kitchen. She heard him moving around, opening and closing doors, finding what he needed. If she had to name Walter's best quality, that would be it. The way he'd been ready, from the very first, to take care of things.

How old had she been the first time he'd knocked on the back door looking for her husband? Not more than twenty-five, already with two babies, and married to a man who didn't have a good word to say about anyone or anything. George and Walter had just started working together, George putting up houses and Walter doing the brickwork.

That first time, she'd come to the door with a baby on her hip, her breasts heavy with milk and pushing against her cotton blouse, her blonde hair wild from the humid weather. She'd caught Walter's look and knew what he was thinking. Oh yes she had. And she remembered what she'd thought, taking in his smile and his blue eyes. Here was a man who knew how to care for a woman. Still, nothing ever passed between them, nothing but looks, until the night she phoned him asking for help.

Walter appeared now with two cups of coffee, saying, "What the hell. I gave us each a splash of Irish." Then he went back for the ginger snaps, which he set on the low table between them. After a deep sip of coffee, he said, "So Dee. Just what sort of problem do we have?"

"They're tearing down my old house." Delilah watched his face for a reaction.

He dunked a cookie into his coffee, as he'd always done, and nibbled off the edge. "Now why is that a problem?"

She gave him a hard look, seeing a cast to his eyes she hadn't noticed before. "Why is that a problem? Christ, man, have you gone mental?"

He laughed, clapping a fist to his mouth to keep from sputtering coffee. After he swallowed, he said, "Oh Delilah, Delilah. You were always the one, that mouth on you, that temper."

"I guess we both know about my temper."

"I guess we do." Another laugh. Then, in a soft voice, "You're still a beautiful woman, do you know that?"

"Save your breath, Walter."

"It's the truth," he said. "If I had my prostate, we wouldn't be wasting our time on conversation."

It was her turn to laugh now, throwing back her head. She couldn't remember the last time she'd done that. Then her laugh died, the truth coming at her like a cold wind. Her old house would soon be a pile of rubble.

Still with a smile, he said, "I know why I'm here."

"That's a relief," she said. "Now why don't you tell me what we're supposed to do?"

Walter rubbed his hand over his hair, white as coconut, clipped close to his scalp. "There's nothing to do."

"What do you mean? We sit and wait for the cops to turn up and haul our asses off to prison?" She was surprised at how calm she felt saying that. The whiskey had softened the edges of her panic.

"Delilah, you're talking about ancient history."

Ancient history? She'd been right. The man wasn't playing with a full deck. "Walter, there's no statue—whatever you call it—for murder."

"Statute of limitations."

She stared, trying to figure out who she was talking to. A loony old man or the Walter who'd stood by her sixty years before.

"Listen to me." He was relaxed as can be, one arm over the back of his chair. "For one thing, it wasn't murder. At least not first degree. You didn't plan to kill George."

"I was just trying to shut him up."

"And you succeeded." Walter's laugh came out like a bark. "I don't believe he spoke another word after you whacked him across the head."

Not another word, true enough. She remembered that November evening, jiggling George Junior, a colicky baby, while she cooked dinner one-handed and tried to keep her daughter from pulling every pot out of the cupboard. Asking herself why she bothered, since nothing she did pleased George. The food was too hot or too cold, too salty or too plain. If she was still in her housedress when he came home, he called her a hag. If she fixed herself up, he asked where she thought she was going, looking like a tart. And he was no better with the kids, complaining about the crying, the mess, the dirty diapers—not that he'd ever seen one close up.

She'd made liver and onions for his dinner that evening, which was what he'd asked for. Started cooking early so it would be ready when he walked in the door. But of course, that day he'd stopped off and had a few, so he was late getting home. Late enough so that the babies were asleep. Thank God for that.

He'd strutted in the back door, walked over to the stove, and said—she remembered his exact words—"You call that piece of dried up shit my dinner?"

No thought passed through her mind. It was as if her body acted all on its own. She'd grabbed that cast iron skillet by its warm handle and swung, clipping him a good one on the forehead, sending the liver and onions flying. He'd gone down like a tree in a storm, spread out on the kitchen floor, eyes staring at the ceiling, mouth wide open. She'd taken him by surprise.

The house had been so quiet, with him dead and the babies asleep upstairs. She'd stood there for the longest time, looking down at him, not knowing what to do. She'd been scared, yes. But sorry? Not a bit of it. Then, she'd thought of calling Walter.

"You came right over," she said to him now. "Didn't even ask what it was about."

"What I *hoped* was old George had taken himself off to Timbuktu, and you were going to try to get me into your bed."

"As I recall, you took it all in stride, him on the floor, me in a flap. You knew just what to do."

"We didn't have much choice. If we'd buried him in the yard, someone might have seen us. If we'd dumped him in the channel, come spring, the cops would have found themselves a floater." Walter drained his cup. "I was a bricklayer, Dee. I did what I knew. Tucked him in that second floor fireplace, emptied a sack of lime on him, bricked it up."

She remembered it all. Walter plastering over the brick, so no one would guess what was behind the wall, opening windows and sealing the bedroom door shut real good, which didn't stop the smell coming through. She'd packed up the babies and moved to her parents' place for a few months, telling everyone that George had run off with another woman. Her family said she was better off. They never could stand him. His family didn't say much, though his father was good about the money, sending a check every month. For his grandkids, he'd said. He'd kept it up until the kids were in school, and she could get a job.

"How about another coffee?" Walter got to his feet. "No Irish this time, or we'll both nod off." Without waiting for an answer, he went out to the kitchen.

The first night she was back home, she'd called Walter and the two of them went straight to bed. He'd made it plain before he even kicked off his shoes that he'd never leave his wife, which was fine with her. Four years of George was enough marriage for a lifetime. She'd have turned down the King of England, Clark Gable and Frank Sinatra rolled into one.

Walter returned with their coffees, set hers down, and gave her a sleepy smile, fighting a yawn.

"You need a nap?" She shot him a knowing look and he laughed. That's how they used to say it, "Time for a nap."

He took his seat and rubbed his face. "What happened to us, Delilah? Why did it end?"

"We had our time. Close to ten years, wasn't it? And then it was over. Better that way than having some priest tell us we had to stay together until we hated each other's guts." *Like you and that whining little pussy cat you married*, she thought, irritation cutting through her whiskey haze. She had to figure out what to do about the house and he was no damn help at all.

Walter, the mind reader. As usual, he knew what she was thinking.

"There's nothing to worry about," he said. "First off, they pull down the house, they find some old bones behind that brick wall. Those bones could have been there since before you and George bought the place."

"You don't know what you're talking about. Don't you watch that show on TV? They got forensics now. They can test those bones and tell you who they belong to, when he died, and what he had for breakfast."

Walter made a face.

"It's the truth." Talking to this man was getting her nowhere.

"Okay. Let's say they figure out it's George behind that wall. The cops come and ask you questions. And you—you're eighty-five years old?"

"Eighty-four," she snapped.

"Same as. They ask you about George and you say, 'Who's George?' They say, 'He was your husband,' and you say, 'Husband? Did I have a husband? What did you say his name was?'"

Delilah stared at him. "You're telling me I'm supposed to pretend I'm a senile old fool?"

He leaned forward, arms resting on his knees. "There's nothing to it. Don't you get it, Dee? They *expect* you to be a senile old fool. They think we're all old fools. You think they're going to prosecute an eighty-five…" he held up his hands "…*eighty-four* year old woman who doesn't know back from front? You're home free, Delilah."

"That's your big solution? Play like I'm mental?"

He didn't answer. In the long silence, Delilah felt her heart bumping the way it wasn't supposed to. She needed to lie down and she wanted Walter, just about nodding off in the chair, out of her house.

"Speaking of cops…" she waited for him to open his eyes "…your keeper's going to call in a missing persons if you don't get home soon."

"I guess you're right about that." He yawned and shook his head. Then, with that sideways look of his, "You know what I was thinking? Maybe I could stop by every once in a while. I've been missing those ginger snaps of yours, Dee." He winked, as she knew he would.

Just what she needed. An old man drinking her whiskey and falling asleep in her living room. "We'll see about that," she said.

Walter stood, then helped her up. She leaned on his arm as they walked to the door. He smiled down at her and patted her hand. "As far as the police go, there's nothing to worry about. I promise you, Dee. Just do what I said." Before he left, he stooped and kissed her cheek, the feel of his lips reminding her how long it had been since anyone had done that.

Delilah limped to the grey chair, pain shooting through her knee, and sank back against the cushion. She'd rest a minute, then take a pain pill. She'd told herself that Walter would know what to do, and what had he come up with? Pretend you're gaga, Delilah, the way your mother was at the end. Her mother, looking at the family as if they were strangers, trying to read the newspaper upside down, taking off after everyone was asleep. And where had they found her? Squatting in the middle of Allen Avenue, in her nightgown, taking a pee.

It wasn't going to happen to her. Playing the fool for a bunch of cops was not the way she was going to leave this world. Neither was prison. Delilah's chest tightened at the thought of a cell door clanging shut, with her locked inside.

There was only one way out as far as she could see—and why not? Living in this place was like being buried alive. The problem was Walter. She let out a long sigh, thinking about him, not the old man yawning in her living room, but the young buck who'd come to her back door sixty years before. In the time they were together, there'd been plenty of talk on the street, with his truck parked for hours in front of her house. The police would put it together in a minute if they got hold of a neighbor with a big mouth and a long memory. Who else would have helped her get rid of George but his partner, the bricklayer?

Well, she'd make sure Walter was left out of it. She shut her eyes, trying to remember. The man who'd worked with George before Walter. Underwood? No. It took a minute, but then it came. Phil Untermyer.

Delilah found paper and pencil in the kitchen and wrote her note, spelling it out, all true except for giving credit for the brickwork to Phil Untermyer, dead a good twenty years now. "He was sweet on me," she wrote by way of explanation. Then a P.S. "If you get here and I'm not dead, do us all a favor and don't even think about pumping my stomach."

She propped the note on her nightstand. Then, sitting on the edge of the bed, she counted out the pain pills, her hand trembling. Only eight left, but that should do it.

Scraps of memory were coming at her, like litter blowing down a windy street. Her father piling the kids into his small boat, heading down Shell Bank Creek with the wind in their faces and a sack of hard-boiled eggs for lunch. Her wedding day, knowing she was making a mistake, then her mother asking minutes before they left for the church, "Are you sure about this, Delilah?" Her kids, both gone. Her son, nineteen years old, in Vietnam, and her daughter to cancer.

Then she thought about Shadow, the dog they'd had when she was a kid, a big black mutt. You gave that dog a bone, and even after the last scrap of meat was gone, he kept chewing. She remembered the wild look in the animal's eyes the night a sliver of bone got stuck in his throat. He died right in front of them on the kitchen floor, her father in tears, saying, "Smartest dog I ever had, and he didn't know when to drop the damn bone."

Delilah sipped the Jameson from the glass on her nightstand, watching the branches of a tree dip and sway outside the bedroom window, the silence broken by a distant car horn. What the hell.

"Drop the bone, Delilah," she whispered, surprised at how husky her voice came out. Then she tossed the pills down two at a time, with the whiskey for a chaser.

∗

Anita Page's story "'Twas the Night," which appeared in *The Gift of Murder* (Wolfmont Press), won a Derringer award in 2010 from the Short Mystery Fiction Society. Other stories have appeared in *The Back Alley*, *The Prosecution Rests* (Little, Brown), *Murder New York Style* (L & L Dreamspell), *Word Riot*, *Mysterical-e*, *Mouth Full of Bullets*, *Ball State University Forum*, *Jewish Horizons* and *Heresies*. She's a member of Mystery Writers of America, Sisters in Crime, and the Short Mystery Fiction Society. She lives in New York's Hudson Valley.

THE DOORMAN BUILDING
BY ANNE-MARIE SUTTON

"Here, Mrs. A., let me grab that before you drop it."

Sarah Armstrong extended her right arm where the plastic bag from the wine shop was cutting into her wrist.

"Thanks, Carlos," she said, as the always-eager young doorman slid the two bottles of wine from her hand and waited patiently while she readjusted the bags of groceries in her arms. It didn't escape her notice that he checked out its contents before handing the bag back to her. She didn't care. There were millions of people living in New York City, and she supposed half of them would soon be settling down to a drink to start their evening.

Upstairs, she unpacked her groceries and put the white wine in the fridge and the bottle of red on the counter. The apartment was sterile, a boxy set of small rooms in a 60s high rise. Her son, Will, a freshman at New York University, lived here, and she was only using the apartment while he was in Florida on Spring Break. Buying the Greenwich Village apartment—convenient to NYU's Washington Square campus—rather than paying for a dorm room had been her husband's idea. Tom made a ton of money as a venture capitalist, and last fall, when Will had started classes, the Manhattan real estate market was in the toilet because of the recession.

"Buying an apartment in the Village will be a good investment," Tom had explained. "In four years we can sell it. Or if Will wants to work in the city, he'll be all set." That was the kind of life they led. Enough money for everything.

She herself had grown up in an affluent environment in San Fernando Valley, a *Val Gal* to the roots of her dyed-blonde hair. Now, she lived in their family's rambling restored farmhouse in equally-affluent Westport, Connecticut. But Sarah had found herself drawn to Greenwich Village from her first visit. Secretly, she had wanted Will to live in a basement apartment like the ones in Hollywood movies, where the neighbors were all lovable eccentrics, and an Italian restaurant with red-checkered tablecloths and straw baskets of Chianti stood on the corner.

Of course, Tom would have none of it. "It's got to be a doorman building. That's a safety feature, Sarah. You don't want to be awake at night worrying."

Now, Will's apartment was her temporary home for a whole delicious week of going native in the Village. Tom was in Asia until the end of the month, and her time was all her own. She was free to spend her days exploring the zig-zag West Village streets with their nineteenth-century houses, trendy clothing boutiques and contemporary art galleries.

"Wait a minute," she said out loud, surveying the groceries lined up on the counter. "Where are the mushrooms? I was sure I put them in my basket." But there were no mushrooms.

Sarah briefly considered doing without. But what was mushroom risotto without mushrooms? Then she began to laugh. She didn't have to drive ten miles to her suburban supermarket. There was a greengrocer on the corner.

~

Returning to the building, Sarah pushed open the lobby door, surprised not to meet the ever-vigilant Carlos. It had already occurred to her that he was expecting a generous tip at the end of her stay.

He was at the reception desk, talking to a tall, young woman dressed in faded jeans and a worn black leather jacket. On her back was a bulging purple knapsack. Seeing Sarah, the doorman stopped the conversation. Alerted, the young woman whirled around, her long red hair brushing her shoulders.

"Is that her?" she demanded. Sarah stared at the woman, examining her flashing dark green eyes. "Mrs. Armstrong?"

Sarah almost said *no*, so much did the woman make her feel ill at ease. But politeness was inbred, and Sarah said, "Hello, how can I help you?"

"I'm a friend of Will's. I need to see him."

"I've just been telling her…" Carlos began, but was cut off.

"Is he lying? He's lying, isn't he? He said Will's gone away."

"Yes, he has," Sarah said evenly. "He'll be back next week." She turned to go and felt the woman clutching her arm.

"Wait."

"What do you want?" Sarah asked, alarmed as the girl began to stagger. Sarah held her up, surprised at the heaviness of the backpack. "Are you all right? Are you sick?"

"I haven't eaten all day," the other woman whispered.

Without hesitation, Sarah guided her toward the elevator. You couldn't make just a little mushroom risotto. There would be plenty for two.

⁓

"Why is it so important that you see Will, Tessa?" Sarah asked after she put the dinner dishes in the dishwasher. Half a bottle of the Chardonnay had made it easier to question her unexpected guest. She'd learned that Tessa Noonan was a scholarship student whose only close relative was an elderly grandmother in Patchogue, Long Island. Going without regular meals appeared the norm in her life.

"I got thrown out of my apartment." The words came out in a rush. "Four of us share a walk-up over on Second Avenue, but I didn't pay my part of the rent this month. It's happened before, so they asked me to leave." She bit at her lip. "It's only four hundred dollars, but my work has been slow."

"What kind of work do you do?"

"I temp. February was a short month, and I…well, I just don't have the money."

Sarah thought of Will and his generous allowance. In the

past, he'd no doubt helped her out with her rent. She wondered where Tessa planned to sleep tonight, but that was a stupid question. She'd obviously expected Will to give her money *and* a bed.

The next morning, Sarah was up early. She started the coffee maker in the small kitchen. Tessa, hearing the noise, came sleepily into the room. She was wearing a faded blue T-shirt and bikini underpants.

"I'm meeting a friend from Westport at the Guggenheim at ten," Sarah said. It was a lie, but she wanted some urgency attached to Tessa's leaving. She reached in the pocket of her robe and took out several folded bills. "I can lend you some money," she said hurriedly, suddenly uncomfortable doing what had seemed so reasonable a decision last night. "Pay it back to Will when you can."

There was no look of surprise on Tessa's face at the offer of another handout from the Armstrong family. She took the money from Sarah's outstretched hand.

"Thanks."

"Do you want some coffee?" Sarah asked. She heard the irritated tone in her voice, but the young woman didn't seem to notice it.

"Don't have time. I need to see one of my professors and get an extension on a paper I was supposed to hand in last week."

After she was gone, Sarah straightened up the living room. Tessa's pillow and blankets were in a heap on the sofa. When she shook out the blanket, an iPod fell to the floor. She hadn't noticed Tessa using one, but guessed it had helped her to fall asleep last night. It was pink, and Sarah read the engraving on the back. *To my girl, Your Chaz.* Well, she thought, Will should know how to get this back to her. She opened the drawer of the sofa table and put it inside. As she turned to go toward the bathroom to take her shower, her foot caught on something under the table. Peering down she saw the purple backpack.

When Sarah returned, the evening doorman was on duty.

"Martin," she said, "I left a backpack with Carlos this morning.

Can you tell me if the owner picked it up?"

Martin looked under the desk. "Was it purple?" Sarah nodded. "It's here, ma'am." And, without asking, he handed it back to Sarah.

"Thanks," she said disappointedly. "If the owner comes for it, buzz me."

Upstairs, Sarah kicked off her shoes, and while she was pouring herself a glass of wine, she was startled to hear a key in the lock. The extra security lock and chain were on so the handle continued to rattle. "Damn," she said, "I wish she had told me that Will gave her a key."

But when she opened the door, it was not Tessa who was standing there. "Who are you?" she asked a slightly built young man she had never seen before.

"Oliver Castello," her visitor said with an engaging smile. "I'm a friend of Will's."

"I'm Will's mother. Sarah Armstrong." Oliver extended his hand, and Sarah shook it. "Will's not here," she said, staring pointedly at the key in the lock.

Oliver looked sheepish. "I didn't know anyone was home. I was going to crash for the night."

"Here?"

"Look, I'm sorry, really I am. I didn't know you were here. Will always lets me use the place when he's away. I live in a dorm. Three of us in a room. My bed is a bunk bed. Can you believe it? For the money it costs my parents? They give me half a bed!"

"Come in for a minute," Sarah said, holding the door open. "You may be able to help me."

"Anything," he said, his eyes resting on the wine glass. "I wouldn't say no to a beer. Will usually has some."

Sarah nodded. "I can see you know your way around the place."

"Will's my best friend," Oliver called from the kitchen.

Funny he's never mentioned you, thought Sarah. Nor Tessa, for that matter. But she smiled sweetly at Oliver when he returned, beer in hand. He was an attractive boy with an unruly shock of black hair and large, twinkling brown eyes. Without an invitation he sat down on the sofa and took a contented swig from the bottle.

"Do you know Tessa Noonan?" Sarah came right to the point.

Oliver frowned. "Tessa? What about Tessa?"

"How can I get in touch with her? Do you have her cell phone number?" Oliver shook his head. "But she's a friend of yours... and Will's, I gather."

"I wouldn't exactly call her my friend, and I don't think Will does anymore."

"Oh? Why is that?"

"She's nuts. An A-Number-One nut job."

"In what way?"

"She's a psych major. They're all nuts. You don't want to know *her*."

"I've already met her. I want to return something that she left here."

Oliver started forward. "She was here? When?"

"Last night. This apartment is like Grand Central Station." Oliver laughed. "Tessa came to see Will and then managed to leave without her backpack."

Oliver's eyes circled the room. When he saw the purple backpack on Will's desk chair, he was off the sofa and opening it in an instant.

"You can't do that," Sarah said.

"Let's see what's in here," he said, ignoring the order. He pulled out a large textbook and dropped it on the desk. Next came a few smaller books, some folders and a thick notebook. Oliver examined one of the folders before digging deeper into the knapsack.

"Stop," Sarah said, putting her hand out to grab a hairbrush from the boy's hands. "Oliver, you must stop."

"Oh ho," he said. "What do we have here?" He held up the unmistakable pink box of a pregnancy test kit.

Sarah stared at it. "Oh," she said and shrank back from the desk.

"Well, well," Oliver continued in an excited voice. "Now what has Tessa been up to, do you wonder?"

"I think we should put all that back, Oliver." Sarah had regained her composure and began to re-pack the bag. She took the pink box from Oliver, who'd grasped it as firmly as a child with a special toy.

"Aren't you the least bit curious?" he asked.

"Why should I be? It's none of my business." And then she stared hard at Oliver. "It couldn't be Will…" Her voice trailed off.

"Oh, no. That all ended before Christmas. Don't you worry, Mrs. Armstrong. Will's not our proud papa. But Tessa does have an appetite, if you know what I mean." He winked. "The list is long, very long."

"Maybe Chaz," Sarah said thoughtfully.

Oliver's eyes narrowed. "Who?"

"Chaz. Could he be the father? That is, *if* Tessa is pregnant. The box, you must have noticed, is unopened."

"Who's Chaz?"

"He's not a student?"

"Nobody I know. Of course Tessa doesn't limit herself to students. NYU's a big place." He paused. "There are… professors."

"Surely that's not allowed," Sarah protested.

"Somebody should have told that to Dr. Findlay," Oliver said with a snicker.

Sarah was unusually tired the next morning. Had a possible pregnancy been the real reason Tessa had come to see Will? Despite what Oliver had said, Sarah knew friends covered for friends. Tessa and Will could still be in a sexual relationship.

Although she wasn't in the mood, she realized she should dress and get out of the apartment. It was too early to call Will and hope to put her mind at ease.

WOMAN'S BODY FOUND IN PETER COOPER PARK in big black letters on the front page of the *New York Post* didn't immediately catch her attention when Sarah left the Strand Book Store that afternoon. It was only after she saw the words *NYU Student* in smaller type over a blurred photo of the victim's face that she stopped to look, and felt her stomach churn. Even in black-and-white, Tessa's abundant red hair was unmistakable.

"Tessa and I broke up before I came home for the holidays in December."

Sarah heard the truth in her son's voice. Now, she had to tell Will the rest of the story, that Tessa Noonan was dead. There was silence at the other end of the connection.

"Will? Did you hear me? Tessa—"

"I heard you, Mom," Will said in a quiet voice. "Are the cops sure it's murder? It couldn't be an overdose, or suicide?"

Sarah looked down at the *Post,* the page open to the story.

"No, honey, she was strangled last night. I'm sorry. If you went out with her, you—"

"It was just for a short time last fall."

Will explained how he had met Tessa in Spanish class first semester. Yes, she'd lived in the apartment with him for a while, and yes, he admitted he'd given her money from time to time.

"But, Mom, I couldn't take it after a while. Sometimes she scared me. Nothing I did was ever enough for her."

After Sarah ended the call, she wished Will were coming home tomorrow. Suddenly, she wanted to hug him, hold her son close to her.

She had to consult her map of the Village to find Peter Cooper Park. When Sarah finally saw it from across the street, she was surprised how small it was. At the north end, a small section was cordoned off with yellow police tape. There were a few benches, some shrubbery, and a statue whom she supposed was Peter Cooper. There was nothing grand or imposing about the space, just a small, pocket park in the middle of a big city. It was an ordinary place to die, and being here made the fact of Tessa's death finally real to her. She knew what she must do.

"We appreciate your coming forward, Mrs. Armstrong," the middle-aged detective from NYPD took the seat Sarah indicated. His partner, who looked nearly as young as Will, sat without speaking. The two had arrived at the apartment within an hour of her call to the local precinct. Sarah had waited for them with trepidation, fearful of any connection they would make between Will and Tessa. But she knew she couldn't hold back information that Tessa had been in the apartment the morning of her death. It could be important in finding her killer.

When she finished her narrative of the time Tessa had spent with her, Sarah indicated the purple backpack on the desk chair.

"Oliver Castello—he's a friend of my son's—and I looked inside." Detective Stamos raised his eyebrows, and she quickly added, "I'm afraid Oliver was curious. I re-packed it."

Remembering the iPod, she walked toward the table in front of the sofa. "And here's something else." As the detective unzipped the backpack, Sarah opened the table's drawer.

The iPod was gone.

"So, you see the name Chaz has to be important."

Stamos nodded. "When you spoke to your son on the telephone, did you ask if he knew who Chaz was?"

"No," Sarah answered, shaking her head. She was still confused as to when the iPod had been taken from the apartment. "I just didn't think of it. But I did ask Oliver, and he didn't know him."

"Chaz," Stamos repeated. He looked at his partner.

"There's that Chazz Palminteri, the actor," the younger man offered. "He spells it with two z's. I think it's short for Charles."

"Yes," Sarah agreed. "But, Charles. Maybe Carl? I don't know." And then she did.

"Carlos."

"What?" Stamos asked.

"Carlos is one of the doormen here. He's young, attractive. The night she came here, I saw Tessa arguing with him."

"About what?"

"I don't know, but Oliver did suggest that Tessa was…" Sarah struggled with an adjective.

"Promiscuous," the detective suggested, and she reluctantly nodded. "If she was here regularly to see your son, she would have had the opportunity to get to know this Carlos. Maybe he called himself Chaz when he was off duty."

"I've seen the doormen take in dry cleaning and other deliveries. The super has keys. I suppose Carlos could get into one of the apartments with a master key."

"We can check that out with the building super."

"There's one more thing," Sarah said. "It could be the motive for whoever this Chaz is. You'll find a pregnancy test kit at the bottom of the backpack."

Stamos stared at her. "The autopsy was done this afternoon."

"And?" Sarah asked, her heart hurrying.

"Tessa Noonan was two months pregnant."

As she closed the door behind the two police officers, Sarah looked at her watch. It was after six, and she deserved a glass of wine.

The Chianti made her feel warm inside, and she wished that Tom was in New York City instead of Tokyo, that they were meeting for dinner in that Italian restaurant with the red-checkered table cloths. Tonight was going to be hard to be alone.

Will returned her call around ten.

"What's the latest, Mom?" he asked.

"I was interviewed by the police earlier."

"Wow, what did they want?"

"I called them. I had to tell them that Tessa had spent that last night here."

"Did they tell you anything about...well, you know, what happened?"

"Not really. They ask the questions. I gave them her backpack. I told you, she left it here."

"That old purple thing. She always had it with her. I'm surprised she left it."

"I think she was upset that day."

"Because you think she might have been pregnant?"

"She was pregnant, Will. They did an autopsy."

"She was going to have a baby? No way. Does Caz know?"

"Caz?"

"Sorry. Oliver."

"Oliver?"

"He and Tessa have been together since we came back from semester break in January. I told him she was trouble. I should know, right? But he was crazy about her. I can't imagine what they were going to do. Tessa was a Catholic. I don't think she believed in abortion."

"Will. Back up. Why did you just call him Caz?"

"It was short for his name, Castello. He never liked the name Oliver so we started calling him Caz."

"And everybody calls him Caz," Sarah said slowly.

"Well, no. Tessa didn't."

"What did Tessa call him?"

"She thought it sounded hip to call him Chaz. She always called him her own little Chaz."

✳

Anne-Marie Sutton was born in Baltimore and graduated from the University of Maryland with a degree in English. She has taught mass communication and journalism at Norwalk Community College in Connecticut and worked as a political consultant in the state. She maintains her own agency, Brick Lane Enterprises, which provides marketing communication services to business. She is currently at work on a mystery series set in Newport, Rhode Island, where she has lived. In May, 2009, she delivered the L. Eugene Rankin Mystery Lecture at The Redwood Library and Athenaeum, located in Newport.

THE SNEAKER TREE
BY TERRIE FARLEY MORAN

On an intensely clear September day, my mother was laid to rest in Calverton Military Cemetery out east in Suffolk County. At the gravesite, my Uncle Eric said Mom would always be there, patiently waiting for my father. My brother Sean replied that Mom waiting for Dad would be a first. A few chuckles and guffaws from the family broke the tension, allowing us to finally move to the waiting limousines for the long trip home to Queens.

By the time we got back to our two-story clapboard in College Point, it was nearly three o'clock. Benateri's on Fourteenth Avenue had a buffet all set up in our dining room, and the mourners scoffed down hot and cold antipasto and sandwiches stuffed with prosciutto, sopressata, provolone, and tomato. They ploughed their way through three different pastas, and then gradually went home to their own lives, leaving little more than green lettuce and black olives behind them.

By dusk, we were down to family members and those friends of our parents that my brothers and I always called uncles and aunts.

I was in the kitchen, wrapping wilted leftovers in aluminum foil, when I heard a quiet tap on the back door.

"Bad day, huh? Just got off work. Want to make a MacNeil run? Visit our sneakers? I brought six friends." And she opened the top of her beach-bag, showing off a six-pack of Coors Light.

We weren't legal, but Miranda Lantoni had only to open

those blue eyes wide enough to match her glorious smile when she placed the six-pack on the counter, and then pout while she searched her pockets for nonexistent proof of age. Without exception, every male convenience-store clerk, young or old, would cheerfully sell her beer and then, as she sashayed out the door, he'd hopefully remind her to come back soon.

We hid the bag on the back porch, while Miranda paid her respects to my father. I left her to dazzle the family, and changed into jeans and a maroon sweatshirt with big white letters that shouted Queens College. When I kissed my father, he tugged my long brown ponytail.

"Not too late, Miss Cat. It's been a long few days."

Miranda and I flew out the back door, grabbed the beer and ran along Sixth Avenue to MacNeil Park, a hill of green jutting into the East River, overlooking a postcard view of the lights of Manhattan.

In third grade, I hit my first homerun on a ball field at the east end of the park. Miranda and I smoked our first cigarettes in a corner of the playground, and to celebrate her twelfth birthday, Miranda kissed Dylan Mulligan on the rocks that led up to the promenade. Last June, done with high school forever, we tied the laces together on our ratty gym sneakers and found the perfect tree—old and wide with a few dying branches midway up. We flung our sneakers high, aiming to wrap them around a branch where they wouldn't be obvious but we could always find them.

We sat under the sneaker tree, hands on our knees, sipping longnecks and watching the planes take off and land at LaGuardia Airport, which pushed into the river just off Flushing Bay.

As one plane began its climb, Miranda said idly, "One day I'll be on that plane flying to Hollywood, because some big producer is making a movie about my life as a struggling, but finally successful, artist."

That was the game we'd played since kindergarten. Where is

the plane going? Who's on it, and what's their story? Since junior high, it had always been one of us on the plane fulfilling a dream.

Watching a plane glide in for a landing, I said, "Mom's on that plane, coming home to tell us the heart attack was a cruel joke."

And Miranda held me while I cried long into the night.

⁓

The next morning, my father pounded on the bedroom door. "Catherine, get up. Come downstairs."

Ugh. I'm not going to school today. He can't make me.

Still, I got out of bed and threw on my robe.

From the bottom of the stairs, I could see Dad and my brother Owen glued to the television, watching smoke pour from each of the Twin Towers. Before I could take in what was happening, the south tower crumpled and clouds of dust blotted out the smoke, leaving the screen filled with swirling gray grit.

A faceless announcer cried, "Oh, my God. Oh, my God."

As the dust on the screen thickened, my father said, "MacNeil."

I pulled on last night's jeans and a tee shirt, and the three of us walked to the park. The streets were crowded with silent people heading to the same place.

The promenade along the East River and the hills above it were filled with onlookers. Everything was still. We looked toward lower Manhattan, past LaGuardia Airport, its runways littered with planes that did not move, and watched plumes of smoke and ash rise. Then, as if they stumbled on the way to heaven, the billowing gray columns made a left turn toward Brooklyn.

I stood with my father and Owen in a small clearing above the promenade. I could see the tree where last night Miranda and I chugged longnecks and loudly sang Bon Jovi's "It's My Life" as if to defy death. I looked for our sneakers, but couldn't see them from this angle. A woman standing a few feet from us dropped to her knees and began to pray. Others joined her. My father, tears running the gauntlet of his wrinkled face, said, "Thank God your mother didn't live to see this day."

After a while, Miranda found us.

"First your mother, now this. Tragedy everywhere." She pulled a pack of Parliament 100s from her pocket, glanced at my dad, and hid the cigarettes behind her back.

We linked arms, walked to the sneaker tree, sat on the ground, our eyes searching until we saw our sneakers.

Miranda mused. "Do you think they'll last longer than we do?"

"With all that synthetic material, those sneakers'll outlast plastic bags."

Miranda stuck an elbow in my ribs. "Let's come back every year until we die or they fall. In honor of your mother, we'll come on September 10th, just like last night, longnecks optional."

"Optional?"

"Sure. By the time we're legal, we'll most likely move up to wine."

We sat for a while longer, then Miranda went off to wait tables at Joey's on the Boulevard. I went home with Owen and my father. We were relieved to find Sean there.

~

That day was the end of anyone outside the family remembering that my mother had died. During all the days and weeks and months ahead, every conversation focused on the World Trade Center. When someone said, "Where were you?" they weren't asking if I was in the kitchen when Mom collapsed on the floor. When classmates asked if I'd lost anyone, they were only interested in the September 11th deaths. A September 7th death didn't count.

People didn't talk about anything else. Everyone was grief-stricken, remorseful, angry, and vengeful, while I was completely numb.

I wanted to shout, "What about my mother? Doesn't her death count? How did she get lost in some terrorist plot?"

During that first year, Miranda was the only friend who

seemed to understand that I was hurting. She'd call or pop up, and do her best to make me laugh or let me cry, whichever matched my mood.

One Saturday, that first winter, we visited our sneakers and sat on a pile of old dried leaves, watching a powerboat do spins in the middle of the river. We were kidding around about some nonsense from back in grammar school, when suddenly Miranda got serious.

"What happens if someone you love does bad things? I mean, what do you do?"

"Ally boosting cars again?"

Miranda's brother had some bad habits. Cost the family in the past.

"Nah, Ally's doing good. It's Mike."

Miranda always loved her boyfriends for the first few weeks, and then the sizzle faded. Mike had been around for months, so I was surprised that Miranda cared what he did.

"Drugs?"

"Nothing illegal like that, it's just…" She rolled down her green turtleneck and I saw marks on her throat. Fingerprints?

"He do that to you?" I clenched my fists.

"I sort of asked for it. He caught me with some soldier at Hector's going-to-Afghanistan party. I was just flirting. It wasn't serious."

"This," I pointed to her neck, "is serious."

"He can't stand the thought of me being with another guy."

"That ain't love. That's possession."

Miranda shook her head as if to end the conversation.

By spring, Mike was gone. Unfortunately, he was followed by a string of jerks. The lazy ones mooched money. The possessive ones shouted threats and waved their fists. The peacocks strutted Miranda around town like arm candy. She may as well have been a cashmere jacket. Guys came. Guys went.

~

We were under the sneaker tree, marking the third anniversary of my mother's burial.

"Here you are, livin' large and we're still drinking longnecks. Never did move up to wine."

"Me, livin' large?"

"Wearing big-girl suits and high heels to that paralegal job. You got it going on. I'm following you to the high life. Got a new job. Day bartender at Izzy's Place. I'll save up money for art school, no problem. Your mom is smiling down on us. You helping folks with legal stuff, and me wearing tight sweaters to rake in those tips."

We clinked our bottles.

The following April, Miranda called all excited. The city was going to put some sort of 9/11 memorial in MacNeil right by our sneaker tree.

"You don't think they'll take down our sneakers?" she fretted.

"We better be there, just in case."

⁓

We were in MacNeil bright and early on a Saturday in late May, 2005. Plenty of bigwigs stomping around our hill, shaking hands, posing for pictures, and speaking in solemn voices to local folks, people we knew who'd lost family on September 11th.

The old resentment welled up inside me. Where were all these people when my mother died? Where was her memorial? She was just as dead as those killed in the Towers.

Always able to read my mind, Miranda pulled me away from the crowd, closer to the sneaker tree. We listened to speeches about how this small circle of newly planted trees, some in bud, some in full flower, would bring healing to the neighborhood. The roll call of the locals lost on 9/11 was somber, more so for me. After each name was read, I whispered: *Mary Catherine McDonough.*

That summer, lots of neighborhood people visited the Memorial Grove, some to say a prayer, most just to see what had changed in the park. Truth was, nothing much. A few scrawny trees, a bunch of flowering bulbs, and a typical Parks Department green wooden sign with the words 'Memorial Grove.'

By the following September, the grove was largely forgotten, except by a few 9/11 family members, who occasionally came to sit. Since the grove was right beside our sneaker tree, Miranda and I were probably there more than anyone.

～

In 2007, my brother Owen got engaged to a really sweet girl from Brooklyn, who asked me to be in the wedding party. I was describing the hideous bridesmaid's dress, while Miranda and I leaned against the sneaker tree sharing a bag of peanuts.

We were laughing about the nylon flounces that rimmed the lilac taffeta, when Miranda asked if I ever thought about the kind of wedding I wanted.

"Only since I was, like, six. We were in first grade, and the music teacher got married. Remember? My mother took me to the wedding. It was so glamorous. I started planning. All through grammar school, I kept a notebook. I designed dresses, picked bridesmaids—you made it on the list in third grade and never got crossed off—I chose songs, catering halls, the whole bit."

"Still got it?"

"I tossed the notebook and the whole idea of marriage in tenth grade. By then, I found out what a pain guys are."

"Ah, Denny Valasco. That was a mess."

"Not just Denny... Well, maybe."

"Well, I kept my marriage plan all these years. I have finally met The One."

I didn't have to pull the details out of her.

"I've been dying to tell you but, well, it's complicated."

"Don't tell me he's married."

"I told you last year, I'll never do that again. No. He's a widower. With kids. And he's older."

"Older? Like thirty-older?"

"Scott's closer to forty. He's the guy that comes in to clean the spigots, you know, for the tap beer. Never on my shift. But one day, he came in to pick up money Izzy left for him. We got to talking. He's The One. I just know it. So, will you be my maid of honor?"

"Sure." I grabbed her in a bear hug. "I can't believe you kept this a secret from me. When's the wedding?"

"Not sure. Scott don't know he's getting married. I have to wait 'til he figures it out. Shouldn't take long."

She was right about that. In less than a year, half of College Point gathered in St. Fidelis Church to watch Miranda and Scott say "I do."

Scott's son, thirteen-year-old Jason, was the best man. If he hadn't had that surly slouch some boys affect right before they move into swagger, I would have been a little taller than him. With him slouching, I towered as we walked back up the aisle side-by-side. His sister, Kerry, excited to be a junior bridesmaid, practically danced along behind us.

I'd worried that Miranda's marriage would crimp our friendship, but we stayed close, shopping, lunch dates, barbecues at her house where I'd bring some guy or another. Afterward Miranda would telephone and say, "Keep looking. He's not The One."

The first year she was married, Miranda was always distracted. I figured she had a lot on her mind, what with being newlywed and playing stepmom to two half-grown kids. If I asked what was bothering her, she'd plead exhaustion and talk about cutting back her hours at Izzy's.

September 10th rolled around as it always does. We were at the sneaker tree. I cried for a while. My mother was gone for eight years, and I still ached for her. Miranda talked about how hard it was to be a mother. How lucky I was to appreciate my mom. Told me she'd never appreciated her own mother until she became a stepmom.

She started to tell me how well Kerry was doing with her singing lessons, and abruptly cut off.

After a minute or two, she whispered to herself more than to me.

"What do you do when you just can't love someone like you want to?"

I was stunned.

"You don't love Scott?"

Miranda started as if just realizing that she spoke out loud.

"I adore Scott. It's Jason."

That I could understand. On Labor Day at Miranda's sister's house, I'd seen Jason tease the smaller kids mercilessly, until Scott noticed and shooed him off. When Scott walked away, Jason aimed such a look of pure hatred at his father's retreating back that I could easily imagine how he felt about his stepmother.

"I can't handle him. He's a bully. A few weeks ago, he had a tantrum and deliberately pushed his schoolbooks off the kitchen table on top of the cat. Last night, I caught him on the back porch striking matchsticks and tossing them at fireflies. Tried to tell me it was a school experiment about light reflection."

"What does Scott say?"

"He knows the kid's wound tight. Took Jason to therapy after Margo died, and the therapist said he was fine. He's a teenaged boy. What do I know about teenaged boys?"

"There was a time…"

We laughed, and then Miranda turned serious again.

"I love Scott. Kerry is a joy, but I can't handle Jason."

Christmas week, Miranda and I shared *moo goo gai pan* and shrimp rolls at a Chinese place in Flushing.

We gossiped about our friends for a while, and then I asked lightly, "How's Jason?"

"Better." Miranda nodded reassurance. "Scott is on top of him. Jason is polite to me, nicer to Kerry." She sighed. "More than I hoped for a few months ago."

A few months later, I met Brian at a Saint Patrick's Day Party. Before the party ended, I called Miranda from my cell and said, "I met The One."

"Tell me."

"Can't. I'm in the ladies room. He's waiting outside."

"Meet me Saturday morning at the sneaker tree, around eleven."

"I'll bring the coffee."

Miranda was waiting, sitting on a folded blanket, her back against the gnarled trunk of the tree. She looked worn, tired, with deep circles under her eyes. Her hair was unkempt, something I'd never seen before.

I bragged about Brian's perfection, and babbled about the future we might have. I could see Miranda was working hard to show enthusiasm.

At last, I asked what was wrong.

"Nothing really. Scott and I had a fight. He doesn't like the way I handle the kids, well, Jason, really. I do my best…"

"He's at a difficult age. And he probably isn't sure how he feels about you."

"That's it exactly. Whenever we're alone he treats me like we're equals. Remember Jon Vitone? How he used to look at us. All creepy like we were naked and he was ready to do his thing? Jason gives me that same tacky vibe."

"Eew. You're his stepmother!"

"Makes it even creepier, right? I'm frazzled trying to make it go away."

That summer, my father hosted a big Fourth of July party to introduce Brian to all our friends and family.

I was in the kitchen, filling the lemonade pitcher, when I felt someone staring. Jason was leaning against the dining room door-jamb, nibbling on the end of a wooden matchstick, his mouth fixed in a grubby sneer. He eyed me up and down. I decided to ignore him, and when I turned back to the lemonade, he moved closer whispering, "Fine, tight boo-ty."

My father stepped in from the yard.

"Need help with the lemonade? Ah, you already have help." Dad nodded to Jason, who instantly replaced the matchstick and sneer with an aw-shucks smile and picked up the heavy glass pitcher.

Miranda dealt with this kid day and night. I guiltily said a prayer of thanks, glad that Brian had no children.

On March 17, 2011, the anniversary of the day we met, Brian proposed and I accepted. Our engagement party, held in the Knights of Columbus Hall, was supremely lighthearted, with my father repeating to anyone who'd listen, "He's a fine lad. Catherine's mother is dancing in heaven tonight."

Near night's end, I walked into the ladies room and Miranda was at the mirror fussing with her makeup. One look and I said, "Either you and Scott have been doing the nasty in the broom closet, or your allergies are really early this spring."

She burst into tears.

I offered tissues and hugged her until she calmed down.

"Scott and I were dancing. When the song ended, Scott went to the bar to get me some wine. I walked back to our table, empty for the moment except for Jason and Kerry. Most of the night, she'd been hanging out with your cousin Annie's kids, but I never thought to wonder why she was back at the table."

"As I came up behind them, Jason said, 'Now you sit here for the rest of the night or I'll burn you again. And then I'll burn your friends.' Then he struck one of his stupid matchsticks on his thumbnail and leaned the flame toward her arm."

"I yelled his name so loud that people at the next table jumped. And the matchstick disappeared."

I cradled her in my arms.

"You have to talk to Scott. Kerry, too."

"She won't. She's terrified of Jason. We both are."

There was no changing Miranda's mind.

～

Finding a catering hall for our wedding, scheduled for the following Saint Patrick's Day, was simpler than I'd thought. With that behind me, Miranda and I spent an exhausting summer shopping for my bridal gown. Toward the end of August, Miranda talked me into going for broke at Kleinfeld's. I spent far too much for a plain spaghetti-strapped gown, which came with a long sleeved bolero jacket for the church.

We were riding home on the 7 Train, when Miranda told me that the city was planning a ten-year ceremony at the Memorial Grove. "Ten years for your mom, too. We'll be there September 10th, just like always."

I entered the park from 115th Street, and spent some time watching the river lap at the edge of the promenade before I walked up the hill to the sneaker tree. I said a quick prayer to my mom and then looked around, expecting to see Miranda coming up the playground path. Someone was sitting on the grass propped against the Memorial Grove sign. I took a step or two. The person never moved. As I got closer, I recognized Miranda's jacket. When she didn't answer my call, I ran to her, but was far too late. Her hair was matted with blood, her face purple and swollen. I fell to my knees, screaming in agony. A couple of dog walkers ran to my aid, but soon realized there was nothing to do but call 911. They tried to lead me away, but I wouldn't leave Miranda.

Two cops took turns questioning me. Finally, they let me make a phone call. It wasn't long before Brian came rushing past the stretcher that the coroner's crew was dragging up the hill.

I think Brian was surprised at how composed I was, but while I stood waiting for him, I'd made a decision. I led him to the sneaker tree, just outside the yellow crime scene tape.

"Boost me up."

He stood still.

"Brian, I have to get her sneakers. They have to come down before Miranda leaves this park. She wouldn't want them to last longer than she has."

He nodded, and I put my foot in the stirrup he formed with his hands. I grabbed the highest branch I could reach, and climbed toward the sneakers. Miranda's pink laces had long faded, but her sneakers looked as though they'd been flung there yesterday. I dropped them to Brian, and began making my way down, more cautious now that I'd done what I needed to do. Suddenly my foot slipped, a branch snapped and I tumbled to the ground. I lay face down, doing a mental check of body parts. Most seemed none the worse for the fall. Then I opened my eyes. Scattered in the leaves, about two inches from my nose was a half-dozen wooden matches. Some had been lit. The ends of the two or three unused matches were cratered, as if chewed.

I pushed myself off the ground, and caught the eye of one of the cops who'd questioned me. I waved him over to the sneaker tree.

*

A life-long New Yorker, **Terrie Farley Moran** is struggling to learn the Irish Tin Whistle, which is not nearly as much fun as hanging out with any or all of her seven grandchildren. Her stories have been published in numerous anthologies and in *Ellery Queen Mystery Magazine*. Terrie's noir short, "When A Bright Star Fades," was named a Distinguished Mystery Story of 2008. Her paranormal mystery, "The Awareness," can be found in the 2010 MWA anthology, *Crimes By Moonlight*, edited by Charlaine Harris. Terrie blogs amid the grand banter of a group of talented New York mystery writers at www.womenofmystery.net

TAKING THE HIGH LINE
BY FRAN BANNIGAN COX

The drone of techno music nearly drowned the words she shouted across our table. They were accompanied by a smile, freshly licked with a flash of tongue. The promise of it seared any doubts I had. Later, up on the High Line, downtown's innovative park, her promise would be delivered. In our special spot two stories above Washington Street between Little West Twelfth and Gansevoort Street, screened by choke cherry trees, we would be alone, floating above the roar of yellow cabs rushing beneath our feet.

Margot moved closer on the red banquette and slipped her hand into the waistband of my pants, proprietary. She sucked the olive from her martini. "Don't look so intense," she said.

"You like it." I knew she did.

"Yeah. That's true. But sometimes I think you live just next door to crazy."

"Crazy about you."

She laughed, scanned the bar and left me.

When I got back from the men's room, Margot was at the end of the bar, silky black hair grazing her bare shoulders, blue eyes intent, red lips whispering into the ear of that night's conquest. No more than twenty-one by the look of him, barely legal, slightly drunk on tequila shots with beer chasers, leaving big tips on the zinc bar top. She sure could pick them. They were the ones who didn't quite fill out their confident expressions, nervously fingered their power ties, twisted their leather wrist bands and probably, I was guessing, my jealousy speaking, were thinking of having their hairy backs waxed.

Ecstasy users find one another effortlessly. They were crazy with love for the whole human race. That told you all you needed to know about the drug. The coke on top of the ecstasy made Margot imagine she was actually capable of loving the whole world. She'd still feel love for the night's mark later when she laughed at him and touched me the way she'd touched him, watching my face like a hawk studying prey.

She'd drive him to kiss her. When his hands belonged to her and he was blind to the rest of the club, game over. She'd excuse herself and saunter to the ladies room, in charge, leaving him to fantasies of more. They always imagined they were in love with her. I did. I still do.

There's no denying I wanted Margot for myself. I wanted to tattoo my initials on her body, inside and out. Sick bastard? Yeah. You could say that. But we're talking about real love here. In me, she'd met her match. It was time for me to settle with one woman. I was an easy kind of guy. If she needed that power trip of hers to love me, I'd watch. I'd never had it so hot. Never mind the acid in the pit of my stomach next to the burn of desire. Bring it on.

I wasn't a day trader on the Street for nothing. That job honed my ability to tolerate tension, the stronger the better. If she could dish it out, I could take it. My martinis and a line of coke just added height to the spiral of desire as it tightened. The predatory game wouldn't last forever. Once she accepted she was mine alone, we'd play only for nostalgia.

Prearranged, I left the club five minutes after she did, and followed her a block to the 14th Street entrance to the High Line park. She always used the elevator up to the garden of native plants and trees laid out along the elevated train trestle. The tracks used to carry freight cars packed with sides of beef, lamb, and pork from the Midwest to the meatpacking companies in the streets below. Carcasses used to hang from hooks on conveyer belts along here, bathed in the ether of bus fumes and cab exhaust. I remembered watching gruff men in black woolen caps and blood-stained aprons hauling the weight of raw meat into the freezers and cutting rooms beyond the plastic strip doors. The sidewalk was treacherous, slick with lard and pieces of offal. It was ten years ago, but I still looked on the sidewalk for greasy smears. Habit. Boutiques have replaced the meatpacking industry, and tourists, the butchers. It was clean where her high heels had passed. Even so, I knew I'd better watch my step.

I kept a half block distance so I could admire her round ass filling the black linen Armani suit. She was an outstanding dresser, cutting an elegant figure in court when she argued a case, which she did often. She was a prosecutor who taught defense lawyers to be wary even as she glad-handed them. She had learned from a master. Her father had been a legendary divorce lawyer. She liked to get him drunk and return his cruelties in spades. Trapped in a wheel chair, like she was once trapped in childhood, he was forced to listen to how stupid he was to have three wives take him to the cleaners, to have a son who was an alcoholic and not to anticipate that she, the ugly duckling, would be his only success. When she described her visits to the assisted living facility, her smile was not pretty.

Anticipation grew as I watched her legs disappear in the glass elevator that rose two stories above the surrounding neighborhood. I took the stairs. A good thing, too. That night I found a nickel on the third riser. It made $156.76 for the year's found money total. Luck. I believe in it. I knew she'd taken her underpants off.

At the top of the stairs, the Hudson River, visible in the distance beyond the Westside Highway, was silver in the moonlight. A cool breeze from the water blew under the new high-end hotel that straddled the High Line. From floor to ceiling windows, notorious for evening exhibitionists, very few people watched Margot or me. Tonight would be special. I had a key for her to my town house on Jane Street a block over from Gansevoort. I wanted her in my neighborhood. Close. My hands were sweating.

She stepped out of a clump of laurel into a patch of moonlight that outlined breasts that shimmered in a see-through blouse. I reached for her. She slipped through my fingers, stepped backward, swung her legs up onto a metal chair like the ones they have in Paris parks. I caught a glimpse under her skirt and moved in for more. She stepped out of reach onto the railing that rims the park. Her smile was triumphant; one bare foot on the black welded steel of the old trestle, the other on the newer stainless steel.

An unwelcome thread of anger wormed its way into my anticipation. She had stolen the initiative. I had to up the ante. Before I could even think what was next, she dropped and disappeared. Goddamned heart attack time. She called from the top of the next set of stairs to the street. "Wait there. Don't follow me."

What could I do? In my worst moments I knew I needed her. I had everything a man could want: friends, sort of, money, a town house to die for, an art collection that was beginning to attract attention from the right people. I had every gadget known to man, plus, my most cherished possession, a reputation for ruthlessness. How had she twisted me around her finger? I'd never let that happen before Margot. I'd never needed anyone's approval. No way. She really loved me. I knew it. I felt it. I am never wrong.

An old couple was staring at me. I recognized them as artists who lived in the subsidized artists' housing, Westbeth, the huge building dominating the southern end of the High Line. I glared at them and they moved on. I was in no mood to be reminded of my dear departed parents. Losers. Made art but never had a penny to call their own. I turned to look over the railing into the street below. Margot was there under the corrugated metal awning of the old meatpacking shops. The bed-headed dude from the bar was with her. She looked up at me as he buried his face in her breasts. She waved. "Tomorrow morning before nine. Be there."

Damn her. It was time for this game to be over. I was the one who went home with her, laid out the lines on her coffee table, undressed her, made her beg. She'd said I was the best she'd ever had. No reason to doubt it.

On the way to my neighborhood bar, I remembered our trip to Cancun, a honeymoon of sorts, although she hadn't liked it when I called it that. No power games for two weeks. What had gone wrong since then? I spent the rest of that night in the bar on my corner, nursing memories and scotch. I texted her again and again. "Where RU?" My rage grew as her silence mocked me. "Where RU? You can only push me so far, girl. Remember that."

I was there, on the High Line Saturday morning, God help me. The sun was high in its blue heaven and all was right with the world. Not! She hadn't answered any of last night's messages. I texted every twenty minutes as the sun climbed higher in the sky.

I saw the wavelets on the Hudson and the daisies in the patch of grass at my feet, but they had no effect on my mood. I lay back on the wooden lounge chair provided by a famous fashion queen's donation to the High Line. I'd had three lattes and a chocolate croissant since I'd changed my clothes and left my house in the wee hours. I couldn't go back. The contractor was there, renovating the back deck, putting in a new Jacuzzi. But just as I was thinking about going to the Tenth Avenue diner for a proper breakfast, I saw Margot strolling down from the 17th Street entrance. Every eye was on her. Even the tourists abandoned their cameras as she passed. She was stunning, hair gleaming, skin translucent like water with a tinge of pink sunlight glimmering on the surface. She was a sight in a gold tube top, grey shorts and sandals. Those blue eyes told me she loved me. She was happy to see me. Yeah, but for how long?

"Don't think you own me," she said, leaning over to kiss my cheek. She pushed my feet aside and sat at the end of my lounge chair.

I'd always been a sucker for conflict. My move. I played laid back, mildly interested. "Whose idea was that?"

Silence as she eyed my offerings: a bagel with a schmear, a latte, heavily sweetened the way she liked it, sitting innocently on the bench beside me. Margot sniffed the bagel. She licked a little bit of cream cheese and held it out on the tip of her tongue. "Bite?"

The cords of resolve to stay away from her, to make her beg, stiffened. I imagined them snapping, whipping through the soft air to break the wings of butterflies.

"Where's your little pal from last night?" I asked.

"Got scared and ran home to his girlfriend," she said. "Are you coming to the club tonight? You want to watch don't you?" She drank her latte.

"Yes, I do," I said. "You know me. I'm a sucker for the game."

"Good." She smiled, got up, stretched so I could see the length of her body, her belly ring pushed out above her shorts. She finished the latte. She came around to the side of the wooden lounge, sat down and pushed me to the edge, snuggling next to me. I had all I could do to keep from reaching for her. Her head fell against my shoulder. "God, I'm tired; too many late nights. Tonight, it's just you and me."

"I know what you mean," I said. I got up.

I took a tube of sunblock off the table. I began to stroke her legs, covering the pale skin with cream.

"Yeah," she said. "Do me." She closed her eyes. "I can't seem to stay awake."

I covered her arms, hands and face, slowly, remembering each contour, memories leaping at me from every surface. I reached inside her tube top smoothing lotion onto her round breasts and stiff nipples. She protested a little but her mumbles made little difference to my excitement. Mine was the touch of ownership. I would be the last to touch her if you didn't count the medical examiner. There was enough Seconal in her latte to put her to sleep permanently. I covered her eyes with a pair of sunglasses I'd brought from home, carefully wiping them clean of prints. She could lie in the sun all day and no one would think anything of it. The windowless brick wall painted with red lips by the fashion designer, a backdrop, smiled down on her. How long it would take for someone to suspect she was dead was anybody's guess. The sun would keep her body temperature high, confusing the time of death. I'd be long gone, no trace, at Belmont Raceway looking for a different thrill.

*

Fran Bannigan Cox is a visual artist and writer with 32 years of experience in creative work, showing artwork at The Brooklyn Museum, The Riverside Museum and other galleries. She holds an M.A. from Hunter College in New York and a B.A. from Manhattanville College. She co-authored *Conscious Life: Cultivating the Seven Qualities of Authentic Adulthood*, published by Conari Press in Berkeley, California. She is currently working on a murder mystery. Her short story, "A Day At A Time" appears in the anthology *Murder New York Style*.

THE BRIGHTON BEACH MERMAID
BY LINA ZELDOVICH

Tanya Kremin, once a respected Moscow lawyer and now a reluctant American call girl, walked into a dilapidated motel on Brighton Beach Avenue, the Russian enclave of New York City. She trudged up the stairs, her heels clacking on the cheap linoleum floor, and found the room. Her stomach churned as she forced herself to knock on the door. The experienced girls had advised her not to look, not to think, and not to panic. She wasn't nervous, but she was disgusted. "God, please don't make him ugly and smelly or I'll throw up," she thought.

Tanya had never dreamed of making her living in a miniskirt and a low-cut blouse, but when a bomb planted in her Moscow apartment had gone off three months ago, she had to run for her life and leave the country. She had signed a dancer's contract with the International ShowBiz agency and landed in the Brighton Beach Mermaids cabaret. The contract hadn't mentioned entertaining clients in private, but the club owner had his own plans for her classic Slavic beauty. He had already threatened to send her back to Moscow if she didn't play by his rules.

The door opened and Tanya surveyed her customer. To her surprise, she didn't find the man ugly, but borderline appealing. He had a high forehead, short, dark hair, and a pair of sharp eyes that took a snapshot of her like a digital camera. Under different circumstances, she even might've liked the guy, but he was a client and that was enough to make her nauseous.

"Come in," he invited her. "What's your name?"

Tanya introduced herself, walked in and stood awkwardly in the middle of the room.

"I'm Simon," he said, and pointed at a table and two chairs. "Have a seat. Let's get the money out of the way."

Tanya sat down. The girls warned her not to touch a button before seeing the right amount. Simon took out two one-hundred-dollar bills, and placed them on the table. That was fifty dollars too much, and she wasn't sure how to react.

"What do you want me to do?" she asked.

"Talk to me," Simon said, with a strangely inviting smile. Something was wrong in the way he was looking at her. His eyes studied her face rather than her body.

Tanya thought he wanted her to talk dirty, but her mind was blank. Simon reached out and patted her on her shoulder, his face so close Tanya felt his breath. She winced.

"I watch your mermaid dance every night," he said. "You're very good. You like working in the club?"

"I'm delighted," Tanya said sarcastically. "My life-long ambition has finally come true."

Simon chuckled.

"You have a sense of humor, and your English is remarkably good. Did you study it in college in Russia?"

The girls told Tanya that clients didn't like educated chicks, because they felt inferior with intelligent women.

"Me try to learn fast," she said, purposely making a mistake.

Simon chuckled again, and she knew she didn't fool him for a second. She wasn't sure what to do, but someone banged on the door, shouting in a language remotely resembling Russian. Simon pulled Tanya up and shoved her into the bathroom.

"Stay here! I gotta settle this."

Tanya locked the bathroom door just as the unexpected visitors stormed into the room. She heard two new voices. She heard yelling, cursing and punching.

"Shit," Tanya cursed, too. She couldn't believe it was happening to her again. She had given up her career and entire life for her safety, and now, she was caught in the middle of a stick-up, maybe even murder! It wouldn't take the men long to figure out there was an unwanted witness.

Tanya heard a knock on the bathroom door and froze.

"Open up," said the man. "Or I'll break the door and kill you."

Tanya lifted the heavy porcelain lid off the toilet tank, flattened herself against the wall, and pushed the latch open with her elbow. The man barged in, and she smashed the toilet lid on his head. He sank to the floor like a sack of potatoes.

"What the hell?" Tanya heard the second intruder roar. She raised the lid again, but he never entered the bathroom. She heard a punch and more cursing. She peeked, and saw Simon deliver a blow to the man's chin. The man collapsed. Tanya shot out of the bathroom, and finished him off with her porcelain weapon.

"He's got the key in his shirt pocket," Simon croaked, and she realized his left hand was handcuffed to the table. He had a red mark under his eye that was already turning blue.

She found the key and un-cuffed her client.

"Let's get out of here," Simon barked.

He grabbed her hand, and they ran till they were out on the street and far away from the motel. They were both sweaty and short of breath. Simon dragged her into a small café, and they piled into a booth.

"Good job," he breathed out with an awed look. "Never thought of a toilet lid as a weapon. Those Bulgarian scumbags caught me by surprise."

"Who are you?" Tanya asked. "Why are they after you?"

Simon's eyes scrutinized her face again, as if he tried to read her mind.

"I'm Simon Doherty," he finally said. "I'm a Federal Prosecutor."

Tanya couldn't help but laugh. "So, in America prosecutors

hire hookers and get attacked in motels? Not quite what I expected from your legal system."

"I work undercover," Simon explained, producing a badge from his pocket.

Tanya examined the picture. "I can't believe I'm talking to a prosecutor who had to haul his ass from some scumbags. It's ironic."

"Why is it ironic?"

Tanya looked Simon in the eye. "Because *I* am a Russian State Prosecutor, and I had to haul *my* ass away from the mafia hit men who killed two other prosecutors I worked with. We had enough evidence to put a Moscow don away for life, and he knew it. He put out a contract on my two partners and me. All three of us were to be killed the same day, but my car broke down, and the bomb in my apartment went off before I reached home. Next morning, the newspapers declared me dead. Before they realized their mistake, I was gone."

"Dancing at Brighton Beach Mermaids?"

"Bingo."

A waiter showed up and Simon ordered two shots of vodka.

"That explains a lot," he said. "You don't look and talk like the rest of the girls. I knew I made the right choice when I asked for you."

Tanya gave him a dirty look.

"It's not what you think," Simon said. "It's not about bedding, it's about bugging. I need you to stick a little mic pin into Pavel Rublev's jacket next time he comes to Mermaids. Pavel does money laundering, gambling and drug trafficking, plus he's suspected in several murders, kidnappings and torture. He wants to settle a cash-flow issue with his drug distributor, so he'll sneak out during the show and return just before the club closes to ensure his alibi. If you bug him before he leaves, I swear he'll never return."

"Pavel's six-foot-three," Tanya said, "he'll snap my neck like a twig."

"Not if you dance off the stage, sit on his lap and give him a hearty hug."

Tanya winced. "Dancing off the stage means you're available for an auction. Drunken moneybags can bid on you. The winner gets you for the night."

"I promise you'll be out of Mermaids before the auction happens."

Tanya grinned. "What else can a guy chained to a table by a couple of criminals promise me?"

The waiter brought the drinks, and Simon belted down a shot.

"How about a good immigration lawyer who'll get you a green card, plus an LSAT book for your law school exam, and your passport resurrected from the depth of Andrei's safe," Simon offered. "Andrei took it from you for an identity check and never returned it, right? You're stuck here, because you got no papers."

Tanya bit her lip. "How do you know?"

Simon pushed the second glass toward her. "He does it to all his girls."

Tanya refused the alcohol. "I drink when I have something to celebrate," she said with a sigh. "Now, why did you choose me? Just because my English was good?"

Simon took the drink.

"You had no fear in your eyes," he said. "It's rare among immigrants, especially women who work at nightclubs. You can do this."

He downed the second shot.

⁓

Dressed in a shimmering blue mermaid tunic, with a low décolletage and a train skirt flowing three feet behind, Tanya descended the stage stairs, gracefully moving to the music. The mic pin was tucked at her waist, hidden inside the folds of fabric. Pavel sat at the center table with his two bodyguards, while Simon watched her every move from the back of the room.

Too nervous to even look at Pavel, Tanya started with the

rightmost table occupied by Boris Rastin, an old, widowed restaurant mogul, desperately sought by every dancer in the club. She made a few provocative moves, and Boris's forehead swelled with beads of sweat. She let him tuck a fifty into her skirt, and moved on to Misha Dubrov, a limo company owner previously married to a stripper who vanished once her green card came through. Misha was said to be dumb, so the girls hoped he'd make the same mistake twice. Too drunk, Misha had trouble sticking bills into Tanya's cleavage and kept stepping on her tail. She shook him off, put on her most charming smile, suppressed her shakes and headed to Pavel.

Pavel had sharp, narrow eyes and coarse hair that started low on his forehead then spiked up like porcupine needles. He wasn't easily amused, but Tanya did a shoulder shimmy inches away from his face, and succeeded in changing his scowl into a sultry smile. She hid the pin between her fingers and wiggled onto his lap. Pavel wrapped his huge hands around her torso and squeezed so hard Tanya caught her breath. She threw her hand around Pavel's neck, and pushed the pin into the back of his jacket collar while he tucked a hundred-dollar bill into her top. She slipped out of Pavel's grip and danced away, never losing her charming smile. She ran up the stairs, and disappeared behind the curtain as the music ended.

The changing room was full of girls dressed in lace, feathers and fake leather. Everybody wore high heels and lots of make-up. Tanya found her bag under a costume pile, snatched her cell phone and texted Simon. "Done." The reply came instantly. "Great job."

"Great job!" she heard from behind and twitched. Andrei stood next to her, arms wide open. "That's my girl! Betcha you're getting an auction."

"I must change for my second Mermaid number," Tanya uttered, escaping Andrei's hug. "Have you seen my pink tail?"

When she entered the stage, encased in skintight rose with five feet of trailing plastic, the center table was empty. Pavel had left.

~

The Brighton Mermaids' living quarters occupied the building's basement, held about forty people, and looked like Army barracks. Tanya climbed into her bunk, stretched out on the ragged sheets, and texted Simon again. "Any news?" She waited, but the answer never came. Either Pavel was still in the middle of his "settlement" or Simon's people were in the middle of Pavel's apprehension.

Tanya pulled a heavy LSAT book from under her pillow and tried reading, but couldn't concentrate. The drunken girls below yapped about their hunt for American husbands. The bookmark she held in her hand was the business card of the immigration lawyer Simon swore would get her citizenship. She pictured herself passing the bar exam and her vision blurred.

"Congratulations, girl!" Lena, their lead singer, shook Tanya awake. "Boris and Misha held an auction on you!"

Tanya rubbed her eyes, sat up and peeled the lawyer's card off her cheek.

"Who won?" She asked hoarsely.

"Boris!" Lena chirped excitedly. "Oh, you're so lucky. You're going to the penthouse. Wanna drink?"

The penthouse was a gaudy version of a honeymoon suite with a mammoth canopy bed and a huge Jacuzzi with a marble mermaid statue next to it. Tanya cursed. She was on the fast track out of Brighton Mermaids, yet not fast enough.

"I only drink when I have something to celebrate," she muttered. "This is not my idea of a triumphant evening."

"Boris is old," Lena consoled her. "If you really hate him, get him to pass out from booze."

"Thanks," Tanya mumbled, sticking her feet into a pair of heels. She checked her messages. There were none. "Damn, Simon, where the hell are you when I need you?"

Already in the penthouse boudoir, Boris waited for her on the Jacuzzi steps, propped against the marble mermaid and enveloped in clouds of hot steam rising from the bubbling water. He toasted Tanya with a champagne flute and pulled her down next to him, pawing her thighs.

"I love your legs, gorgeous," he said drunkenly, as he poured champagne into Tanya's glass and tucked the Dom Perignon bottle into a corner. He banged on the statue. "See, tails ain't good. What can a man do if a woman's got no legs—there ain't much in between?"

Tanya watched Boris laugh at his own joke and wondered how much alcohol it would take to knock him out cold. Her nausea surged, but Boris's foreplay was interrupted by a heavy slam on the door, which Tanya had forgotten to lock. Misha stormed in.

"Get outta here," Boris shouted. "I won!"

"You c-can't g-get it up, you old c-castrate," Misha stuttered, dead drunk. "This lady n-needs a r-real m-man!"

Boris shrieked. "Get out!"

Misha kicked the door shut and rolled up his sleeves. "L-let's settle this like m-men!"

He threw his fist forward, but lost his balance and hit the statue instead.

"Andrei!" Boris hollered. "Help!"

Tanya heard a heavy man's steps outside, and the door burst open once again. Boris assumed an insulted scowl, but it was short-lived.

In walked Pavel Rublev.

Tanya dropped her flute. The glass shattered.

"Out," Pavel mouthed to the two rivals. He was dripping with sweat, and his right sleeve was torn and bloody. Boris dashed out of the room like a rabbit, but Misha was so drunk his self-preservation instincts failed.

"You didn't bid," he yelled, but Pavel drove his elbow into Misha's solar plexus, and the man collapsed on the floor. Pavel picked him up like a kitten and threw him into the penthouse's hallway.

"I don't have to bid," he muttered hoarsely, as if he were a touch drunk, yet his eyes were sharp and sober. He turned to Tanya. "You danced so wonderfully today, I had to see you. Mind if I sit down on the steps?"

Tanya was frozen in horror. She managed a nod.

"Champagne." Pavel brushed away the fragments of broken glass. "I heard you drink only when you have something to celebrate. What are you celebrating?"

"Nothing," Tanya whispered.

"Nothing, just a beautiful night?" Pavel asked with a strange smile, inching over to Tanya. He threw his arm over her shoulder. "Nights are always beautiful at Brighton Mermaids. I'm a romantic, regardless what people say about me."

Tanya shivered, despite the hot steam rising from the Jacuzzi.

"Why are you trembling?" Pavel questioned. His narrow eyes traveled up and down Tanya's body. "Are you afraid of me? You shouldn't be...unless you have a reason."

His fingers dug into her shoulder. "Do you?"

Tanya stopped breathing. Pavel scrutinized her. Misha moaned in the hallway, but Pavel's eyes never left Tanya's face.

"You can be intimidating," Tanya managed.

"Then you must have a reason," Pavel concluded. His fingers moved to Tanya's throat. He pulled her chin up so their eyes were level and asked, "Who do you work for?"

Tanya gasped. "Andrei."

"I had thought so too," Pavel said with a frightening smile. His hand touched Tanya's cheek, brushed across her ear, and grabbed the back of her hair like a pair of pliers. "Until now. I was on my way to a meeting, but instead I walked into a shootout. The Bulgarian brothers decided tonight was a good night for a stick-up. How did they find me?"

"The Bulgarians?" Tanya echoed, vaguely remembering Simon's description of his attackers, one of whom had met with her porcelain weapon. "I don't know anything about them."

"Don't lie to me!" Pavel snarled. He pushed Tanya's face down into the Jacuzzi until hot bubbles tickled her skin. "Wanna see if you can breathe under water, my little mermaid?"

"I'm not lying!" Tanya spat out, but her cry died in the chlorinated stream. Pavel watched her thrash and gurgle.

"I know the Bulgarians want me dead, but I didn't expect them to hire you for the trick!" he said as he brought Tanya out for a breath. He grinned at her gasping, then pulled her head back, exposing her throat. "Maybe this will help you talk."

Pavel reached behind his neck, and snatched the mic pin from his collar. The mic's head was smashed. Simon's crew was no longer taping Pavel. Neither could they trace his whereabouts.

"Is this the reason you're trembling?" Pavel questioned, holding the pin to her throat. He pushed it in slightly, and dragged it across, leaving a deep, red cut in Tanya's skin. "Tell me, what is it?"

"It's a pin," Tanya forced out. "It's a mi…"

Pavel smacked her head against the mermaid statue's tail.

"It's a tracker!" he snarled. "The Bulgarians followed me because you stuck a tracker in my jacket! Who do you work for? Answer me!"

"Simon Doherty, Federal Prosecutor," Tanya blurted. From the corner of her eye, she saw Misha rise to his knees and pull himself up behind Pavel's back. Misha was no match for Pavel, but he'd make a good distraction. Tanya looked Pavel in the eye to keep his attention and continued talking.

"It's a mic. The Feds got you on tape. Bulgarians have nothing to do with it."

"The Feds?" Pavel let out a chilling laugh. "Andrei's slut is a Fed's agent? You got a sense of humor, mermaid, but now is not the time."

"You can kill me, but I'm telling you the truth," Tanya insisted. "The Feds are on your back, and I'm under their protection."

Misha stood up straight, and let go of the wall. He let out another moan, but Pavel didn't care to turn his head.

"Cut the crap. Feds don't bother us as long as we don't bother them," he growled at Tanya. "I can kill you fast or I can kill you slowly. And painfully. The choice is yours. I'm gonna ask one last time. Who sent you?"

Misha bellowed, and dove onto Pavel with a knife in his hand. Caught by surprise, Pavel let go of Tanya's hair. He seized Misha's hand, but the drunk's momentum carried them forward into the mermaid statue headfirst. The sculpture teetered on the Jacuzzi's edge, and tumbled down the marble steps shattering to pieces.

Tanya rolled away from the fighting men, grabbed the mermaid's tail, and aimed for Pavel's head. Pavel swerved, and the marble piece barely scratched his temple. He grasped at Tanya's ankle and pulled hard. Tanya fell, bringing the rock onto Pavel's chest. Pavel roared. Still clutching the statue's tail, Tanya stumbled to her feet, hopping up the Jacuzzi's steps to gain an advantage in position, but her heavy weapon threw her off balance. She slipped on the wet surface, and plunged into the spa, sending a wave across the tub.

The penthouse door burst open, and Simon stormed in with four police officers in tow. He was drenched in sweat and breathing like a winded horse. His clothes were torn and smeared with dirt. A bloody gash crossed his left cheek.

"Tanya!" he shouted while the cops handcuffed Pavel. "Where are you?"

Tanya emerged from the whirlpool with the mermaid's tail in her hands.

"You lied to me," she screamed at Simon. "Pavel almost killed me!"

"We lost him in a shootout!" Simon reached forward to pull her out of the water. "The Bulgarian brothers got trigger-happy and screwed up everything."

Tanya swung her rock at him. "You set me up! You didn't tell me about the Bulgarians!"

Simon jumped back, avoiding her strike. "You've met the brothers," he objected. "You took Ivanko out with the toilet lid."

"Well, now it's your turn!" Tanya roared as she stepped out

of the water and followed Simon around, swinging the tail. The officers started closing in on her.

"Don't touch her!" Simon shouted, dodging Tanya's blows. "Hold your weapons. Guns, lids, tails... Ouch! Damn!"

Simon stumbled over the marble fragments on the floor and fell. Tanya raised the rock over his head. "I want to know the whole story. Everything about you, the Bulgarians and Pavel."

"All right," Simon yelled, looking up from the floor, his hands raised in a defensive position. "The Bulgarian brothers hired me as a hit man to take Pavel out. They saved me months of work by supplying his schedule and hangout places—like Mermaids. But I took a long time to do the job. The brothers ran out of patience and gave me a black eye the night you and I met."

"I'll give you another one!" Tanya promised. Simon seized the moment and grabbed Tanya's arms from below so that she couldn't maneuver the marble.

"After that, the Bulgarians swore blood," he continued as he got up slowly, firmly holding Tanya's hands while her fingers still clutched the tail. "Mine and Pavel's, both. They followed me tonight, wrecked our van, wreaked havoc, and screwed up the entire operation. We shut them down, but lost Pavel. Pavel didn't realize there was a third party to the shootout, and blamed it on the brothers. He found the mic that he mistook for a tracker and returned to settle matters with you. Got it?"

Tanya unclenched her fingers, and the marble rock fell on Simon's toes. He bellowed and hopped among the pieces of ruined statue. He stumbled, and backed up the steps to the Jacuzzi to avoid another fall. Tanya grabbed the tail and raised it again. Simon hopped a step higher. Tanya summoned all her strength and thrust the heavy tail upward. Simon leaped back again, not realizing he was on the top step, and landed in the hot bubbles, sending splashes to the ceiling. Tanya's hands buckled at the last second. The tail fell on the floor.

Drenched and angry, Tanya felt taller than she was. Her long blonde hair was plastered to her face, her wet dress clung to her like a second skin, and the water streamed down her body making a puddle around her feet.

Simon arose from the tub, soaked clean and with a peace proposition. "Now that we're even, wet, and done, let's go rescue your passport from Andrei's safe."

"Let's," Tanya said as she kicked at the tail, venting the last of her fury. The tail rocked back and forth, and settled at her toes.

"You look just like a mermaid—wet, beautiful and mysterious," Simon told her while he stepped down onto the floor, and picked up the Dom Perignon that had miraculously survived the cataclysms in a safe corner. "Can I get you a drink? Today you sure have something to celebrate."

*

Lina Zeldovich is a bilingual writer who grew up on the classics of Russian literature, started writing at age five, and switched languages at twenty-one. Since then, she has published over a dozen short stories and more than forty theater reviews, and won three Writers' Digest fiction awards, including first prize in the memoir genre. Her latest works are scheduled to appear in *Ellery Queen Mystery Magazine* and *Writer's Digest Collection 2010.* She is looking for a home for four novels, including her latest belly dancing murder mystery, *Death by Scheherazade's Veil.* Lina writes for a travel magazine and blogs about her adventures at http://noveladventurers.blogspot.com. Her passions are traveling off-the-beaten-path, all things poisonous, and, of course, belly dancing!

JUSTICE FOR ALL
BY CATHERINE MAIORISI

Wow. Seeing was believing. People really did live on boats in Manhattan. Fantastic. But no time to gawk at the picturesque scene—yachts and houseboats and sailboats bobbing in the blue-green Hudson River at the 79th Street Boat Basin. I clipped on my shield, waited for an opening in the stream of bicycles, joggers, dogs, and baby strollers, then dashed across the path to the uniformed officer stationed at the gate. She logged me in and pointed to the knot of humanity gathered on the boardwalk to the left. I paused to get the big picture before diving in, so to speak, and saw Detective John Quinn, the primary, standing with his back to the scene, staring across the river at New Jersey.

As I approached Quinn, the boardwalk undulated in the wake of a passing ferry carrying early-to-work New Jersey residents to their jobs on Wall Street. The walkways moaned and screeched with each wave. My stomach lurched.

"What do we have?" I asked.

"Body of a girl pulled out of the water at dawn this morning." Quinn avoided looking at me. Nothing new. He wasn't happy partnering with a woman, especially an African-American, but anyone with a choice avoided working with him, so he was stuck with me. It was a toss-up as to which of us would celebrate more when he retired six months from now.

He tilted his head toward the body. "Get the details."

The ME looked up. "Ah, Jones, saddled with Quinn again, I see."

I focused on the battered body of the young Asian woman lying on the blood-soaked boardwalk in front of me. Her pearly skin and blunt-cut black hair a sharp contrast against the red-stained wood; her gaily printed halter dress bunched around her waist, one breast exposed; no panties. I fought the urge to cover her. Looking away, I took a minute to wrap my professional heart around the sad and caring heart, so I could concentrate on the business of finding whoever did this.

"We have an angry killer. I count ten stab wounds so far," the ME said. "Call me later for details."

I flashed a grateful smile. He knew Quinn gave me all the scutwork but didn't share anything that might help me do my job. And his.

I opened my notebook, wrote the date, time, weather, and place, sketched the scene and jotted down the names of the near-by boats: *Road to Life, Dream Boat, Sweet Sal's Gal, Tide Ride, Justice for All.*

"Speak to you later," I said.

The ME lifted his hand, but his eyes stayed with the woman.

Quinn seemed mesmerized by New Jersey. I didn't see the attraction myself. I edged around him to talk face-to-face, but he pivoted north, looking toward the George Washington Bridge. "We have a witness, a Mr. Carter, on the *Justice for All*," he said, throwing an arm in the direction of a large houseboat behind him. "Take the lead. You need the experience."

I climbed aboard the *Justice for All* and knocked. "Detectives Jones and Quinn to speak to Mr. Carter," I said to the woman who opened the door.

As we stepped into the room, the woman reclining in the lounge spoke.

"It's *Ms.*, detective. *Ms.* Carter Stanhope."

Oh, my. Not just *Ms.* Carter Stanhope, but *Detective* Carter Stanhope. I straightened and fought the impulse to salute. My hero. The cop I aspired to be—honest, dedicated, successful. Stanhope had lost weight, and her face was all sharp points and shadows, but her voice was strong and throaty. A metal walker stood near her chair, and a wheelchair with a crocheted throw draped over the back lurked in the corner. How long since Stanhope was raped and brutally beaten? A month? Six weeks?

"Detective Stanhope. Sorry. I was told… I had no idea." How are you feeling, I wanted to know, but I kept it professional. "We'd like a few minutes of your time."

A smile played at her lips. "Hello, Quinn. Still at it, I see."

"Stanhope," he said. His voice made it clear that he wasn't thrilled to see her.

The place was all teak and windows and vibrant colors. Nice. I took the seat she offered, facing her. Quinn ignored her and walked to the window.

Stanhope's eyes bore into me like gold-pointed lasers. I swallowed and hoped my voice wouldn't betray me. "What happened this morning?"

"I was on the deck with my morning coffee, watching the dawn break when I heard moaning," she said. "I went to the railing and saw a woman clinging to the boardwalk, clearly in trouble, so I pulled her out."

She caught my glance at the walker and smiled. "I went down on my rear end."

"How did you manage with the casts?"

She shrugged. "They made it harder, but she's small."

"Did she say anything before she died?"

"She only lived a few minutes, but I think she said 'ma' and 'free.'"

"Did you know her?"

"No."

"Any theories about how or why she ended up at your, um, gangplank?"

"If you're asking whether it was related to the attack on me, I'd say no."

Quinn coughed. I froze, expecting an inappropriate remark, but he controlled himself.

Carter confirmed that she usually had coffee on her deck around dawn, that she hadn't heard the woman go in the water, and the only person she saw beside the victim was the neighbor who helped her pull the woman out. I stood. "Thank you, Detective Stanhope."

The woman placed the walker in front of her, but made no move to help, so I curbed my impulse to dash to the rescue. Carter pulled herself up and hobbled to the door. I remembered that in addition to her broken arm and leg, her pelvis was fractured. If she was in pain, she hid it well. I gave her my card. "You know the drill, detective."

Quinn mumbled something and slipped past us.

"Still has problems with women, I see. How did you get stuck?"

"Low detective on the totem pole."

"Leave him behind when you come back."

Repressing the urge to whoop, I followed Quinn off the boat.

The body was gone, but the techs were still working. Men and women, some in suits carrying briefcases, streamed toward the gate.

"People are leaving for work. If we hurry, we might catch some at home."

"Good idea. Get started. I have things to do." With that, Quinn headed for the gate.

After the dockmaster assured me that the woman didn't live in the boat basin, I spent several hours climbing aboard boats questioning anybody who answered my knock. But no luck. And I was starving. On my way to the gate, I spotted people sitting under umbrellas on a terrace overlooking the boat basin. An outdoor restaurant. Perfect.

The burger was good. The coffee so-so, but I sipped and made a to-do list: request uniforms to finish canvassing the boats tonight, confirm that SCU checked the underground garage, get a picture of the young woman, and come back to the café later this evening to question the help and the patrons.

～

Eleven o'clock on a weeknight, and the Marina Café was hopping. Groups of drinking and flirting patrons waiting for tables filled the wide staircase up to the outdoor terrace. I went inside, or sort of inside, to the cave-like, brick-ceilinged area without walls. The din was unbearable. Yet the tables were all full, and the bar was invisible behind a ten-deep wall of men and women clumped into groups, leaning in close to shout in each other's ear. I elbowed my way to the bar, and nobody even noticed the elbows. When I finally got the barmaid's attention, I shouted my order for a San Pellegrino. A second later, she slammed the bottle down and did an impatient tap dance while I retrieved my money. I flashed the girl's picture.

She shook her head, grabbed my cash and the picture, which she showed to the three male bartenders as they flew by. Three nos. As fast as they moved, the customers were probably a big blur. She handed the picture back and leaned close to my ear. "Ask Marie, the manager, or Frank, the assistant manager. They keep tabs on people." She indicated a man in a long-sleeved shirt standing alone.

I sauntered over with my fizzy water and pointed outside the echo-chamber. He nodded and followed me. The noise level was a few decibels lower, but out here we had to deal with the sounds of cars whizzing by overhead on the West Side Highway. I introduced myself.

"What's up?" he said.

"Ever seen this girl?"

He took the picture and stared a long time before handing it back. "She comes in a lot. Her name is Susan. Susan Liu. Not a good picture."

Yeah, not too many people look good dead. "When did you see her last?"

"Last night. What she do?"

"What do you think she did?"

He shrugged. "I figure if a detective is looking for her, she's in trouble."

"Who was she with?"

He made a face, like he smelled something bad. "This guy, Terry, thinks he's Frank Sinatra, a real ladies' man." He chewed his thumb. "Haven't seen either of them tonight."

"What's Terry's last name?"

"Don't know."

"Did they leave together?"

"I didn't notice. Marie would know, she keeps her eye on Terry. I'll send her over."

He pulled out a handkerchief and mopped his face. "Need another drink?"

I handed him my empty. "Another San Pellegrino would be great."

After he left, I realized I never told him Susan was dead. A minute later, Marie arrived with a bottle of San Pellegrino and a glass of ice. She was striking: nearly six-feet tall with tons of dark curly hair haloing her heavily made-up face. Despite the heat, she was wearing jeans, a jacket, and cowboy boots. Just looking at her made me sweat. I identified myself, showed Susan's picture.

"Did you see her last night?"

She lit a cigarette, took a drag, and exhaled before answering. "Yes."

"Who was she with?"

She took another drag. Her eyes met mine. "Is Susan in trouble?"

I didn't say anything.

"A sleaze-bag named Terry. I warned her about him."

"What's his problem?"

"Likes to put roofies in girl's drinks. I told him, next complaint, he's eighty-sixed."

"And?"

"No more complaints, but I don't trust him."

"Did Susan leave with him?"

"Yes."

"Know his last name and where he lives?"

"No to both. So what's going on?"

"Susan was murdered."

"Oh, shit. Last night? In the park?" She swayed, grabbed my shoulder. "It was him. I knew he—"

"Right now we're tracing her movements. But I would like to talk to Terry. Call me if he comes in." I gave her my card.

She nodded, wiped a few tears, and went back to work.

I found Frank. "Now what?"

"Susan was murdered last night."

He paled. "Oh, God. Where?"

"In the park."

He wiped his face. I couldn't tell if it was tears or sweat. His eyes followed me as I showed her picture as best I could in the mob, but it was a waste of time, so I left.

It was late, but Carter's boat was lit up, so I took a chance.

She was alone on the deck. She smiled and invited me to sit.

"Her name was Susan Liu. She hung out at the café, and last night she left with a guy named Terry."

"Good work."

"Now that I have her name, I'll find her apartment. And I'll get some help tomorrow night to talk to the customers at the café, see if we can find Terry."

"Have you talked to the homeless people in the park?"

"I haven't seen any."

"It's not unusual for them to witness something, because they fade into the landscape and people don't notice them. They're afraid of cops, but if you approach them with respect, you might get cooperation. Just don't let Quinn near them."

～

I spent the next day in court waiting to testify on another case, and when I got back to my desk at five, I almost missed the tiny sticky note that said, 'killer in cell 2, process him.' No signature. Quinn had arrested someone for the murder? I was flabbergasted. Quinn, of course, was gone, and I couldn't reach him to ask what convinced him this guy was the killer. I scrounged around, and found the reports hidden under a grimy pair of shoes in his desk drawer. An officer canvassing in the park noticed a large purse around the neck of a homeless man called Buffalo Dog. When asked about it, Buffalo Dog refused to answer, just repeated the question, so they brought him in. The purse contained Susan's wallet with credit cards and four hundred in twenties. When they searched the many bags Buffalo carried, they found a pair of size-six spiked heels. Susan's size. So Quinn wanted him booked for murder. Simple.

Too simple for me. I called Carter.

"Hi, it's Cappy Jones. I've been in court all day, and I just found out that Quinn arrested a homeless guy, um, Buffalo Dog. He had Susan's pocketbook and a pair of high heels in her size."

"Talk to Buffalo. See what you think, Cappy."

"Do you know him?"

"Yes."

I sensed a story behind that yes, so I kept quiet.

Carter sighed. "Buffalo was one of the homeless people who chased my attackers and saved my life."

As I stepped into the interview room, I was assaulted by the reek of putrid vegetables; wet dog; moldy mattress; crusty, un-washed body; and clothes so filthy they may have never been ex-posed to water other than rain or snow. I adjusted my breathing to shallow and began, hoping I wouldn't vomit before I finished interrogating him.

He was standing nose to the wall, arms extended.

I stared at his huge back. One swat of that powerful arm and I'd be dead. I glanced at the two-way mirror, then reminded my-self that this man saved Stanhope's life. I moved closer and spoke to his back. "Buffalo, I'm Detective Jones. I'd like to ask you a few questions."

"Ask me questions, ask me questions."

"Did you see," I slipped the picture between his face and the wall, "this young woman Tuesday night?" I was encouraged when he tipped his head back to look at the picture.

He spun suddenly, and I did a quick two-step to avoid being trampled.

"Come fly with me. Come fly with me."

"Buffalo, did you see this woman?"

"Come fly with me. Come fly with me."

Try as I might, I couldn't get anything else out of him. I sent him back to his cell, and after holding my head out the window for five minutes trying to get the stench out of my nostrils, I moved to Quinn's desk. Maybe because Buffalo saved Carter's life. Maybe because he didn't hide the evidence. Or maybe because his clothes looked and smelled as if they haven't been washed in years and, he didn't seem to have a spot of blood on him, I was still on the case.

I picked through the reports. No address book or cell phone in her purse. The ID in her wallet wasn't current. No help there. As I shoved the reports back, I noticed a stack of pink telephone messages. I thumbed through them. Hah, a friend of Susan Liu's called at four-thirty. I'd have bet a week's salary that Quinn was long gone by then. I copied her address and headed out.

When I arrived at Ricki Leung's Seventy-third street apartment, I learned that Susan was something of a free spirit, a non-monogamous bisexual who lived with her latest hot-sex partner only until she found someone else. Then she changed partners. Recently, she had a problem with someone who wouldn't let her go, but Ricki couldn't remember who. The only names she remembered were Tony, Carol, Frank, and Terry, a guy with a boat. I thanked her and drove to the boat basin.

When I mentioned Terry, the dockmaster buzzed me through and pointed me to the *Come Fly with Me*. Buffalo wasn't so crazy after all. I boarded.

"I was expecting you," Terry said.

"But you didn't call?"

"I left a message for a Detective Quinn as soon as I heard."

"You were with Susan last night?"

"Yeah. We came here, had fabulous sex, then fell asleep. When

I woke up a couple of hours later, Susan had almost finished a whole bottle of Bourbon. I said I would shower and then drive her home, but she was gone by the time I got dressed. I figured she'd be at the café but I found her sleeping under a tree near the stairs. I couldn't wake her, and rather than leave her, I went up to the café to tell Marie and Frank where she was. I knew one of them would take care of her."

"Then what did you do?"

"I drove to my, ah, to a friend's to spend the night."

"I need your friend's name and contact info."

He looked away. "My fiancé will be upset if you call."

"How upset will she be if you're charged with murder?"

"Can't you ask Marie or Frank?"

"The name and number please."

His fiancé confirmed his story. I warned him not leave town, then I went to the café to talk to Marie and Frank. But she had taken the night off, and he had called in sick, so I chatted with the maitre d' and a couple of waitresses.

On the way back to my car, it dawned on me. If Buffalo was nearby, then perhaps others were as well. After an hour of wandering around Riverside Park, I saw a guy on a bench with two mangy dogs and an empty whisky bottle next to him. He had really long dreads, but looked more pulled together than Buffalo Dog. And he didn't smell nearly as bad. It's all relative though. I sat, so I wouldn't tower over him.

"Excuse me, are you Gentleman Gerry?"

"Who's askin'?" He sounded like he had a mouthful of marbles.

"Detective Cappy Jones. Detective Stanhope suggested I talk to you."

He smiled, and his false teeth popped out. He pushed them back.

"Were you around last night when that girl was murdered?"

"They arrested Buffalo Dog. I told the cop Buffalo wouldn't hurt nobody but you know cops."

He closed his eyes.

"Um, excuse me. Do you know how Buffalo got her purse and shoes?"

"Found 'em."

"Where?"

He stretched out on the bench, and I scrambled to avoid having his feet in my lap. In a second, he was snoring. Back at the house, I found a message from the ME: left-handed killer, a couple of bloody prints found on the railing along the Hudson. NYPD Harbor Patrol divers retrieved a switchblade from the water that could be the weapon, but no prints. I settled in to research my suspects. Finally, late as it was, I called Ricki to see whether I could jog her memory. I was sure who did it. I just needed confirmation.

The next morning, Quinn didn't show. I called his cell. He didn't pick up. I called his house. His wife said he had left for work a few hours earlier. Nobody knew where he was. I waited and waited. Finally, Paul Becarelli, a senior detective, noticed my agitation and took me under his wing. Together, we went to our lieutenant, presented the case, and got approval to proceed without Quinn.

I found Gentleman Gerry wandering in Riverside Park. "If you come to the station and tell me how Buffalo got the woman's things, I'll let him go." He agreed, but only if the dogs could come too. Talk about smelly. I gagged as I drove, but managed to avoid embarrassing myself.

At the house, I sat with Gerry and the dogs and took his statement. "We was sitting on a bench, and her and the guy that's always singin' were staggerin' toward the boats. He dragged her through the gate, and it were hard to tell if she was crying or laughing. We went to see if she needed help, but she weren't screaming or nothing so we figured she was okay. Buffalo found her stuff on the ground and took it so nobody could steal it."

"Did you see her leave the boat?"

"A couple hours later, she came out the gate and went to sleep under that tree by the stairs. We watched her and kept her things safe. Then the boat guy come, shook her, and went up to the cafe."

"Did you see him again?"

"Yeah. Couple minutes later, he went into the garage."

"We waited till somebody came to take care of her, then we went to our sleeping place. We forgot Buf had her stuff."

Detectives brought in Marie, Frank, and Terry and took their statements. After Buffalo and Gentleman Gerry signed their statements, I brought them into the room one at a time and asked them to point out the person they last saw with Susan. Gerry pointed, but Buffalo walked over and put a paw on the shoulder of one of the three. Detectives and suspects jumped up. I heard gagging, and there was a rush to open the windows as I escorted the two homeless guys out.

I took a call. The lab had a match on one of the bloody prints.

Becarelli spent some time on the phone with the café's bank. We huddled. "Let's do it," he said.

According to their statements, Susan was screwing all three of them and living with one. We strolled over to the where they were seated. I hesitated, then aware that the room was watching me, I moved in front of the murderer.

"Marie Torelli, you are under arrest for the murder of Susan Liu." As Becarelli chanted the Miranda warning, Marie jumped up. Becarelli grabbed her. I stepped behind, pushed her sleeves up, and cuffed her. Lots of scratches under those sleeves.

"You got the wrong one. Terry did it."

We took her to an interview room, stated names, etc. for the recorder, and started. "Didn't you serve time a few years ago for slicing a girlfriend who wanted out of the relationship?"

"You have no right—"

"Two waitresses saw Terry speak to you right before closing."

"So, I forgot."

"Two other witnesses saw you with Susan under the tree."

"Liar. Nobody's in the park that late."

"The bank said you deposited the night's receipts at six that morning, not four-forty-five, as you claimed. We're testing the deposit bag for blood."

She started to stand, but Becarelli placed a hand on her shoulder.

"Oh, and we have your bloody fingerprint on the railing where you tossed Susan in."

Marie suddenly stilled, her eyes wide. "Okay. Okay. She was dead when I found her. I was afraid I'd be blamed, so I threw her in the water."

"Good try, Marie. Susan was alive when she was pulled out. Her last word was 'Marie.'"

With that, I led her to a cell.

Carter Stanhope, my hero, called to congratulate me. Besides great press coverage, I got promoted. I'm no longer low man on the totem pole. Oh, and Quinn retired earlier than planned. As it turned out, I was happier than he was.

*

Catherine Maiorisi lives in New York City. Most often, she can be found writing in her Starbucks office. Catherine has completed two mysteries, and is currently querying for book one of her series starring NYPD Detective Chiara Corelli and her sidekick Detective P.J. Parker. Her short story, *Old Cape Cod*, received an honorable mention in the Al Blanchard Short Story Contest held annually at the New England Crime Bake. "Justice for All" is her first published story.

A Morbid Case of Identity Theft
by Clare Toohey

In a fourth-floor Brooklyn walk-up, summertime is a battle for survival, and the computer where I edit video and my apartment's overloaded A/C refused to co-exist electrically. I've known Joanna since my first crop of peach fuzz, concurrent with my first failure at sneaking into a Roger Corman horror movie marathon, so I wasn't suspicious of her offer. Free computing in her climate-controlled library of unusual tomes and oddities. I didn't even have to open to the public, she said, just 'babysit the curiosities' while she took her first week's vacation since founding the place. That seemed overprotective for a bunch of junk, but I was grateful anyway.

The Morbid Anatomy Library stands within a sprawling warehouse of art galleries. The industrial building hosting this cooperative is a former box-factory squatting beside the historic and toxic Gowanus Canal. July's heat enhanced the canal's olfactory pleasures, but that wasn't the most revolting aspect of my trudge to the library. All the way down Union Avenue, I was obstructed by sweating throngs assembled for a parade. No summer Saturday in New York City remains unblemished by lame public events. As a cinephile, I adore the medium of film, but not necessarily audiences, if you get me. I couldn't wait to escape the heaving scrum.

Upon reaching the library's inner threshold and unlocking the door, simple relief was replaced with a tingle of illicit discovery. I felt as if I were sneaking into an explorer's most private, strangest trophy room or breaking into Houdini's prop closet. I began to understand some of Joanna's feeling for it, and wondered why I hadn't visited earlier.

If the crowded room that composes the Morbid Anatomy Library isn't quite a library, it isn't purely morbid either. The subject matter isn't hamstrung to the anatomical or even the human. The bookshelves contain art and legend, metaphysics, superstitions, and the mysteries of death. Medical marvels share space with unapologetic frauds and freaks. I dumped my gear bag and found a delectable lemon muffin in a string-tied box on the desk. I noshed blissfully in the dry, impersonal mustiness.

I hadn't anticipated how much of the beautiful and bizarre I'd find worth filming. All I had with me was my mini-cam, but I got straight to capturing incidental imagery. A filmmaker of the macabre never knows when he might require a few frames' worth of empty prosthetic legs. And what about a miraculous saint figurine, a plaster cast of the inner ear, convicts' teeth, an empty hive, antique syringes, dangerous toys, or a reptile skull? As I panned and zoomed, the back of my neck prickled with a sense of being observed in return, of vague movement just beyond the lens.

I stopped filming and jerked my head up fast to catch whatever it was, but found only a flea-bitten, stuffed squirrel sneering at me from the top of a bookshelf.

I had the immediate, distinct feeling the collection didn't appreciate my collecting it.

Of course, a certain, twitchy sensitivity on my part might be explained by the number of energy drinks I'd had, but that doesn't explain what happened next. The room flickered with venomous green light and filled with the sudden smell of ozone. At least, I thought it did. I could've been hallucinating, I guess, like Nicholson's epic breakdown in *The Shining*. Who can say whether a place is truly haunted or its observer is going insane?

In any case, I took the hint to stow my camera, and pretend

nothing unusual happened, like any New Yorker would. I settled into my computer editing, the reason I'd come in the first place. I was re-working a stubborn scene transition, but the seeping bagpipe corps from the parade outside disrupted the ambience of menace I wanted to achieve. I only looked down for a second, really, just to dig out my earphones and a fresh orange soda. But when I looked up, a gray-haired stump in a pink cardigan had sprouted in front of the desk.

"We're not really open, and the bathroom's not public. Sorry, ma'am." Insincere remorse makes us city-dwellers seem civilized.

"I'm a victim of identity theft, putz! Where's Joanna?" For a relic, she had surprisingly clear elocution. The little ragbag didn't sound like a tourist either. In that wadded Kleenex of a face, intensely black eyes twinkled, as beady and untrustworthy as a ferret's. Even a squirrel's.

"Identity theft's more of a cop issue than a library issue," I said. "There are loads of nice officers leaning on blue sawhorses just a block away."

"Can't you see I'm an eighty year-old woman?!" She seemed overly excited about the obvious. "I got…lost somehow." Was that moisture gathering in those ball-bearing eyes?

I scooted out of my chair, patted her shoulder, and ushered her toward the door. "You must've been trying to find the South Brooklyn Casket Company and gotten confused. My sympathy on your bereavement, or on picking out your own coffin, whatever. Parades are monstrosities. Just go out to the corner at Union and take a left."

Ungrateful, she stuck a surprisingly painful fingertip in my sternum. "Stop talking down to me, or I'll kick you in the ankles first and work my way up. I can't believe you didn't hear anything. It was like an explosion!" She sank into one of the reading chairs, staring at her gnarled hands as if she'd never seen them before. I retreated behind the barrier of the desk. "I'll forgive you for being an ass, because you think I'm a lunatic, *Randolph*."

"If we'd ever actually met, you'd know I prefer being called Dolph now."

She snorted, but her eyes had gone cold and sharp, diamond-tipped drillbits. We glared at each other, stalemated. A knobby finger tapped her temple. "Oh, I know lots of things about you, *Randy*. What I'll mention aloud is your stash of pirated Hong Kong vampire movies." My open-mouthed expression seemed to make hers soften. "That's part of my condition. Somehow, I know the dirty secrets of everyone I see. I sense people's misdeeds and what they're capable of doing. I had to get away from those crowds, and I thought maybe this place... I only wish I knew how to stop knowing all this stuff...and what the hell's happened to my body!"

I didn't comprehend, but as she retracted further into her sweater, I felt compelled to help the sad, pink turtle.

"Joanna's out of town. If the answer's in here somewhere, I don't know enough to find it, um, ma'am." Then, something more important caught up with me. "Did you say explosion?"

"That's right, Sherlock. A statue on a float went poof in a cloud of plaster dust. The horses freaked! I was standing right next to it when it happened." She raked vigorously through her snowy hair, releasing faint puffs of dust.

I groaned. "Don't tell me something actually worth filming happened!"

The crone leaped from the chair with unexpected agility. "You self-centered jerkwad! Listen to me! Half an hour ago I was out there, my normal self, with bakery samples. And then—blammo! Everybody was yelling and running. I wasn't me anymore. I had a pounding head full of other people's sins, and I looked like this!"

I fired up the internet. "Maybe my awesome skills can be of some help after all."

"Really?" Smiling briefly, her teeth were unexpectedly white and even looked real. The youthful glee in that wizened face was disturbing. As my fingers flew, I realized she had a different notion of what I was researching.

"The name's Melanie P. Fitzroy." She sucked in a quick, deep breath. "Born June 18th, 1980."

The girlish first name poorly suited that prehistoric corpus. "Hold on a minute. That would make you only…"

"Thirty years old." She offered it as a dare, her jaw jutting like a dog's I'd cross the street to avoid. "I opened the new bakery down the block. I dropped off those muffins yesterday." She pointed accusingly at the crimped paper cup at my elbow, empty but for microscopic lemony crumbs. More frighteningly, she advanced toward me, holding her crabbed, road-map hands before her like battle flags.

"They look perfect to me for kneading pretzels," I said to mollify her.

"Moron! I can't even reach my top oven now! This is not *me*!"

Before I could formulate an intelligent reply, she aimed a bent fingertip over my shoulder. The monitor now displayed a screen shot from the parade at the intersection two blocks away.

"There!" she yelled like a mad scientist says *Eureka*. "Everything went crazy after the plaster woman disintegrated. You found it!"

"Sure I did. With that many spectators, figures someone would've posted by now." My search had returned a video from less than ten minutes previously. Hot off reality's presses. "Now we can relive the magic without leaving climate control."

Unfortunately, Granny Mel tottered around the desk, leaning a scratchy woolen forearm across the back of my neck to watch along.

The clip's disembodied narrator sounded like a proto-nerd, however, the establishing shot of the crowd-lined sidewalk was stable enough to assume he'd used a tripod. Go, go geekdom. A tall, shapely woman with a long, dark braid and a blue chef's shirt crossed in front of him.

"There I am, Randy. Or was. Just look at me," said a cracked voice that had, inexplicably, acquired a British accent like my college roommate after his semester abroad.

"1777, Excelsior!" The video's narrator cheered as what he identified as the Great Seal of the State of New York rolled into view. I'd never seen the thing before, but the fifteen-foot plaster circle was elevated above the street on a chariot-style cart drawn by two white horses with feathered hats.

The dark-haired woman re-entered the frame balancing two trays full of paper cups like the one I'd emptied. In seconds flat, her freebies were cleaned out. Two guys scuffled over the last sweet morsel: a slick, young Asian dude, who I thought had the edge, and a paunchy, balding guy who obviously had the experience. The nerdy narrator wished aloud that the visual impediments would am-scray, and the woman in blue edged out of the picture with her warring admirers as if she'd heard.

The plaster Seal was as garish as a kindergarten art project. Against the navy background, a giant pair of Grecian goddess-types were sculpted in relief on either side. They hovered barefoot, painted in pale blue and yellow togas, with official-looking symbols molded in their free hands.

The nerd, who must prefer his ladies inanimate, glossed over Liberty and her pole on the right, or 'dexter.' He saved his painstaking description for the blindfold and disheveled hair of leftmost, and therefore, 'sinister' Justice. The shield centered between the goddesses depicted a Hudson River landscape. A full-color globe was its cherry topping. If that weren't enough understated heraldry, a golden eagle spread its wings over the whole kaboodle. "The Seal was last revised in 1882," the nerd continued, "but we're cheating to celebrate its quasquicentennial!"

That's the 125th anniversary. I had to look it up, too.

Suddenly, the narration and equine clip-clopping halted with a concussion of sound. Nothing like the pyrotechnic boom I'd hoped, more like the ear-bursting pop of a giant metal cap off an enormous soda bottle. A pale cloud blanked the scene.

After an eternal five seconds, the haze cleared, revealing blurred bodies zipping across the camera's sight line. Even that close to the chaos, the nerd kept rolling frames with a dedication I had to respect. The pair of horses reared, all hooves and teeth, while a handler tried calming them back to earth. It would've been better footage if he hadn't succeeded, but finally the chariot settled and exposed the damage.

Liberty was going to have to look for solo gigs. The colorful Seal's leftmost two-thirds ended as raggedly as torn paper. The entire figure of Justice had been obliterated.

"Cool!" I said. "Not that it wouldn't be simple enough to fake with digital editing, or even in real-time with stage magic."

"Did you not just see the whole figure vaporize into nothingness?" Granny Mel asked.

I shook her off my shoulders and rotated to face her accusatory stare.

"I don't know what you expect. I wasn't there. I only have your word."

The kicked-puppy look on her face shut me up. "Randy, I can't return to my home or to my shop, because I can't explain my appearance to anyone I know. I have a craving to go to the police and volunteer to investigate open cases. Every two minutes, I feel like unraveling this sweater and re-knitting the whole thing." She yanked miscellaneous shreds of paper out of her pocket, finding one to blow her nose. "I've never been crafty in my life! Now, I'm a full foot shorter and decades older. I need a bra with a waistband, not shoulder straps!"

Imagine the Queen Mother's voice saying all that, and you'll have some idea of my cognitive dissonance. Curious, I picked up one of her discarded pastel scraps.

"I didn't think they made pound notes anymore," I said.

"I'm getting worse!" Granny Mel unleashed a firehose of profanity, truly admirable in both its hipness and filth.

It was that spontaneous, heartfelt outburst that convinced me. At minimum, the woman contained multiple personalities warring for dominance. Or, she was possessed. Was the diagnosis more of an *All About Eve* or *The Exorcist?* No wait, I had it.

"Identity theft isn't really the best description of your situation," I said, doing the finger point and shrieking Donald Sutherland face from *Invasion of the Body Snatchers.* She wasn't tracking with me. "Look, if you want to find yourself, maybe you should return to the scene of the crime." I retrieved the mini-cam from my gear bag. "I hate the public as much as anybody, but I'll even go with you. Just in case there's some traumatic aftermath worth recording for art's sake."

Granny Mel's eyes glittered with hardened purpose, and she cackled. "To the scene of the crime! And you'll be my sidekick!"

I hated the 'associate producer' sound of that term, but as I locked up, I ridiculously warned the squirrel I'd hold him responsible for hijinks. I couldn't shake my weird suspicion that the varmint would come out to play the instant this cat shut the door.

When Granny Mel and I rounded the corner toward Gowanus canal, she looked dazed by the dispersing crowd. I took her elbow to keep her from stumbling while she muttered pronouncements about everyone we passed. Men, women, children alike.

"Embezzler. He stole a hotel robe, too."

"*Thirty* parking tickets?!"

"Forged his report card. 2 D's and an F."

"Returned her prom dress after wearing it. Yuck."

This last was loud enough that the lady-in-question overheard, and I'd swear she looked guilty. I can't prove it though, because I didn't have my camera rolling while I gallantly steadied the listing H.M.S. Melanie. An annoying voice in my head reminded me of the impossibility of even an imaginative lunatic guessing out-of-the-blue about my cache of martial-arts bloodsuckers. I told that voice to shut up.

Suddenly, Granny Mel halted again, gasping, and I wondered whether she was having a grabber in the stinking heat.

She yanked my arm and my attention toward a pair of over-dressed, middle-aged men, who were jamming fedoras onto their heads like they had oozing brain tumors with a side of migraine gravy. Other passersby didn't seem to notice, and there weren't any police idling nearby. In fact, the thinning herd of pedestrians avoided that whole section of sidewalk where the remaining half-lozenge of the Great Seal was propped against the canal's railing. However, I couldn't let another second elapse without filming it and its hungover-looking sentries.

The much-shorter man had a fish face and a dark suit. Though weaving on his feet, obviously distressed, he firmly gripped a glowing cigar that smelled like a burning latrine even from across the street. The taller man was Asian. His suit was as white as melted marshmallows and he sported a tight Fu Manchu. In recent years, Brooklyn's attracted ever more artsy eccentrics, but these two were armpits-deep in character. With a stab of certainty, I knew I'd seen them before.

I backed up the footage to review what I'd just shot. I always think better when I can see things on screen. But, with both my hands thus occupied, Granny Mel was unanchored to dodder across the street toward them. I yelled a warning as she barely missed being flattened by a street-meat cart evacuating the area. I hustled across to follow, alternately glancing down at the LCD screen, until I realized what bothered me about the men I'd filmed.

"You're not black and white!" I shouted at the confused-looking trio.

The fish-faced man spoke, waving the his cigar at me, "Your closet is overflowing with illegal copies of Hong Kong..."

"Fine, fine. I admit all that, dude. Or should I call you Barton Keyes?" Melanie looked sharply at me, snapped out of her daze. "I don't consume as much noir as horror these days, so it took me longer to recognize him." Her eyes were clearer, but not comprehending. "Barton Keyes was the tenacious insurance investigator, right? Closing in on his murderous, adulterous colleague, Walter Neff. You know, Keyes! Played by the immortal Edward G. Robinson! Can't you see this guy is the spitting image?" I prodded. "*Double Indemnity*, anyone?"

"Oh, the movie? I've always been more of a reader," Granny Mel said.

I could've screamed in frustration. I hate readers and their superiority complexes. The fish-faced man goggled like he was trying to breathe black mayonnaise from the canal. And instead of congratulating me on my astounding insight, Melanie looked distracted again.

"That isn't enough?" I asked, robbed of glory. "Then you *really* won't care that the other guy's probably Charlie Chan." I shrugged toward the ice cream man without nearly as much zest. "Zanuck produced a lot of those at Fox, but they were no Billy Wilder films. Sorry. Anticlimax."

But it was at that moment Granny Mel cracked a horrible grin, like a prune giving birth to the Cheshire Cat. "That's it, Randy! This is all a frame-up." She turned that incredibly scary face to the sky, stretching her arms overhead like she was calling down lightning. "Hear me, Justice! The jig is up! Olly, olly oxen free!"

The street around us hazed pale and winked out, just like in the parade video. The only thing still in sharp focus was one, amazing girl, coming toward us in a gauzy yellow gown.

Wavy, black hair floated under its own breeze. Glossy lips pouted, manga red. She wore a windshield of tinted shades that would make me look like a praying mantis. I did find myself praying for a sudden downpour, however, as every unimpeded curve swayed beneath ridiculously thin fabric. I decided my Xena and Whedon-girl fantasies were merely the tasteless infatuations of youth.

"How was vacation, Justice?" Granny Mel asked.

Lifting the hem of her gown, the goddess revealed a pale foot with white wads between the toes, freshly-pedicured nails as red as her lips.

As crimson as the arterial spray when she pierces my heart beneath the stilettos of her gorgeous contempt.

"Randy, do you realize you're speaking aloud?" Granny Mel drew everyone's attention back to herself by knuckle-rapping the Great Seal's intact plaster goddess. "I see *Liberty* didn't take a powder, did she? Maybe that's why the saying goes 'liberty means responsibility.'" She cocked her fuzzy gray head like she was listening. "Who's being catty? You bailed!"

The other two guys seemed to be included in the conversation, satisfied to hang out in this weird bubble-cloud and let Granny Mel duke it out as their spokesperson. Hearing no voice except the ancient one's, I felt left out.

"But you didn't exactly hire temps, did you?" she continued. "Your playing hooky created an instant vacuum of justice… Yes, I *do* think every woman deserves to feel pampered occasionally, but… Oh, yeah? Well, I got shrunken like an apple head and stuffed into a Marple-shaped hole in the universe!"

"Marple's a funny word," I said. Granny Mel glared at me. "Sorry to interrupt, but I'm still trying to understand what you're talking about. Plus, I'm blanking on the movie you're from."

"They're mostly novels, Randy, except for programs on PBS." I shuddered and winced. "Agatha Christie's detective lives in *books*."

Now, that was horrible. But I thought I was getting the picture.

"So, when the goddess ditched her role for a mani-pedi, the unmet need for justice sucked in whoever was closest to fill the job? And, since you don't watch movies, your pathetic subconscious had precisely *zero* cool crime-fighting identities to work with. Oh man, if only you read comic books, you could've mutated into something awesome!"

At my explanation, Justice's ivory shoulder raised with the tiniest of acknowledgments. That scintilla of remorse made me want to weep forever.

Granny Mel concurred with another assertion I couldn't hear. "…but what about the serious crimes that didn't get handled, because we didn't know we were supposed to be covering for you? Can you fix them all?"

The glistening cherry lips quirked. Justice drew the bad-ass shades down her nose like she had her own television series.

Shark's eyes swirled metallic black.

Oil slicks.

Galaxies.

In that endless moment of awful, I felt like I'd been smeared onto a glass slide. Everything I'd ever done or thought about doing was inspected and dissected from the inside out. Justice wears her blindfold as a mercy.

As fast as that, the fish-faced guy paunched back into the parade video's bald guy in a golf shirt. Chan was transformed back into a model for hair gel. Out of habit, I looked downward for the withered gnome to find she'd gained height and lost years. The woman beside me was a real Melanie.

"One last question?" asked the rejuvenated Melanie in a whiskey voice straight from the Bronx, not Buckingham Palace. "Why today, on the quas-qui thing, and why right here, of all places, did you get the uncontrollable impulse to go AWOL?"

Justice didn't seem to reply, but before she concealed her all-knowing orbs, they flicked toward the library. I'd swear it in court.

Melanie moved between Chan and Keyes, her arms bridging their shoulders. "Gentlemen, might we arrange to give Justice a spa day every so often to avoid such mayhem in the future?"

The goddess bounced up and down, clapping her hands in delight. I nearly had an aneurysm.

No one had asked whether I was available, but Chan and Keyes agreed like bobble-heads. The new J-league members leaned together, best buddies, hands-in. I felt totally disposable.

The goddess sashayed away, scented like the best fabric softener ever. I decided watching her shimmy up the canal's railing was more than adequate recompense for my inconvenience. She positioned herself across the plaster, and then…

The Great Seal of New York was perfect again.

The cityscape cleared and regained its crisp edges.

Part of the surreal magic, I guess, but none of the suddenly visible passersby even slowed their strollers or texting to notice. Except for capturing two wobbly guys in fedoras, none of my video survived.

For all of this, I blame Joanna.

It was her doing that placed the uneasy contents of the Morbid Anatomy Library in their dangerous hinterland between hoax and science, industry and art, history and modernity, water and land. Where nothing's clearly defined, anything goes. That's what happened Saturday.

For an orange soda, I'll tell you about Sunday.

*

Clare Toohey was educated in studio art and music, but often buys her greeting cards and plays the ukulele poorly. Unnatural curiosity is her main qualification for working in laboratories, restaurants and bars, technology and data companies, financial services, retail and inside sales, adult education, and factory floors; never mind the executive adventures, which might also have benefitted from steel-toed shoes and frequent disinfection. She aspires to hack-dom, and hopes this story is a step forward. Online, she's clare2e and blogs at Women of Mystery (.net)

Only People Kill People
by Laura K. Curtis

For eight years, it was my honor to serve and protect Sam Bradley, his family, and his employers. Sam took care of me, and I took care of him. He kept me clean and dry and safe. Every morning, he would take me out, check to be sure I was in good shape, and snap me into a leather holster beneath his jacket. Then, he would kiss Consuela and the children, take the bagged lunch she had prepared, and head out.

Sam and I worked at Goldmark Jewelers, in the diamond district of New York City, where most of what glitters is compressed carbon and the rest is platinum. We would take the subway down from our Harlem apartment, stopping on the way for coffee and a bagel with cream cheese from the deli near the station. The subway was always crowded, but even with all the jostling, I remained secure in my leather case, Sam's jacket tightly buttoned so that no one could see me.

At work, Sam unbuttoned his jacket, unsnapped my holster, and stayed by the door, letting people in and out. Often, shoppers eyed us nervously, even though we were there to keep them safe. As long as the shop remained open, Sam stood guard. Even at lunch time, he ate in a back room, keeping an eye on security monitors.

In the evening, Sam and I would ride back uptown with the crowds of commuters. Sometimes, we'd stop at a supermarket or deli, but most nights we went straight back to the apartment, where I would be locked up once again.

Week in and week out, very little changed. Occasionally, on weekends, Sam would take me out to a firing range and practice. Not that he needed to be such a good shot in the close confines of Goldmark Jewelers, but he was conscientious.

One weekend, Sam had to work because the store had a big sale. He told Consuela he wouldn't be home much, so she decided to take the children to visit her parents in New Jersey. She made him two casseroles for dinner while they were gone. There was a lot of teasing and tickling that morning before we left for work, and when we got home the house was unbearably quiet.

Sam flopped onto the couch with his feet up on the coffee table, a habit I'd often heard Consuela nag about. He unstrapped my holster and laid me next to a pile of decorating magazines, quite a different view than the usual gun safe. Using a worn remote control, he began flipping channels on the television. Before he could settle on one, the phone rang, and he levered himself up with a groan and headed into the kitchen.

"Sure," I heard him say over the voice of a woman confessing something to television detectives. "Come on up."

A few minutes later, the buzzer rang, and Sam pressed the intercom button to open the downstairs door.

"Hey, Sammy." The guy at the door was skinny, looked shifty. Even his smile flickered on and off like Sam's old television did before it went dark forever. But Sam welcomed him with a slap on the back and his usual broad grin.

"Where you been, Tommy-boy?"

"Here and there." The man shrugged. "Consuela and the kids not home?"

"Nope. Jersey, visiting her folks. I managed to dodge that bullet by having to work this weekend. Can I get you a beer?"

"Yeah, sure, that would be great." Sam stepped back into the kitchen, and the man eyed me for a minute, before settling on the couch right by where Sam had placed my holster.

"So," Sam said, taking a spot on the couch, popping a beer for himself and one for Tommy, "what brings you by?"

"I need to borrow some money."

Sam sighed. "You know I can't lend you any more. Consuela would kill me. I thought you were in Gamblers Anonymous."

"I was. I am. I wasn't really gambling. It was just a couple little poker games."

"Right. And how much do you owe?"

Tommy mumbled something.

"What?"

"Nine grand."

"Nine thousand dollars? Jeez, Tommy. If I wanted to lend you that, I couldn't. I don't have that kind of cash."

"Your bosses do. Hell, one little diamond from Goldmark would cover my debts and then some."

"What are you talking about?"

"They trust you. There must be times no one is watching you, times when they leave the stuff in the back room or whatever."

"No, there aren't. Mr. Janowicz is careful to put the diamonds in the vault whenever the store isn't open."

"So, trip or something while he's laying them in the displays. Make a mess and swallow one or two while helping clean up."

"It doesn't work that way." Sam shook his head, and little wrinkles formed around his eyes.

"Sammy, these guys, they're going to kill me. I'm telling you, I need your help."

Sam stood and began to pace. "I could help you get a loan, maybe. You got anything to put up as collateral?"

"No. And I…I lost my job. That's why I went to the poker games. I just wanted to make enough to get by. And you know if I don't bring in a steady paycheck, Cheryl will leave. You gotta help me, Sammy. You're my only hope."

"I can't. Look. I'll take you to see a guy I know at Midtown North. Maybe they can do something for you in return for you ID'ing the guy running the games or the guy you borrowed from."

"The police? That's your idea of help?"

"Calm down, Tommy," said Sam. "We'll get through this."

"I only have four days! Four fucking days! How are we going to get through it?"

"They only gave you four days?"

"No. They gave me two weeks. But I couldn't come up with it. And I then I saw Goldmark's ad in the paper, and I knew you'd be working this weekend, so I took the chance I could catch you alone. But what good does it do if you won't help?"

"I won't steal for you. I can't."

"You can!" Wildly, Tommy snatched me off the table and wrenched me from my holster. Shaking hands pointed me at Sam. "You just won't! High-and-mighty Sam! So much better than the rest of the family!"

"Jesus, Tommy—" Sam raised his hands to ward Tommy off, but it was too late. In an instant, Tommy pulled the trigger. A harsh yank rather than a smooth squeeze, but with the same result.

Two lives are over: Sam is dead and I have become a killer.

Tommy's hands sweat, shake even more than when he first picked me up. He leans over Sam, who is lying still, so still on the floor, a huge stain spreading across his chest. His fingers clench reactively, and I think he may fire once more, but he does not. Instead, he shakes Sam's body with his free hand.

"Sammy? Sammy! Don't do this to me, man, please. I didn't mean it, Sammy." After a long minute, he stuffs me in the pocket of his windbreaker and takes off. As he runs, I bounce up and down, longing for the security of my leather holster. Everything is foreign and frightening. I have just killed my only friend.

After a few bouncing, bobbing minutes, the air changes and I recognize the gritty, oily humidity of the subway. Tommy's hand settles tightly over me, forcing me deeper into the slick fabric of his jacket pocket. He fears that one of the many bodies pressing around us will discover my presence. If only I had the power to call out and accuse him!

We stay on the train as others leave. The conductor's voice—which I've never been able to make much sense of, and which is even less clear with a clammy hand pressing me into the depths of a pocket—announces stops that have names, not numbers. We have abandoned Manhattan, with its neat grid of comforting, rectangular blocks.

Eventually, Tommy stumbles out of the subway. He climbs a long set of stairs, not releasing his hold on me until we are above ground. His walk slows, but his steps remain jerky. We enter a building and a heavy door slams behind us. Tommy jogs up flight after flight of stairs. When he stops, he is out of breath. Heaving. He hesitates, and then I hear the click and snick of a key in a lock and the creak of an un-oiled hinge.

"What did he say?" The woman's voice is like the hinge, scratchy and metallic. "Is he gonna lend you the cash?"

"No."

"I hope you told him where to get off."

"I... I killed him, Cheryl." He pulls me out and holds me toward the woman. "His gun was lying there on the table. I didn't mean to do it. I was just so pissed."

"And you brought the gun home with you? What kind of fucking moron are you? Never mind. I know what kind of fucking moron you are. Give it here. It's not worth much, but someone will give us a couple bucks for it."

"I thought about that on the way home. Little Joe will take it."

"I said, give it here." He hands me across, and she stuffs me into the waistband of her jeans. I hear a smack, and realize she has hit him.

"Little Joe? That's your idea? Yeah, he'll want it, all right. And he'll use it. And then there'll be a murder in Morrisania with a bullet from the same gun as killed Sam. And who would an upstanding citizen like Sam know living in the south Bronx? Why, his lowlife cousin, Tommy, that's who."

Tommy mumbles something I cannot make out.

"Go take a shower. I'll call a bouncer I know in the meatpacking district. He's always looking for a little extra firepower. That way even if it's used, the damn thing shows up back in Manhattan where it belongs."

Cheryl pulls me out and examines me. Her long, thin fingers are cool and steady as she carries me into a kitchen reeking of old food and desperation. She grabs a cloth off the counter. It is dingy and spotted with unidentifiable stains, and when she rubs it over me, I wish I could shrink away. She is particularly careful to wipe off fingerprints around my trigger.

The sound of water running in another room seems a signal, and she lays me on the table and picks up a portable phone. She pokes her head out of the kitchen to check the hallway before dialing, then taps her foot impatiently until someone picks up on the other end.

"Serge, it's me. Yeah, I know you're working. But I have something for you and I want to get rid of it tonight. Yeah. A nine."

I know she is talking about me, for that is my size, though more accurately I should be called a "point nine."

She walks to the door and checks to be sure Tommy is not nearby.

"I told him I knew a guy who was a bouncer. That's it." She paces as she speaks. "Of course I didn't give him your name! For Christ's sake, d'ya think I'm stupid? I can be there in an hour."

Obviously, an hour is not to Serge's liking, for she huffs angrily at his response. "Why can't I just meet you in the club?" Impatient and nervous, she checks Tommy's whereabouts again while she listens to Serge. "You have a girlfriend, don't you? That's why you don't want anyone to see me." Her voice drops. "I told you I'd leave him. All you have to do is ask. But you never do."

Her voice drops even lower. "Fine. I'll be there. Be sure to have the cash."

She hangs up, puts the phone down next to me, and leaves the room, only to return a minute later with a small purse. She wraps me in the dirty cloth, and I feel her stuff me into the bag. A few minutes later, she calls out goodbye to Tommy. My new receptacle is dark and close, scented with fruit gum and tobacco, but at least this time when the shifting and jerking of the subway begins, I am secure.

When she takes me out at last, shadows surround us. Buildings rise on either side, obscuring the view. Cars pass rapidly, lights flashing past the mouth of the alley, illuminating Cheryl and her companion in strobes. Music pulses nearby.

"Give it here," says the tall man I assume to be Serge. She hands me over.

"It's got a body on it?"

"Yeah, but it's no biggie. Guy's a nobody. Tommy's cousin."

Sam was not a nobody! He was my friend, my protector. But these two don't care.

"Where's the money?" she asks. "I can't go home without it, or he'll know something's up."

He hands her a wad of bills and she begins counting while he checks my magazine. Like Sam's, his calloused hands are practiced in the motions. But they are neither respectful nor attentive.

"Hey," she protests. "There's only a hundred bucks here. We agreed—"

He fires three times, then watches as she sinks to the ground.

"Serge?" She reaches out for him and for a moment I think he's going to help her, but he just leans over and picks up the money she has dropped. He wipes me clean on his black t-shirt, drops me next to her, and walks away.

Night fades into day, and I lie there in the cooling blood of my second victim. A man comes by with a huge black and tan dog. The beast begins to howl before he even gets to the mouth of the alley, and pulls his master towards us as soon as we are in sight.

"Get away from her, Cujo!" The man has his cell phone out, and is trying to make a phone call. "Yeah," he says into the receiver, "I—my dog found a dead body. A woman. Thirteenth just east of Tenth Avenue." He continues to drag the dog away, until I can no longer hear him speaking.

Before long, the alley is filled with cops. A ginger-haired man in a blue jacket with N.Y.C. POLICE CRIME SCENE UNIT on the back picks me up and squints at my registration number. He calls it out to another man, who copies it into a notebook before

Ginger secures me in a cardboard box with plastic zip ties. I wish he would wipe me off. My victim's blood has coated me, and is crusting the grooves in my grip as it begins to dry.

Notebook man is on a radio, and after a minute, his slouching posture straightens and he waves Ginger over. "Hey, Mike, check it out. That gun belongs to a murder victim. Guy was shot to death last night up in Harlem. More 'n likely, same weapon."

"Dumbass," opines Ginger Mike. "Another civvie who shouldn't have a gun."

"Nah. Guy was a security guard. Worked in the diamond district. Needed the gun for work."

"Really?" For the first time, Mike sounds interested. "Any leads? He ever take the diamonds home?" He stares at Cheryl's body as if she might be hiding a stash of precious gems.

"No leads. And no on the diamonds. His bosses took full inventory. Nothing's missing."

"Well, shit." Mike pops my box open and looks at me as if I should explain the puzzle of a gun traveling all over the city to him. I wish I could, but at least I know as soon as they identify Cheryl, they'll connect her to Tommy and him to Sam.

For hours, nothing seems to happen. At last, I am tucked in a box with other paper and plastic bags containing wet and dry evidence and placed in the back of a van. The bags rustle and bounce each time the van hits a pothole. Though I am desperately uncomfortable, I am also relieved: no more evil acts will be required of me.

In the following days and weeks, without Sam's routine or even a window on the sun, I lose all sense of time. I spend most of my time in a cool, dark box along with the rest of the evidence gathered at Cheryl's murder. Occasionally, I am taken out to be swabbed or dusted, but I have no idea how long passes between these brief flashes of light. I am fired three times, and I understand they will be comparing the bullets to those that killed Sam and Cheryl.

In the darkness of my box, I can hear the whispers of others.

They are alternately proud and despairing. Some glory in the destruction they have wrought, numbering their kills in the dozens, but just as many whimper with fear of what the future may bring, and wish to be returned to their owners. Old-timers explain that we will be required to tell our stories in court. For some, once will be enough. Others will testify repeatedly, as their defendants appeal convictions. What happens after that is a mystery.

I have heard stories of a massive warehouse in a place called Queens where all of us go when the testifying is done. Alternate tales tell of giant fires and crucibles where we are melted down. It is all speculation, for no one who has gone to Queens has ever returned, at least as far as the collective memory of the evidence locker is concerned.

I think I would prefer to die immediately, to be melted down, than to live indefinitely with my sins, but I suppose I will find my fate soon enough. It was not only Sam I killed. I betrayed Consuela as well, and the children. She insisted, the day she found herself pregnant, that Sam get in the habit of keeping me in the safe. Did she foresee the terrible things I would do? How will she survive without him? How will the boys grow up without a father? These are the questions that haunt me in the dark.

Whatever happens to me will be no more than I deserve.

*

Laura K. Curtis lives in New York with her husband and three Irish Terriers, which is enough to make anyone occasionally dream of murder. When she's not indulging her bloodlust by writing fatal fantasies, she's playing with fire to create glass beads. She can be found online at http://www.womenofmystery.net.

THE GREENMARKET VIOLINIST
BY TRISS STEIN

We poured out of class buzzing about the complex assignment we had been given. I am as dedicated to pursuing my history degree as anyone—there is a Ph. D somewhere far down the road—but didn't these professors realize we had other courses? And jobs? And families?

My friend didn't care about any of that. She grabbed me and started babbling about the morning drama at her job. She had arrived at the small historical house museum where she worked, where nothing had ever happened in this century, and found an ambulance and cops swarming all over the tiny park.

Even half-listening as I was, I thought it was a crime that made no sense at all. An old man was beaten badly enough to put him in the hospital, late at night in a Brooklyn park. Sadly, not an entirely unknown urban tale. But this park was just a single square block and bordered a busy avenue at one end. There were no hidden leafy glades where evil might lurk. It was just a small playground, the charming colonial stone house behind it and a playing field behind that. And in this once bleak neighborhood, the biggest daytime danger now was a collision with an SUV-sized baby stroller. The only nighttime gangs were crowds of office-casual young people leaving the chic bars and restaurants.

I wasn't really listening. Then she mentioned the empty violin case they found on the ground.

~

The first time I saw him at the friendly little farmers' market in the park, he was glaring at the tiny children running and screaming in the playground. Like any New Yorker, I reflexively registered the wild gleam in his eyes and the clothes that might have come from a dumpster, and just as reflexively classified him as someone to avoid.

The second and third and fourth times I saw him, he was wearing a Santa hat and playing a violin. Ok, guess he wasn't as crazy as I thought. In the weeks around Thanksgiving, as the market offerings shrank and segued from fall grapes to wreaths and holiday cookies, he was there every Sunday, playing the same clichéd Christmas tunes over and over. Judging by the violin case full of dollar bills at his feet, quite a few people enjoyed his third or fourth rendition of "Santa Claus is Coming to Town." I wasn't one of them.

Then, one hectic, chilly day, I didn't get there until it was nearly dusk. The only produce, so late in the day and late in the year, was the last of the apples and a few pumpkins. I was disappointed. I had become addicted to this market because of the tomatoes and beans that actually had flavor, the corn as sweet as sugar, the homemade baked goods, and the cheerful interaction with the vendors. The unexpected bit of history was a bonus.

That day, though, I was kicking myself. I'd stolen an hour from the paper that was due tomorrow, for this? A few apples and the last whole grain bread in the entire market? My hands were cold; I had stepped in a puddle and that annoying violin kept on and on, one chorus of "Jingle Bells" after another.

Usually this place was a peaceful retreat in my too-busy life. I'd found it when I decided to reform a lifetime of deli meats and an extensive collection of take-out menus.

There was a giant greenmarket at Grand Army Plaza. I tried it just once and learned I didn't have the time or patience for the locavore frenzy, and the bikes, the dogs, the baby strollers. Even with the huge choice of foods and the location, between the grand and grandiose memorial arch and the lovely entrance to Prospect

Park, one sweaty, claustrophobic visit was enough for me. Here, at this little strip of stands, I could pick up a winter squash, grab the last of the summer tomatoes, sample some homemade chutney, buy a pumpkin pie, and be done in ten minutes.

Sometimes, I could even steal a few extra mental health minutes to sit in the playground and enjoy the ecstatic children running under the spray on hot days. I would give a moment to the young soldiers who died right here in 1776, losing the Battle of Brooklyn as part of Washington's brave, rag-tag army. I could look over the sweet, old-fashioned herb garden surrounding the stone house, refresh my memory of the modest exhibits on colonial life inside, and see what community programs they offered this weekend.

I also got a kick out of knowing this was a spot sacred to all true Brooklynites. That shuttered Dutch colonial house was, later, the original home of the team that became the Brooklyn Dodgers, and was managed by the original Mr. Ebbets himself. So what if the final layer of history is that the house is a 20th century rebuild from the original stones and plans, a project of city planning czar Robert Moses? Now, it has become its own piece of history. It all speaks to me, when I have time to listen.

That day, I did not have time. The last of the merchants were breaking down the stalls and I was digging in my purse for warm gloves, when the music in the background finally stopped. I don't think I realized, until I heard the silence, how tempted I was to rip the violin from his hands.

When it started again, it was something different, delicate and precise. And it was soft, barely audible. Was he playing just for himself? The music changed to scattered phrases I almost knew. Was that "I'll Be Seeing You"? Then it became something else, classical again but now full of feeling. I don't know anything about music, but his playing seeped into my tired body and overstressed mind.

I moved closer to hear the muted sounds. His eyes were closed, and he seemed lost in the music. When he stopped, I was so moved I surprised myself—my street smarts must have succumbed to the December cold—by walking right up to him, and saying, "You can play real music. What are you doing here in a Santa hat?"

And to think my family sees me as too impulsive.

He stared at me, unseeing, and then blinked and said slowly, "I play what makes money." He turned away, scooping up the bills from the open violin case on the sidewalk, and packing up the violin. He was done, but I was not.

"That was beautiful. It was—it was like a hot cocoa…it made me feel…better." I stopped, embarrassed. I didn't have the right words. I speak history, not music.

"Can I give you something to say thank you?" I was fumbling in my purse for a stray dollar.

"Next time. Not for me, for my boys." Then, money packed away, violin packed away, Santa hat replaced by a wool cap, he walked away himself.

My boys? He was old, not just elderly, really old. Too old to have children, easily old enough to have grown grandchildren and maybe some great-grand babies.

I caught up with him and said, "I don't have much, but I'd be happy to help your boys. Are they very young?"

"Even the young ones aren't very young. And the old ones are old. Like me."

Then he disappeared down the subway steps.

∼

As soon as I told an officer at the local police precinct that I knew the old man who played a violin in Washington Park, he told me to come right in. On the way, I thought about the last Sunday, when there was almost no produce left to buy.

I really went there to see him. He'd presented me with a mystery; I wanted to solve it. When he took a break, I handed him a Christmas cookie and a cup of hot cider from a vendor, dropped several bills in his case and said "Tell me about your boys."

He looked surprised. Did he even remember me? I wasn't

sure, but at least he wasn't glaring. Finally he said, "I take the money over to Fort Hamilton. The VA hospital. Holidays are hard for them. My way to help." His words were slow, as if he didn't talk much.

He moved away as he picked up his instrument, but I said, quickly, "So you were in the Army?"

"Hell, no. Navy." His expression softened just slightly. "I discovered this park when I was at the Navy Yard. Before I shipped out. Not many of us left now, and less who can still get out and make a buck."

My eyelids pricked.

"My granddad used to tell me how he helped build the battleship Missouri there, at the Yard." I swallowed. "He's gone now."

"Like I said…"

"You can really play."

"I used to be able to play some. Stiff fingers now." He paused and then said, softly, "Navy gave me that, my chance to go to music school. After."

The few words merged in my mind with grandpa's stories and what I knew myself, and I had a picture of Brooklyn as it was during World War II, when these very blocks were filled with boarding houses for the 70,000 or so Navy Yard workers streaming into town and the city was humming again, round the clock, after the despondency of the Great Depression.

I tell my students history is happening all around us. This strange derelict of a man was a living time machine.

⁓

At the precinct, an officer showed me a photo of the man they found, and even with the terrible bruising, I could see he was my mystery man. His wallet was gone, and his violin, but they had a possible ID. The abandoned violin case had a rusty, ancient nameplate in it. Jacob Willard. They were looking for more information on him.

And they were interested when I told them he was at the Greenmarket every week and about his connection with the VA hospital. They were already canvassing the neighborhood for witnesses, and now they had more places to ask questions, but the next market day was four days off. What was he doing there, I wondered, on a weekday? In the middle of a cold night?

"Does he have any family?"

"Not that we've found. We're looking. Hospital's supposed to let us know if he has any visitors."

"Can I visit him?"

The two officers glanced at each other and one said, "No reason you can't, if he's up to it. But you'll let us know if he says anything at all, okay?"

The nurse on the phone said he had moments of consciousness, and I could visit briefly. I knew I would have to make that tedious trek to the trauma hospital in spite of the responsibilities pulling me in all directions. Somehow, he had become my project. I wanted to hear the rest of his story, just as I'd wanted to hear my grandpa's.

After twenty minutes trying to find my through the maze of color-coded corridors, I was finally in the right department. The nurse at the desk said, "Are you family?" When I said no, just a friend, she said, "Poor guy! He's had no visitors except cops." She pointed down the hall toward his room and added, "Just stay a few minutes. And be prepared—he looks pretty bad."

That was an understatement. He was asleep or unconscious, attached to machines, with purple bruises on his face, and bandages on his head and hands. His hands. Oh, God. His hands. He was a violinist.

He began to stir. His eyes fluttered a little, opened then closed again. He croaked out something that I finally understood to be water.

With my help, he sipped from a cup with a flexible straw, stopped, sipped some more. He squinted at me and croaked out "Who you?"

"I heard you were hurt. I know you from the Greenmarket at Washington Park."

He squinted some more, and then said, "Girl...questions."

I'm hardly a girl, but I smiled, and took a chance that touching his arm was not overstepping a boundary. "That's me. The lady with questions."

"No questions. More water."

I said, gently, "EMS found you. You were hurt. They're trying to find out what happened to you."

Tears trickled out from under his eyes. "Met a girl there. All those years ago. Prettiest girl in Brooklyn...prettier than Iowa girls..." Then he seemed to fall asleep again. A nurse came in to check his machines and told me it was time for me to leave.

The police officers were not too excited by what he'd said, but they told me they had confirmed his identity and had an address. When I promised I wouldn't interfere with the investigation—I would stick to some public record searching—they gave it to me.

I assumed he was homeless, or at best, expected his address would be in a low-income project, or in one of Brooklyn's most distressed neighborhoods, the kind of run-down, illegal multiple-residence that a man with almost no income could manage.

Imagine my surprise to see he lived at a well-known, modest, but highly-respectable co-op complex in downtown Brooklyn under the shadow of the Manhattan Bridge. Hmm. Not a derelict then, in spite of his frightening clothing.

I knew very well how to find the paper trail, but it would not be fast or easy. Those lucky folks on *History Detectives* have a lot more time and funding than I did.

I went straight to a source for basic military records. Yes, there he was. His draft record showed he'd lived in Iowa. I wondered if he joined the Navy because he longed to see an ocean. More detailed records existed, but I couldn't get them today.

The Social Security records I needed are closed to the public. The mid-century editions of the late, great local newspaper, *The Brooklyn Daily Eagle*, are digitized only in an oddball source. I took a deep breath and prepared to struggle, and—aha!—my patient looking paid off. There it was: a blurry wedding photo, the bride in a street dress and veiled hat, and the groom in a Navy uniform. Ensign Jacob Willard of Ames, Iowa to Mary Pat Tierney of Brooklyn, at St. Augustine, 1944, with a reception in the church social hall.

St. Augustine's is still there, just a few blocks away from where I sat. She must have been a neighborhood girl. Was she that prettiest girl in Brooklyn? The one he met in the park?

I couldn't find his name again, so I tried a long shot and went into the online archives of the *New York Times*. And hit pay dirt. He was mentioned in an article from 1990 about a wave of retirement at the New York Philharmonic. He had been in the violin section for 35 years.

Yes, I guess he could play some. Now I had the man's life in the blurry pages I was printing off the computer screen. I'm not a detective who solves crimes, but I am a kind of detective.

I called the crime-solving detective and told him what I found.

～

This was the week before Christmas. Chilly winter air, with the moisture off the harbor cutting right through winter clothes, and it was already dark as people left their offices. Much as I wanted to be home, with hot soup or a warming glass of Scotch, I impulsively left the bus many blocks away, where it stopped right in front of the playground. I sat on a bench in the cold dark, thinking about Jacob Willard and wondering why he had been sitting there, uncomfortably, so late at night. Through the dark, I heard a crying child insisting from the bordering sidewalk, "Playground now! *Now!*" and an exasperated parent saying, "It's too cold. We are going home *now!*"

Then it was silent, except for the constant murmur of traffic coming from the avenue.

No one at all was in the playground itself. The stone house was closed, windows covered by immense red colonial shutters. It was too cold to sit still, so I walked around the park. I could not have said what I was looking for. I was just looking. I found the playing field behind the house was dark and empty. No one was there, in the park or on the adjoining sidewalks. I shivered.

There were no answers—what had I been expecting?—and it was time to go home myself.

My eye was caught by light from a street lamp reflecting off a shiny jacket. Then I saw them: two teens or young men, in dark pants, bulky black winter parkas, black caps. I looked harder while stepping deeper into the shadows under a tree.

They moved furtively, trying to stay in the shadow of the building. I could barely see them, but I could hear them more clearly than they would have wanted. Their voices were weirdly loud and excited; I was sure they were high on something.

"This time we get in, get stuff to sell. Always stuff to sell in a museum, right? Try not to do anything stupid this time."

"Shut the fuck up. Hey! I need that thing. Not that one—*that* one! Now, come on," he said to the tool, "just let's get this blade in. Right. Here."

My street-smart brain told me to leave right now, immediately, but I was not sure I could without attracting their notice. And the real truth is that my curiosity got the better of my brain and glued my feet to the spot.

I caught a clanking sound and the gleam of metal. Not a gun. Tools. They were under a window at the back of the museum, furthest from any sidewalk. They were wrestling with those wooden shutters.

My mind whirled with a jumble of thoughts. I was scared, sure, but also outraged—they were robbing a tiny, struggling, history museum—and puzzled. Why were they robbing such a modest place, where the only value was the history? There was no priceless art or jewels.

I looked for the nearest park entrance. On the street, in the light, up on the busy avenue, I could call 911.

They fumbled, cursed, worked on the window frame. One of them said, "That old guy, ya know, ya didn't need to go apeshit like that."

"Me? *Me?* He was the one... Hold it, yeah, give me an extra hand here..."

I should go around to the other side of the building. As soon as I turned that corner, they would not be able to see me, and I could slip out the gate, up the dark block next to school and to the safety of open stores and restaurants.

A clanging sound and a stream of curses. Someone had dropped a heavy tool on a toe.

More curses, but this time, the curser was looking at me. I froze, willing myself to be invisible.

He punched his companion, who looked up, and now they were both walking towards me.

I walked away briskly, acting as if I had not seen them and was just going about my business. I heard them running up behind me and knew they did not buy it.

I ran. Who knew I could run this fast? Fear had completely overcome curiosity. I was far from an entrance, but here, there was only low, stone wall dividing the park from the sidewalk. I could scramble over it easily. I could leap it if I had to.

I passed a trash can at the edge of the patch, and slammed my arm into it without stopping, in some panicked hope that it would crash onto the walk and slow them down.

I was running so fast, and breathing so hard, I wasn't even sure if I heard it hit the ground. I headed for the avenue, and lights, and safety, afraid to stop to make a call, and burst into the sleek bar on the corner. Lungs burning, I gasped out to the bartender, "911. Right now!"

~

The cops eventually found them. The tools were left behind and identified. Someone else had seen them running. They were, in the end, not so hard to track down. As the nice detective told me, most criminals are actually pretty dumb. I will probably have to testify at a trial eventually.

I went to see Jacob a few times, and sometimes, I would catch him when he was fully there.

Bit by bit, he told me all about the pretty girl he met ice skating in Washington Park, introduced by a Navy buddy who knew her from their block. The hurry-up wartime wedding. The ecstatic few weeks they had before he shipped out. The cold-water tenement they shared while he was at Julliard. All the long happy years when he made music and she made their life.

I could read between the lines to see what happened when she died. There were no children, old friends were dying, she was the sociable one. I guessed that days went by when he did not talk to a single soul.

The night he was attacked was their anniversary. He was sitting there all alone, remembering, feeling her presence in the place where they had met, and he went into a blind rage when some young thugs tried to hurt that place. It felt like sacrilege.

I made him a book, a kind of scrapbook with his own words typed up, printouts of his draft record, the newspaper stories, and old photos of the park. He was fully awake the day I brought it over, and he could not get over seeing his memories made tangible on paper. It seemed to bring out a flood of stories, and when he drifted off he was holding the book and murmuring, "We are… still here…remembered…in here."

He passed away a few days later, sitting up in bed with the book open to his wedding picture.

And I do remember.

*

Triss Stein is thrilled to be included in the newest New York Sisters in Crime chapter anthology and thought it fun to write about her own Brooklyn neighborhood. She has published two mystery novels, *Murder at the Class Reunion* and *Digging Up Death,* as well as a short story in *Murder New York Style.* Triss is presently working on a new series about Brooklyn neighborhoods, featuring an amateur sleuth who is a historian and mother. She describes it as "urban cozy." Triss is currently chairing the national Sisters in Crime/Bowker survey analyzing mystery readership.

THE UNDERSTUDY
BY LOIS KARLIN

They met at a Talking Heads concert at CBGB, both of them five-foot-eight with hazel eyes that connected above the crowd. Colleen Morgan and Jenna Strickland were skinny brunettes, hair spiked with wax. Funny how lookalikes found each other. Funny how wealthy Jenna-from-Greenwich wanted to hang with a stray from Pittsburgh.

It was '78 and they were twenty-four, living in a squat on Avenue C. The neighborhood people couldn't tell them apart. Colleen thought Jenna was prettier, lips full and eyes outlined, but the two of them were close enough to mess with peoples' heads.

They shared Alphabet City with junkies and artists who came for the same reason they had: to live cheap in a place the rest of the world had forgotten. Neither of them minded the rusted appliances and stripped cars that lined the streets, or the burned-out tenements. As near as Colleen could figure, Jenna stuck around convinced that Alphabet City was the way to the writer's life, and that someday Joey Ramone would return her love.

But Jenna hadn't expected to be leashed to a dealer. Even though she admitted the junk settled her crazy moods, she resented Colleen for getting her hooked. She took out her anger by pulling rank, treated her low-class friend like scum, rubbed salt into a wound that envy had opened. When Colleen couldn't take the abuse, she disappeared until Jenna came begging, coaxing her back to the seedy digs they shared.

Colleen taught Jenna to use her wits on the street. Street-smart meant blending in with the neighborhood, keeping the corner boys in business. Once, outside a record store, Colleen saved Jenna's ass when a couple of creeps tried to toss her. She took care of one with a plank she found on the curb and kneed the other in the balls. After that, the girls were accepted in the neighborhood, and Jenna followed Colleen's lead. To get money they operated as a team, working Bloomingdale's and Saks grabbing wallets, perfume, jewelry they could sell on the streets. They pulled scams on Wall Street junkies, cleaned out pockets, ripped off credit cards.

Jenna's parents had divorced when she was little, and her half sister Margaux—her mother's kid from a second marriage—grew up on the West coast. Jenna was raised in Connecticut by a father she hardly ever saw. Colleen thought it was kind of pathetic how Jenna combed the society pages for events at the Met where her father was a member of the Board. One paper showed him stepping out of a limo, arm around a woman not much older than Jenna. Colleen would have killed for the woman's sleeveless satin.

Colleen pegged Jenna's father as a major-league con artist cashing in on investment fraud. She found herself admiring him, and didn't really get why Jenna had walked away from all that money. Jenna never even went to visit her sister when the society pages reported their mother's death. If her father tried to find her, he didn't try hard enough. But Jenna never gave up the notion he wanted her back.

"He'd take me in, if I cleaned up," she insisted, lifting the pointed chin that matched Colleen's, intent on the lie she was telling herself.

Colleen rolled her eyes. "Ever try getting off smack?"

Jenna crossed the room and gave her what amounted to a kick. "Why the hell couldn't you leave me where you found me?"

When Jenna was in a mood like that, she would go on a tear through the cruddy room they shared. When it was over she'd collapse, get that haunted look in her eyes, curl around Colleen, tell her she was all she had in the world.

Colleen was always scared that Jenna would go back to the

father she hated or the girls from Vassar she used to hang with. Colleen depended on pretty, once-rich Jenna. More, maybe, than Jenna depended on her.

~

Shit-head ten-year-olds with sticks were shoving junkies into line behind a bricked-up building. Heroin sold at a premium there because the nearby fire department was handy for drug overdoses. Colleen was turning into the alley when she spotted guys with FDNY across their shirts working on boys who'd overdosed. When spotters on the roof shouted, "Puerco. Pigs," she looked frantically for Jenna among the scattering druggies, then took off alone, her fist full of unspent twenties.

She would have tried to stop Jenna. She would have told her take it easy with such a strong batch. When she came back to the building ten minutes later, Jenna was limp on the concrete, the strap still around her arm. Colleen watched the kids drop their sticks, followed them as they carried Jenna up the alley and down the block, dumping her in front of the firehouse door.

Colleen hid in a stairwell that smelled like urine, trying to stop the shakes. She watched through an iron railing, while a fireman in unlaced boots worked on Jenna, pushed on her chest, gave her mouth-to-mouth. He shouted to someone in the firehouse, and then it was the two of them watching her, faces grim, sirens threading through the streets. Colleen stayed long enough to know Jenna was gone.

She left Avenue C a week after Jenna died, when their tenement went up in flames. She swung Jenna's duffle over her shoulder and walked across the Williamsburg Bridge, leaving Alphabet City and her own name in the ashes. She was in and out of a Brooklyn rehab. It took a year and a half before she finally got clean, and counselors helped her get a job washing dishes. She would have started again with the scams, but she'd lost her nerve. She needed look-alike Jenna.

She stayed on in Brooklyn, companion to an Italian lady in a gloomy house with small windows and big furniture. She supplemented her income by pawning a couple of the old lady's rings. The woman had no family, and nobody noticed or cared what Colleen took. She had a plan, and forced herself to be patient.

She forged references, watched for ads in the papers, and in '84, got her first job as a housesitter. She was nervous moving back to the Lower East Side, trading the relative security of the Brooklyn neighborhood for an artist's loft on Bowery and Rivington. The old industrial building—skid row with a touch of whitewash—was a little too close to Alphabet City for comfort. But the loft itself blew her mind.

The three thousand square-foot space was lined with wide, arched windows. Light flooded the rooms on three sides, the ceiling supported by cast-iron columns. The rent-controlled loft was paid for by a sculptor who spent winters in Santa Fe. Colleen was well paid to maintain the place, babysit her landlady's expensive artwork, and feed the squirrels on the fire escape, for God's sake. Jenna would have wigged out over the tile bathrooms and twenty-foot ceilings. Hell, she would have wigged out over the second-hand silk around Colleen's neck.

Colleen kept to herself. Over the years, she had got to listening to a voice in her head, the one that said *trust me*. She knew it was Jenna talking. Jenna telling her to take care of herself. With makeup, the furrows in Colleen's face relaxed. Her skin drank up water and the cream she smoothed in using her landlady's lighted mirror.

She was moving up, but at first, it wasn't about the money. She just wanted to *be* Jenna. She tried to talk like Jenna, dressed in Jenna's clothes. She realized she'd been acting the role since Jenna died.

Colleen was crossing the Bowery in the early winter dark. Steel gates covered every storefront, and the broad street was nearly vacant. A bum whistled and waved a bottle, and his foul odor greeted her as she steered away from his legs. He wore a filthy sweatshirt and a big, leather cap, visor and ear flaps pulled down around his face. She didn't think he was one of the flophouse regulars who forked over a few bucks a night for a cubicle with a chicken-wire ceiling. She tried to make out his face under the cap, but he kept turning his head. When she crossed Rivington he crossed behind her, against the light.

Never show them where you live. She stepped into the lighted interior of Marie's Deli, and nodded to the graying Puerto Rican man behind the counter. She paid for a lottery ticket and the *New York Post*, stood awhile by the bodega's glass door then went back out into the night.

The bum was behind her, face in shadow, as she fumbled with her building's lock. She shoved and bolted the door against his boot, then waited, shivering, for the keyed elevator to stop a few inches above the lobby. When she reached the sixth-floor loft, she stood outside the elevator and let her heart slow down.

No feet on the staircase. No sound from the rear fire escape.

She bolted every one of her security locks, hung her coat, and pulled off her high boots. She glanced at the newspaper's headlines. The year's projected $180 billion deficit was a meaningless number, but she was sort of sorry to learn that subway vigilante Bernie Goetz had been arrested. She was about to toss the paper onto her landlady's Bauhaus table when she caught a full-page obit with the name Strickland. The page was full of photos of Jenna's newly deceased father, his late wife, and her daughter Margaux—and Jenna herself, presumed dead.

According to the paper, when Jenna disappeared in '78 the Stricklands had pulled out all the stops, fearing she had run off to join the Moonies or Jim Jones' Peoples Temple. After so many years, Colleen read, the family had come to terms with its grief.

Dear God. Her luck turned, at last.

She pulled Jenna's duffle bag out of the closet. The poems and letters were still inside, carbon-copied, as if one day Jenna expected to be famous. She pored over the journals, recalling details about Jenna's friends and relatives.

She deserved some of the Strickland money, and she planned to go after it the only way she knew how; the same way the two lookalikes had survived Alphabet City. If the family challenged her, Colleen would explain any memory gaps by confessing to the drugs. Dope had damaged her brain. The lawyers wouldn't find anything crooked so long as no fingerprints of Jenna existed, and she saw no reason they would.

With a calligraphy pen filled with purple ink, she practiced Jenna's script, not for the first time, copying the irregular loops and noting again the crazy mood changes reflected in Jenna's penmanship. She tried to think what to say. "I'm Jenna. I read about my father's death. I would like to meet with Margaux." She sealed the envelope then changed out of her jeans. She shut off the lights and stood at the window long enough to make sure the bum was gone.

She took the staircase and let herself out the building's back exit. A cab took her uptown for a glass of champagne worthy of her victory. She craved light and music, but the bar's crowd gave her the creeps. The voice in her head told her get out of here, and she splurged again on a cab, spending a little more of the fortune she could almost taste. On the way home, she planned her new life. She'd rent one of the luxury lofts in Soho, fill it with elegant Japanese furniture and real art.

Colleen spent the weekend noting every detail she could remember about Jenna. The constellations Jenna glued to her bedroom ceiling and the blue streak she put in her best friend's hair. The Opium perfume her mother wore. The joint trips to the islands that lasted until Jenna was fourteen. Her father's three Afghan hounds.

Inside Colleen's head, Jenna barked instructions. *Don't slouch, wear your hair up, wind the landlady's pearls through a scarf. Cross your ankles and rest a hand in your palm. Don't forget St. Martins where little Margaux nearly drowned.*

The call came on Monday, an invitation to meet for lunch uptown with Margaux and the family lawyer. Colleen hardly slept that night, afraid she'd be expected to order off the menu in French.

On Tuesday, she was ready. She downed one of her landlady's valiums to ward off a panic attack, and carried Jenna Strickland's birth certificate and the driver's license Colleen had renewed with her own picture. When she saw the creep get up off the sidewalk to trail her, she ran down the subway stairs and ducked into a train.

Colleen snuck a look at the restaurant's tiered mezzanine, then turned her attention to fifteen-year-old Margaux. Other than being model-thin, the kid looked nothing like Jenna. It wasn't just her coloring or the sweater dress straight off the cover of *Elle*. It was the confident way she moved, swinging her hair to show off the diamonds she wore in her ears. Before they sat down, Colleen endured Margaux's hug and double air-kiss.

"I can't believe I have you back," Margaux said, tearing up the way Jenna used to.

"Me too, baby." Colleen had rehearsed Jenna's favorite endearment. "You're all grown up." She tucked a strand of Margaux's silver-blonde hair behind the girl's ear. Just the right touch.

She greeted Stuart Whitmore, the lawyer, an older man with a receding hairline. He offered a hand, and his brief examination of her chipped nail polish mortified Colleen. What a telling lack of class. Unnerved and groping for conversation, she asked Margaux about their mother's illness, and apologized for not coming to the funeral.

Margaux tossed off the apology. "I had Nana and the family. Anyway, your father…" Margaux trailed off. "He was supposed to look for you again. I don't know if he really tried."

"I made myself scarce in those days. I was hard to find."

Margaux gave her a doubtful look. "You look thinner. Sad, or something. You're different from before."

Colleen forced a smile. "Well, it's been awhile. I'm just older and wiser." She paused while the waiter placed steaming rolls on their plates. "It's not pretty out there. It gets to you no matter how long you're straight."

"But why didn't you go home?" Margaux reached for her arm, resting a hand there long enough that Colleen's annoyance changed to fascination. Her new sister wore a three-banded diamond ring that quietly said Tiffany's.

Whitmore kept his eye on Colleen. She was grateful that Jenna had taught her which fork to use. She ordered the same meal Whitmore did, minus the cocktail. He laced his conversation with comments only the family would recognize as truth or fiction. Unfortunately for Whitmore, Colleen was good at reading lies. Margaux, who didn't understand the game he was playing, cued Colleen without realizing it.

Only once did a blunder cause Colleen to choke on a forkful of deviled crab. She didn't know Jenna had taken a semester off in her freshman year at Vassar. When Whitmore asked about it she froze, well aware of the alarm on her face. She reached for her water, and Whitmore waived a waiter to the table. In the commotion, she found her wits.

She cleared her throat and set down the glass. "That was when—well, if you must know—I had to get an abortion."

Whitman nodded, apparently satisfied, and sat back in his chair. They began talking trusts and accounts. She and Margaux planned dinners and plays.

The three of them left the restaurant together. When Whitmore handed her into a cab headed downtown, Colleen waved her fingers and watched her new little sister cross the street. Her heart nearly failed when she caught sight of her stalker. He must have caught the train she'd taken to the restaurant.

He set off after Margaux with a sure stride. His shuffle was gone. Off the junk? She watched with relief when Margaux climbed unmolested into a cab and shut the door.

She was afraid to go home. There wasn't a person in the city to welcome her, celebrate her good fortune, or advise her in a situation like this. Cops were out of the question. When the cab stalled in traffic, she paid the driver and took the subway to Chinatown to prowl her regular haunts. She wondered whether the two planets that she and the overindulged Margaux came from were ever likely to converge.

On Canal Street, at an outdoor kiosk, Colleen won a free-for-all for a "Louis Vuitton" handbag, and tossed a wad of cash at the vendor. She was browsing the storefronts for jewelry, high on the thought she'd soon be able to buy what she liked, when she caught sight of stained sweats and an overlarge leather cap reflected in the window. She bolted for a subway entrance, wasting precious minutes finding the platform for the Nassau Street Line. By the time she was through the turnstile, the bum was right behind her.

The cars were almost empty. She moved toward the middle of the train nearest the conductor, trailing him when he changed cars, hearing the strain in her voice when she asked for help.

"Lady, you got one more stop. You want I should call the cops?"

"No cops." She sat down.

Bowery & Delancey was the seediest station in Manhattan. The newsstands and restrooms were long closed, a couple of tracks unused. She'd planned to race up the three-flight staircase, assuming she was in better condition than the junkie chasing her. But he got out near the stairs, and stood with his arms spread, ready to catch her.

She turned, took off at a run toward a closed exit on the south end of the platform, slipped on something foul-smelling, and almost fell. She slung her new bag over a shoulder, and kicked off her shoes, started to shimmy up the fence's vertical rails. Only she wasn't fast enough.

Her foot was within his reach when he caught up, and he was stronger than he looked. She screamed when he pulled her off the fence, and she fell onto unforgiving, filth-encrusted tile. The visor of his cap had slipped sideways and he tossed it to the ground, shaking out a mane of dirty brown hair. Colleen gawked. Hazel eyes. Pointed chin. Wide mouth in a sneer.

Her mouth. Lips that belonged to Jenna.

Colleen screamed again, and Jenna straddled her, a knee on each arm pinning her to the platform. Colleen kicked and bit while Jenna wrestled off one of her coat sleeves then fumbled in her own sweatshirt pocket, pulling out works and a bag.

"Jenna. Christ. I'm clean." Colleen watched the needle in horror as Jenna bent forward to strap her arm. She jammed her knees hard into Jenna's back, but Jenna just clamped her own knees tighter.

"You think I give a shit you're clean? You left me to die," Jenna said.

"What are you talking about? By the time I found you no one could bring you around."

Arms still pinned, Colleen raised her hips to unbalance Jenna, who swore and slapped her face. The second she had one arm free, Colleen aimed her fingers at Jenna's eyes, but Jenna swatted her away like an insect.

"I thought you were dead," Colleen said. "I swear it. I never would have left you."

"You thought I was dead, because you made sure I would be. You sent me to stand in line for a noon delivery way stronger than I could handle. You practically handed me the needle."

"I wasn't anywhere near when you shot up, Jenna. I loved you. I still do."

"You never even tried to find me." Jenna gave the strap a vicious tug.

"Why in God's name would I look for you? You were on your way to the morgue."

It's been years, Colleen thought in dismay. Alive. Had Jenna been right across the bridge?

"So where were *you* all that time?" she demanded, mustering a defense. "How come you never looked for me?"

Jenna's eyes were vague. "Hospital. Detox and mental wards, I couldn't tell you how many. I kept going back on the streets— I need air to write. I need dope to write." She paused. "Anyway, nobody knew if you came out of that fire alive."

"So you never called home? You never told anyone who you were?" *If she could get away, it was dark by the tracks, no one to see.*

"Only you, baby," Jenna said with a smile.

"That first night you followed me…"

"I'll admit it was luck you moved down the street from the Sunshine, but it didn't take a genius to figure out you'd be playing my role. You were fun to watch."

"You knew it was me?"

"How could I miss, asshole? You showed up on the Bowery in my blue fox coat. I trailed you to figure out if that tall chick in the boots with four-inch heels was really you. Then I saw you with Whitmore and Margaux, moving in on my family. Who're they gonna believe? A washed up junkie with no ID, or a slick, fake Jenna Strickland?"

When Jenna pulled a knife, Colleen sank back, her eyes tracking the weapon. "I'll give you everything. Anything. Let me go."

"All I want is my damned ID." Jenna slapped the inside of Colleen's arm, raising the veins Colleen had so carefully nurtured back to health.

"Take it. You can have the bag."

Jenna ignored her. "I've got a sweet mix for you," she said with a smile. "1000 milligrams and a speed ball."

"I don't use anymore. It'll kill me." Colleen heaved against the legs that held her arms like a vice, twisting for a view of the platform. Empty.

"Give it up," Jenna said. "You're the one who taught me to fight, remember?"

Colleen braced her bare heels on the gritty floor and wriggled backward. Jenna lost her balance, and when one of her legs splayed out, Colleen trapped it with a foot. Driving an elbow at Jenna's throat, she rolled her and tried to pry away the knife.

Jenna's grip on the weapon was like iron. Colleen strained away in rage and terror, but the wild-haired junkie only sliced through her shoulder strap and yanked off her bag. Relieved, Colleen scrambled to her feet just as Jenna's blade drew a deep and crooked path down her thigh.

Colleen howled and fell to her knees, clutched a column as if its solid weight would save her. She watched her own blood add color to the black graffiti some street artist had sprayed. Mouth open in horror, she turned her head to watch Jenna come at her.

As the needle bit her vein, Colleen relived the torment of detox. Her crawl out of the nightmare. Her struggle for a real life. And now, wealth within her grasp...

Spinning out, she tried to drag in breath. Her lungs didn't seem to work. Darkness took her as fast as the kick that sent her over the platform. She surfaced briefly when her body hit the tracks. She felt their vibration, but, curiously, no pain.

A laugh sounded, far away.

Blackness, when it swallowed her, was warm and welcome.

*

Copyright © 2011 Lois Karlin

Lois Karlin is a professional writer and educator who writes and publishes computer help systems, web copy, and video training scripts. She blogs with Women of Mystery, and recently taught writing to war veterans through the Orange County Council of Arts. She is currently revising her second novel, speculative fiction set along the Upper Delaware River. "The Understudy" is Karlin's first published short story, inspired by reminiscences told round a neighbor's campfire by seasoned veterans of the FDNY. She lives in New York's Warwick Valley.

MURDER ON THE SIDE STREET
BY STEPHANIE WILSON-FLAHERTY

Summertime, Bay Ridge, Brooklyn.

The view down each avenue includes the steel-gray silhouette of the Verrazano Narrows Bridge. The cuisine has expanded from the traditional pizza places and Chinese food takeout joints to Mexican, Lebanese, and Thai. On the side streets, the Korean women carry umbrellas to guard against the sun, and the Middle Eastern women sweat under their headscarves and *burqas.*

Yep, we've got it all in Bay Ridge. From some pretty classy Italian restaurants that make the grade in Zagats, to Irish pubs with microbrews and decent grub, to basic working-man dives serving Bud and shots, to hookah parlors with curtains in the window to hide whatever it is they actually do in there.

I'm a native, you see, who's rapidly becoming a stranger in her own land. I'm not the latest model; there are quite a few miles on my odometer and, if I have my way, I'm going to clock quite a few more before the engine goes. Got an older, limestone-kind-of-attached house with a floor-through layout. Since I retired, I spend a fair amount of time at the window, watching everybody, being nosy, yelling at the kids when they make too much noise and looking in people's windows.

That's my favorite. I'm sort of like a Peeping Thomasina. But you can call me Sadie. I think there's a song out there somewhere about a Tattooed Lady—you did get the rhyme there, I hope—but for me, no tattoos. Nothing exotic. I'm regular folk with a nosy nature, and I've got a story to tell about the goings-on behind the windows at number 366, down the street a bit and across the way.

So, a year or two back, a moving van pulled up across the street where Old Man Gemenelli lived before he died, and a couple of husky fellows moved in these gigantic pieces of furniture. We're talking huge old mahogany wardrobes and massive brocade sofas. The kind of furniture you don't see any more. Stuff my Granny had. The kind with lace doilies.

Well, that naturally got my curiosity going into high gear. I parked my butt into my front parlor chair, got out my binoculars and settled in until the new neighbor showed up. Mentally, I put my money on a wealthy older woman. Silvery-white hair in a bun, elegant walking stick, flowery dress flowing around her ankles. Of course, I've seen too many old movies, because what I eventually got was an obese slob covered by a circus-tent sized muu-muu in chartreuse, who climbed clumsily out of the back seat of a stretch limo. Her hair was a sickly yellow kind of greasy-gray. It was wiry and coarse, and I could've cut it better with a bowl and hedge clippers. The limo sped away. She leaned heavily on what I recognized as a genuine Irish *shillelagh*, and gasped her way up the six stone steps to her front door.

While there is an eleventh commandment in New York that goes something like "Thou shalt not know thy neighbor," I've never been one for rules, so I was across the street and down the block before she made it inside the house.

"Hi, there. I'm Sadie. Welcome to the neighborhood. Can I help you with anything? Need a cup of sugar? Quart of milk? I would've baked a cake but I didn't know when you were coming."

She leaned on her stick, half turned, and glared at me. Just as if she actually knew that I've never so much as baked a cupcake in my entire life. A lesser woman would've withered under her evil eye, but the not-so-domestic me persevered.

"Okay, okay. A cake would not be such a good idea, I'm sure, as you're probably trying to watch your weight. Did you know they now say that there's more health risks from obesity than smoking? Of course, no one's ever died from second-hand fat. But still, I could've offered you a salad, or maybe carrots. Carrots are good for you and they help your night vision. Did you know that?"

It was as though I had said "open sesame" to her emotional cave. The fire in her eyes tamped down to embers as a rueful, little smile chunked up the fat in her chipmunk cheeks.

"I did know that," she said, a sad note to the words. "About the carrots, I mean. The fat part is not my doing." She glanced upward. "He has made me this way. I used to pray it was different, but now I know from all the doctors that it's not my fault. That leaves Him."

Holy macaroni. I thought I'd heard it all, but this was a new twist in the chubster debate.

That said, I don't do politics or religion. Each to their own on 77th Street.

"Well," I said, "I just live down the block a-ways and across the street." I pointed. "And I wanted to welcome you to the neighborhood."

"I surely do appreciate that, Sadie. You did say Sadie, didn't you?" She waited for my nod. "I'm Margie and I just moved here from Kansas. Wichita, in fact. A great uncle of mine died and left me this place. I have no other family back in Kansas, and I didn't really have any friends, either, so I decided to try life here."

Thank goodness she didn't tell me her name was Dorothy. Poor Margie really wasn't in Kansas anymore. She and I got to be pretty good buddies over time. It turns out that Marge is not the sharpest thorn on the rose. She grew up bullied and picked on. Always chubby and never very bright, she picked up that evil eye business as a defense mechanism to mask one of the sweetest souls I've ever known.

Using the resources Old Man Gemenelli had left her, seems he was actually something like a third cousin, twice removed, Margie signed on with a domestic help agency to hire an aide who could come in a few days a week, shop, cook, do some light cleaning, and polish up the mahogany furniture that had been in Margie's family for generations.

That was how Olga came into the picture. Apparently, Olga emigrated from Russia and lived two neighborhoods away in Bath

Beach where a lot of Russians live. Bath Beach and Brighton Beach are the big ones for the Russians. Interesting people. When I was kid, we were taught to hate and fear them and hide under the desk in case the Big Bomb came. Now, we're taught to hate and fear their Mob. The *Cosa Nostra* of the Black Sea since we don't have so many Italian wise guys any more. The Italian Mob—what's left in New York—has pretty much moved on to greener fields, like Staten Island and New Jersey.

So, Olga was a pretty blonde. Young. Well, younger than Margie and certainly younger than me. It's hard to tell ages these days what with self-help Botox and buy-on-time plastic surgery. She tended to wear these sky-high shoes, thigh-high skirts, low-cut huggy tops, and she carried an enormous satchel-like purse. I understand those things can cost more than a thousand bucks, and much as they might look like Mary Poppins' magic bag, they mostly seemed to tote flat shoes for when the sky-highs hurt too much.

Of course, I always kept my eye on things. I cased the joint on my daily five-mile hike around the 'hood, where I kept up my sources, nosed my way into the shops, and gossiped with anyone who would stand still for five minutes. Then, I sat my butt in the front parlor chair and watched the comings and goings, and occasionally used the binoculars to peek into other parlors and kitchens.

Kitchens were always my favorite. Since I can't cook much myself, I'm endlessly fascinated with those who can. And even though I'm not much for rules, I do have principles. No bedrooms. Never used the binocs for bedroom windows. I'm a busybody, not a voyeur. And, I'll have you know, I happen to have a pretty satisfactory sex life of my own. One day, when we have the time, maybe we'll chat about him. Meanwhile, Olga was keeping company with some shady looking characters. Your basic big, black Lincoln Town Car glided up to the curb when she came out of the house of an evening. The windows were tinted so dark, that even eagle-eyed me couldn't get a glimpse inside. And I'll tell you, it made me *so* frustrated. I just knew that tinted car windows meant trouble.

Which meant it was time for a Plan B, which is what always follows a situation where simply peeping doesn't get me the desired result.

"So, Olga. How's it going these days?" I said one day, real casual-like as she was taking out the trash, and I popped over from across the street. We haven't talked much, but we did have the occasional social conversation.

"Is good," she said in her throaty Boris-and-Natasha-cartoon way. "Margie is good and I make money."

"Yeah," I said with a glance at her feet, "I noticed the new shoes. Must give you, what, six or eight inches more in height? Must make you tower over the new boyfriend."

She looked startled. "New boyfriend? New boyfriend? Why you think new boyfriend?"

"Oh, you know, the guy with the Lincoln Town Car. Picks you up. I assume you go on a date."

"No, no. No date. No boyfriend." She actually looked a little frightened and threw a glance to the left and then the right. "Is brother. Brother comes, takes care of sister."

"Okay, okay," I put a soothing little croon into the words. "It's your brother. That's okay. As a matter of fact, you ought to introduce me to your brother. We could chat about Russia. Just like I chat with you. I love Russians, you know."

Now that was not-so true. I mean, it wasn't exactly false, but it was a stretch. I don't actually judge any nationalities in particular, except for the Irish. I actually do love the Irish. I'm part-Irish, but only a little bit, so that's not it. I haven't really analyzed it but I think it has something to do with beer. On second thought, make that the real thing—you know, something like a Guinness. Dark, malty, room temperature, and sippable. No guzzling your stout. Just build it and sip.

"No, no," she said, louder this time. Then, she dropped her trash bag into the receptacle and slammed down the lid. "No meet brother. He not like people. He not like you. Goodbye now."

She raced up the steps and slammed her way back into the house. So much for that Plan B. Margie appeared then in the front window and waved a happy little wave. She looked much better. Had cleaned up pretty nicely with some time and attention. Even lost a little weight. Not much, mind you. But a little. She said that He had heard a little bit of her prayers. I said to just keep eating more carrots. We each work in our own mysterious ways.

The Lincoln Town Car stopped coming to the house. I noticed that right away, but I was suspicious. Sure enough, after a few days, I had it figured out. My surveillance tracked pretty little Olga as she tripped her way on tottering heels to the far side of Third Avenue where the Town Car picked her up.

So, it was no surprise to me when I heard the news that Olga had been murdered.

Russian Mob. I knew it. Had to be. It made the local paper. She'd worked late one night at Margie's. Left on those tottery high heels in the dark. Had not quite turned the corner onto Third Avenue and was shot.

In the head. Close range.

Some rumors said a mugging. A robbery gone wrong. But she still had the $500 shoes, the $2,000 purse. Her rings. Her Rolex. I mean how does a domestic house aide get the money to buy all that designer trash? Use your noodles, people. It was the Mob. Had to be. So, now Margie had to hire a new domestic house aide. She called the agency, and some girls and some older women came to be interviewed. Margie asked me to help. And after a batch had come and gone, we sat in her kitchen and had tea. I can boil water, you know. I just don't bake.

When the subject of Olga came up, and I don't really remember why it did, all of a sudden, Margie turned a sheepish look on me.

"You know," she said, "you're my best friend in the whole wide world except for Him." She gave that little upward look she does. "And of course, He already knows, but you don't."

"Huh?" I said, really pretty surprised by now. "Know what? What's up, sweetcakes? Something bothering you?"

"No," she said with a serious look and slightly lowered brows. "Nothing is bothering me. I'm perfectly happy. I just wanted to tell you that I shot Olga."

Well, you could just blow me down and roll me into New York Bay. Marge may not have shot either the sheriff or the deputy, but here she was telling me that she had shot our Russky.

"Are you sure?" I asked, and don't remind me about how dumb that is, because, of course, she would have to be sure to say something like that. But I had to ask. I really had trouble believing it. "Yes, I'm sure. He told me it was okay." Little look upward. "And, well, I'm pretty good with a gun. I am from Kansas, you know."

That *really* was the story. Olga was involved with the Mob, but they and she were going to kill our little, okay, not so little, Margie, knowing she was not a rocket scientist and knowing she had money. They were going to break into the house, rob her, and kill her. No witnesses. Apparently, more than one older or disadvantaged person has been targeted by these kinds of thugs. The girlfriends seem to be happy to put up with a little domestic drudgery for the greater gains at the end.

How did Margie know about this plot? She overheard them talking on the cell phone. And our Margie thought it was pretty funny, because she said that people think that dumb means you're deaf. It turns out that Marge was a bit smarter than most of us. I don't have problem with her decision, at all. Okay, folks, read my lips here. That's *at all*. No *problemo*.

I mean, let's face it. This is a Darwinian tale at its finest and its simplest. The strongest will survive.

So, Marge and I are still best buddies, and occasionally we take a stroll where the view down each avenue includes the steel-gray silhouette of the Verrazano Narrows Bridge. And, when there isn't a murder on the side street, Korean women carry umbrellas to guard against the sun, and the Middle Eastern women sweat under their headscarves and *burqas*.

*

Stephanie Wilson-Flaherty has been actively writing for publication since the mid-1990s. As a member of Romance Writers of America, she has a long association with its Mystery Suspense Subchapter and e-published her finalist novel in its Golden Heart Contest's Romantic Suspense division, receiving 4 stars from RT Book Reviews upon its release. Her association with Sisters in Crime began in the later 1990's and more recently, she also joined MWA as her focus has settled into writing mysteries with a humorous touch, set in her native Brooklyn habitat and starring a busybody, older-woman sleuth.

Out of Luck
by Cathi Stoler

In the end, it's desperation that screws you every time. Johnny shook his head, taking in the scene on the crowded sidewalk across the street. Pedestrians streamed by—fat-assed tourists in New York tee shirts and shorts, theatergoers pushing through the crowds to make a curtain, strolling shoppers blocking the way with too many bags—the usual Times Square mob out for some action in The Big Apple on a warm summer night.

Except for the guy. The one he'd passed in the dingy hoodie and filthy jeans skulking along the side of the building trying to hold it together.

Johnny had eyeballed him right away. Early 20s, stringy hair, sallow complexion, twitchy mouth. He looked wired enough to light up the block, hands clenching into tight balls, head bopping up and down, bouncing hard on the balls of his hi-tops. But it was the eyes that were the real tell. They never stopped moving. Back and forth. Up and down Forty-first Street. Man, his eyes were jumping.

If I were a betting man, Johnny told himself, fingering the lucky silver dollar in his pocket, I'd lay odds Rhineman is gonna bust him in the next ten seconds.

Slipping the coin out of his pocket, he tossed it high in the air. Heads, the guy gets busted. Tails, the Uniform had developed tunnel vision, and he walks. Johnny snatched the piece as it spiraled on its downward arc and slapped it on the back of his hand. He waited a beat before he called it. Heads. He smiled. Rhineman had got it right. He'd already cornered the guy and was asking for ID. The guy was fumbling around, patting his pockets, talking up a streak, digging himself in deeper and deeper with every word. The cop waited, face neutral, his right hand resting lightly on the butt of his gun, ready for anything.

Don't worry, bro, Johnny nearly called out, *the guy isn't running.* Nowhere to run to in the new Times Square. Uniforms and Mounteds were everywhere, undercover D's, too, not to mention the security cameras on every street. A "presence," as the Police Commissioner would say, to deter would-be terrorists and make the tourists feel safe. No more porn shops, pimps or pros. But there was still plenty to watch out for—it was in his face every day. No amount of Disneyfication could get rid of all the crime, or drugs, or the con artists and grifters that had had the run of these blocks for more than fifty years.

Johnny had seen enough. Silver dollar safely back in his pocket, he walked west toward Eighth Avenue, checking his watch. He had forty minutes until his meeting with Joey 'Bones' Biscottini. Not nearly enough time to catch a break and come up with what he owed. He was fucked. Big time.

～

Johnny was pacing the length of the coffee shop that fronted onto Fortieth Street and sweating enough to make the polo shirt he was wearing stick to the small roll of fat that was slowly building around his middle. At five-ten and just over one-ninety, he knew he'd have to watch it, especially now that he'd turned forty. Six-pack abs were a fond memory. He pulled the shirt away from his skin and cursed the heat, but the knot in his stomach told him the sweat was coming from somewhere else.

Johnny reached the end of his path, swiveled back and noticed the couple arguing quietly in the mouth of an alleyway a few buildings down. Her head was moving back and forth, shaking a definite *no,* her shoulder-length blonde hair whipping from side to side emphasizing her actions. The guy was holding her by the arms, murmuring softly, his mouth close to her ear, trying to convince her…of what?

Not your business, he reminded himself, an image of Joey

Bones filling his mind and supplanting the one of the couple. Bones, his bookie, was a vertically-challenged bruiser who imagined himself to be a modern-day entrepreneur. Hey, he had a Blackberry that never left his hand and sported a diamond stud to match his pinky ring and sweat suit, didn't he? A guy who had come up from the neighborhood in Little Italy, he had a standard reply when people asked what the Bones meant. "I could tell you, then I'd have to kill you," he'd say with a huge, throaty laugh and a slap on the back at the old line he'd appropriated as his own. Only somehow, Johnny noticed that the person who'd asked the question never laughed along.

He fingered the roll of bills in his pocket tucked up close to his lucky silver dollar. He'd toted it up three times at the apartment, spreading the cash out on the old wooden kitchen table, smoothing each crumpled bill flat with his hand. But no amount of counting could parlay it into more. Eight hundred even. It might as well be Monopoly Money. He was short twelve C notes. Bones was expecting two large tonight and, it was a sure bet that after he heard Johnny's news, he wouldn't go for anything less.

The irony of the situation wasn't lost on Johnny. He was a good customer—horses, baseball, football, Vegas fights. The two grand was just the tip of the iceberg; this week's vig plus what he was shy from last week. Bones had been letting him slide every now and then and Johnny had been making good in other ways; protecting his runners on the street and slipping the Desk Sergeant, Gonzales, some bookie cash to look the other way when one of them got picked up. Gonzales was starting to get twitchy and wanted out. Johnny was going to lose his leverage. He needed to make other arrangements and make them quick. Man, he didn't want to have to tell Bones the deal had gone south. Who knew what the crazy bastard would ask him to do instead.

Johnny swallowed hard and thought about the two muscle heads who bracketed Bones' every move like misplaced parentheses. They'd make sure he delivered, one way or another. His gut clenched tight and the taste of acid filled his mouth. Without the cash, no way was this was going to turn out right.

The voices from the alleyway had risen in pitch and pulled him back. *What the fuck's with those two?* He cut his eyes to the couple. Kansas. He imagined miles and miles of cornfields and long, flat roads as he checked them out. Clean cut, farm-fed, maybe eighteen, or younger. Maybe runaways and a little the worse for wear after landing in the big, bad city. He looked closer. No luggage that he could see. Probably just off the bus at Port Authority with only the clothes on their backs.

The girl was beautiful. The kind of beauty that reached him even from where he stood. It looked natural too, with clear blue eyes and a fresh-scrubbed face that didn't seem to need makeup. She was in jeans and a short-sleeve print blouse, rumpled like she'd slept in them. The guy was okay. Not a stud, but tall and slim, with short brown hair and wide-set brown eyes that skewed a little confused, a little out of his comfort zone. He was in jeans, too. Not that home-boy-crotch-around-the-knees-with-Calvin's-hanging-out-look that made Johnny want to puke. Just regular Levi's with a long-sleeve button-down stripe shirt. Kansas, for sure. Or, could be Indiana, Ohio—one of those places.

The girl caught him staring and tugged on the boyfriend's sleeve. She jutted her chin toward Johnny and looked up at the boy. He shook his head *no,* but she was already moving in Johnny's direction. The boy reached out to pull her back, but she shook him off like rain from an umbrella and walked out of the shelter of the alleyway.

"Shit," Johnny muttered under his breath. "What the fuck!" He started to turn away, but it was too late. The girl had reached him and planted herself in his path. She glanced over her shoulder to see if the boy had followed. He had and sidled up beside her.

"Excuse me, sir," she clutched the handbag she was carrying to her side, "I, um, I'm sorry to bother you but, I…saw you…looking at us." There was no accusation in her words, just a statement of fact. "I, um, hope you can help." Her voice was soft and sweet, younger than he'd thought, and matched the sad look in her eyes.

Johnny couldn't break their hold. Deep blue pools, they drew him in and made him want to swim all the way down, like a sailor lured by a mermaid. A little voice in his head started whispering to him to leave it alone; forget those eyes and think about Bones. No luck with that idea. He couldn't get away from their pleading.

"Yeah, I noticed you over there," he replied a little gruffly, finally rousing himself enough to speak, embarrassed that he'd been caught. "And..." his voice trailed off, not really knowing how to explain why he'd been watching them, "... I figured maybe something was wrong." It sounded lame even to him.

She lowered her head and spoke with a shyness Johnny hadn't heard in a long while. She paused for a moment, gathering her thoughts and concentrating on what to say next. "We, um, have a problem." She lifted her face then, searching his and looking for something Johnny knew she'd never find there.

"Em, we shouldn't do this." The boy squeezed her shoulder and tried to turn her away. "This man's a stranger," he added, his voice wary. Then more apologetically to Johnny, "No offense."

"Stop it, Tyler." She pulled away, not letting her gaze break contact with Johnny's. "I think we can trust him. He was ready to help me when he thought you and I were fighting." She saw the flicker of surprise cross Johnny's face. "Your eyes gave you away," she said with conviction. She turned to look back at the boy and nodded.

"Guess we'll have to." The boy's tone was sullen, a note of warning weaving its way under the simple words.

"Sir,"—Johnny winced at the title he'd always reserved for older men—"my name is Emma and this is my...this is Tyler." She began to tell her story, her voice losing some of its tentativeness as she spoke. "We just arrived in New York from Columbus and...and...we don't know what to do."

Johnny listened intently, now unconsciously looking for the tell that would show the girl was spinning him a tale. The words were spoken in a way that felt real and didn't make him wary. She sounded honest and sincere, but that didn't mean she wasn't trying to play him.

"We found this on the bus." She removed a small piece of paper from her bag and held it out to him gingerly with her fingertips, like a priest offering the host at communion. The boy's hand was back on her shoulder, squeezing harder this time, trying to stop what it was already too late to undo.

Johnny didn't take the paper. He looked down at it fluttering from her long, slim fingers. He could read the printing at the top: it was a New York Lotto ticket. He waited silently for her to continue.

"Shit, Em. Let's go!" The boy's tone had gone from sulky to belligerent. "We'll find someone else. He's not going to help us."

"Tyler!" The girl spat at him angrily. "Watch your mouth." She shook her head and turned back to Johnny. "I'm sorry, sir. He didn't…"

Johnny cut her off. "The name's Johnny, not sir."

"Nice to meet you, Johnny," she replied, then seemed at a loss for what to say next.

Johnny jutted his chin toward the ticket now clutched in her fingers. "Why don't you just tell me what's going on…you know, about your problem." He'd spoken without thinking, involving himself in their shit, the words out of his mouth before he could stop them.

A specter of hope turned the corners of her mouth into a tentative smile. She looked at him eagerly and cleared her throat. "Well, like I said, we just got here from Columbus. This ticket was on one of the seats up front when we were leaving. We tried to find the person who was sitting there. I thought it was an older woman I'd noticed when she went to the restroom. But we were way in the back and by the time we got outside, she was gone." She nodded at the boy, as if to make sure she was remembering things exactly as they happened.

"Inside the station, we passed one of those stores selling newspapers and sodas and stuff. They had a sign out front with the winning numbers and the prize amounts. Well, since we had the ticket we thought we'd check and," she stopped for a moment, choosing her words carefully and spoke more softly, "it's a winner."

She moved the ticket closer to Johnny, unconsciously inviting him to see for himself. *That's luck for you. Right off the bus and they scored.* "Okay," he shrugged, "so what's the big deal? You guys won a few bucks. Just bring it to any place that sells lottery tickets and turn it in. You can probably get your cash right there." He pointed to a bodega across the street where he'd met Bones a few times. He knew they sold lottery tickets to all those suckers who believed that 'dollar and a dream' bull. At least that wasn't one of his vices.

"You got it wrong," said the boy. "It's more than a few bucks. It's worth twenty thousand five hundred and thirty dollars. I don't think they're gonna give us that over there." The boy cut his eyes toward the bodega.

Yeah, right. Johnny would lay five-to-one that they were the ones who'd got it wrong. "You sure about that? Over twenty grand?" he asked, unable to hide the skepticism in his voice.

The girl nodded yes. "It's got five out of the six numbers. See." She stuck the ticket up under his nose as if the numbers would speak out for themselves. This time Johnny took it from her.

Jeez, could this be happening? A hot flash streaked through him, setting his body on fire at the thought of what he could do with that much money. *Pay off Bones and get him off his back until he could replace that piece of shit, Gonzales.* Slow down, he told himself. It's not your ticket.

It had gotten dark while they'd been talking and the streetlights had come on. Johnny held the ticket up toward one of them to see it better, his hand trembling slightly. It looked legit, like every other lotto ticket he'd ever seen. He ran his thumb over the printing and it didn't smudge as if it had been altered. "Well, good for you," he said with bravado, his voice sounding false, even to himself. He hoped they couldn't hear the longing in it. "That's a lot of money but I don't see the problem." He held the ticket out to the boy. "Just bring it down to one of the lottery offices and turn it in. They'll give you a check and you can cash it at the bank."

"We can't," the boy spoke hesitantly, taking the ticket from Johnny and tucking it into his shirt pocket. "We asked the guy at the bus station about getting the money, and he said the same thing that you just told us. Plus, he was sure that you have to be eighteen and have ID and all to claim a big prize."

"So, neither of you can, right?" His first instinct was right: they were underage and probably runaways.

"It's not like we're doing anything wrong," the girl jumped in before Johnny could utter another word, seeming to catch the drift of his thoughts. "We just want to be together and…"

"…And this is a whole lot of money to us," the boy finished for her. "We could sure use it to make a start."

Johnny lifted up his hands in a questioning gesture. "Guys, what exactly do you want from me?"

"Maybe, you could turn in the ticket for us," the girl said softly, those baby blues tugging at him again. "We'd pay you. Really. Even split it with you, if you think that's fair," she added quickly. "We'd just need some money to get us through the next few weeks, or so. We'd trust you to do the right thing."

Are these people for real? Is everyone from out of town so naive? Still, ten thousand had a nice ring to it. Like a long shot at Belmont paying off big time. "I don't know," Johnny shook his head and the girl's face fell. "I'm just some guy you met ten minutes ago. You don't know anything about me. I mean, I could just get the money and you'd never see me again."

"Tyler," her voice rang with an authority that startled Johnny, "I think he's lying. He's the one who doesn't trust us. Go with him to that store," she lifted a slim hand and gestured to the bodega across the street. "Let him check it for himself. I'll wait here." Her eyes blazed at Johnny. "Then you can decide what to do."

They were back three minutes later, astonishment flooding Johnny's face. The ticket was legit. He'd checked it against a printout of the winning numbers and it was good for the second prize, over twenty thousand, just like they had said. Luis, the bodega's owner had eye-balled it too, and cursed in Spanish lamenting the fact that he hadn't sold it and scored a commission, or at least a tip.

Johnny's heart was galloping as fast as a pony flying down the home stretch. *Maybe, my troubles could be over.* He'd take the ticket and show it to Bones, explain what had happened. Promise to pay what he owed as soon as he visited the lottery office, got the check and cashed it at his bank. Hell, Bones could even come with him. It would all work out. No way it couldn't.

The girl was standing exactly where they'd left her, the anxious look on her face flipping into a smile as soon as she saw Johnny's grin. "Okay, okay, you were right. It is a winner. I'll do it. You got yourselves a deal."

The girl reached up and hugged him. The boy fished the ticket out of his pocket and handed it over. "How do you want to work this?" Johnny asked, tucking it away.

The girl took the lead as she had before. "Well, if it's okay, once you get the check, maybe we could meet you at a bank or after, at your house and split up the money there. Whatever you think is best."

Johnny nodded in agreement. "At my place is good. Here, let me give you my info." He took out his wallet, removed a card from it and handed it to her.

"The only thing is," the girl hesitated a moment as if embarrassed to continue, holding Johnny's card close to her chest. "We need some money now, for somewhere to stay until we get settled and to buy some food. Do you think, maybe, you could help us with that?" Her voice was small and plaintive again.

"We're good, don't worry. I have cash on me." There was the eight hundred he was carrying for Bones. He could hand it over as a down payment of sorts. After all, he had the winning ticket. What did he have to lose? "Here's what we'll do," he said as he reached for the money, his fingers brushing against his lucky silver dollar, which had finally paid off.

Johnny was all smiles, watching the girl and boy walk away when Bones lumbered up to him, his two apes a half-pace behind. "So, my friend, Detective Walker, you got something for me tonight? I hope you didn't make me come all the way down here for nothing." He shook his finger in Johnny's face in a bad DeNiro impression. "You know how much I hate being disappointed."

"Bones, you're not gonna believe this." Johnny's excitement was palpable as he reached for the winning ticket. He glanced down the street and realized that the girl and boy had disappeared. All he could hear was a low laugh echoing back from where they'd been.

It hit him in an instant. *Shit, I've been played.* A red-hot anger filled his mind, and he began to shake all over.

"Hey, Detective, you look like someone just pissed on your shoes. What the hell just happened?" His eyes bored into Johnny's. "I hope we don't have a problem here."

Johnny didn't know how'd they'd done it, but whether they'd switched the ticket or forged it, the one he was holding was bogus—a fucking worthless fake. His hand jerked out of his pocket, sending the ticket and his lucky silver dollar flying into the gutter. He felt Bones' hand snake around the back of his neck like the knot of a noose ready to be tightened. He was shit out of luck. And that was only the beginning.

*

Copyright 2011 Cathi Stoler

Cathi Stoler, an award-winning advertising creative director/copywriter, has written two mysteries featuring P.I. Helen McCorkendale and magazine editor, Laurel Imperiole. *Telling Lies*, her first novel, published in April, 2011, takes on the subject of stolen Nazi art. The second, *Keeping Secrets*, delves into the subject of hidden identity. She is working on the third book in the series, *The Hard Way*. She has also written several short stories and is delighted that "Out of Luck" is part of *Murder New York Style*. Cathi posts at the www.womenofmystery.net blog and you can also visit her at www.cathistoler.com.

Tell Me About Your Day
by Lynne Lederman

He was flicking the old Zippo and thinking it needed a new flint, before he was even aware of the cigarette he'd plugged into the corner of his mouth.

Damn. Can't smoke with the kid here. He removed the cigarette and contemplated it. Can't go outside, can't leave her. Really too cold to hang out the window, let alone sit on the fire escape. She'd know, anyway. He shredded it into the ashtray. Have to get rid of that, and the matches. Weren't little kids always playing with them, starting fires?

Kids, and also drunks passing out on the couch with a lit butt in their hand, he thought, glancing at the charred hole in the rug. He got up and edged the couch over the spot. That re-exposed the worn path behind it, but hey, can't have everything. He turned to the window and looked down to the street four flights below. Not high enough to escape the traffic noise from Roosevelt Avenue, the El that roofed the avenue, or the Long Island Railroad trains squealing into the Woodside station just down the block.

Several men were loitering in the glow from the spotlights illuminating the front of Ernie's Elbow Rest across the street. Could go out for a quick smoke. No, can't leave her. Tomorrow, then. No, poor little girl didn't even have a coat when that witch from Child Protective Services showed up with her. She hadn't said a word yet, not to him, not to the cops, not to that so-called social worker. Probably heard the whole thing, whatever happened. Maybe even knew who it was. Then doing what? Cowering behind the bedroom door, hiding in the closet in case someone came back for her? Phone jack ripped out of the wall, and no one heard a thing. Nothing in the kitchen either, except her mother lying there with her head bashed in. Didn't that little girl deserve some kind of help? And now, today, not Monday or whenever they were planning to come back and check up on her.

How do people do it? He asked himself out loud. He could see the bar patrons talking across the street, first one frosty exhale, then another in response. How do you take a kid out in the cold to get a coat? How do you buy the coat without the kid? His hand sought his breast pocket and cradled the pack of unfiltered cigarettes within—just one to think with. No.

He paced. He looked at the shreds in the ashtray. Did snuff look like that? He was pretty sure it did not. Maybe he could chop it up. This is ridiculous, he told the pack.

It's only for a weekend. Well, maybe it's a sign I should finally quit. Crumble them all up? But then I'd probably just get out the rolling papers or the hash pipe. Have to get rid of those, too. The hash pipe. Why did I keep it? To prove how strong I am? His Narcotics Anonymous sponsor had told him he was just asking for a relapse. Some sponsor that guy was, he thought. I'm clean, he's out on a street corner, selling crack, last I heard.

Matches. Well, have to keep some of those around. What if we have another blackout and have to light a candle? I guess you lock them up somewhere. But where? That old trunk? Then what do I do, carry the key around until I lose it and I have to get the kid to pick the lock? Bet she knows how, too.

He emptied the pack of cigarettes into a trash bag. This is why we need garbage disposals in this building, he told the cigarettes. Get rid of things while you have the strength. He sprinkled their shredded colleague over the cigarettes and anointed them all with several, generous shakes from the bottle of Louisiana hot sauce that sat on the kitchenette counter next to the remains of what had passed for dinner.

A coat. Food. What else? He turned to the window in time to witness that unmistakable glow in the cupped hands of one of the loitering men. As he watched, a big man shouldered his way through the group and into the doorway. The door opened, and the neon glow from the Elbow's interior flared briefly before the big man continued into the bar, blocking the light almost completely as the entry absorbed him. Even from this height, you could tell you wouldn't want to come up against that guy, especially not after spending a few hours at the Elbow.

Why is tobacco any different from the drugs or booze? He thought of all those AA and NA meetings, the chain smoking, the endless pots of coffee. Coffee. Surely I can still have that, can't I? Just one bad habit. Anyway, maybe it's just until Monday. Sure, she was his niece's only kid, but still, who in their right mind would leave a kid with him for any length of time? True, he'd lost track of the rest of his family, but he couldn't be the only one left, could he? He didn't remember his niece mentioning which of her many boyfriends was the little girl's father, and no one in her building knew, that's for sure. They hadn't even noticed she wasn't around until the smell got so bad.

His niece had been lying in the kitchen for days, the medical examiner said. Thank goodness someone remembered about the girl, remembered his weekly visits, knew enough to get the cops to search for her address book and his number. They found the girl cowering in the bedroom closet behind a pile of old clothes and rags. You'd never even notice there was someone there under all that junk, the cops said. They sure hadn't seemed motivated to look around much, although they'd mentioned the empty bottles that they'd knocked over when they'd pushed open the slightly ajar bedroom door. One of them had sneered. Your niece always let the kid play with wine bottles? Just another loser who got no worse than she deserved, his tone implied.

Maybe we'll eventually figure out who did it, he'd said. But we can always use more information, and the sooner the better, because the kid ain't talking. It just gets harder as the trail grows colder. Almost half the homicides in this city are never solved, the sarcastic cop said. With all those men coming and going, we can't count on fingerprints and fibers being much use here. Maybe she'd surprised a burglar, hard to tell what might have been stolen, though. Was her place always such a god-awful dump? They had talked to several guys in particular. The current boyfriend, some mousey little guy. He and the kid didn't seem to get along. You could say that for most of them, like the one before the Mouse, that bodybuilder who lived downstairs. And a couple of delivery guys in the area, identified through the take-out containers littering the kitchen counter. Someone from the Chinese restaurant they were sure was an illegal, but it wasn't their concern. A gawky teenager from the pizza parlor, seemed really nervous, lots of reasons for that. But the dates on the receipts were from too long ago. Did they come back on their own? Who knew? Not enough evidence to hold any of them. None of the neighbors seemed to recall who else had been around recently, but then they hadn't heard someone beat his niece to death with fists, maybe feet, either. The Mouse seemed real shaken up, sure, but he'd seen the body, walked in while the rookie who was waiting for the detectives was forgetting to secure the place, standing there in shock, his first homicide. A sight like that was not something you ever got used to, take it from me, the sneering cop had said, tossing him his card on the way out.

That bodybuilder, he thought, eyeing me like competition, until I'd made my relationship with my niece perfectly clear. What had his niece seen in that gorilla, anyway? Not his personality, certainly not his appearance. You didn't see a lot of men with skin that bad. Maybe he had qualities that weren't obvious. She was always looking for someone to help support her and the kid. However much he'd promised his sister he'd look after his niece, he'd never been all that helpful. That was back when he was using and boozing. He knew the gorilla was, too. Easy to recognize a fellow traveler. Maybe not booze, but something.

How relieved he'd been when she'd said she'd finally broken it off with him a few weeks ago. Sure, she kept running into him, and he was always calling, trying to get her to take him back. She said he was always putting down her new boyfriend, what did he call him, the runt? And she'd laugh about it, say he didn't scare her, no one did, most guys were all bluff. Anyway, her new boyfriend could take care of her. He's your size, that's not so runty. Plus he does some kind of martial arts thing, but it's only for self-defense, she'd said. He'd never hurt anyone if he didn't have to. I just need to convince him the old guy's really history. Sure, she'd gotten into a couple of screaming contests with the new guy. He was jealous, but he was all bark. Anyway, she'd say, have you seen how skinny my ex's legs are? Some bodybuilder, just works his chest and arms, legs like toothpicks. Couldn't take a joke about it either, she said. That's why she broke up with him, no sense of humor. Although, come to think of it the new guy didn't have such a sense of humor, either, when she'd found out the martial art, some Brazilian-Afro-American thing, was done to music. What happens if there's no sound track when someone attacks you? she'd asked. For a minute there, she'd thought he was about to show her, but since then, things had been okay. And he had a job at the post office. A boyfriend with a job, that was progress for her.

He should have been more insistent about her moving out of that dump in Corona and living somewhere around here. Could have kept an eye on her and the kid, could have gotten her a waitressing job at the Stop Inn on the corner, maybe. Being a dishwasher there had to be good for something besides minimum wage and dishpan hands. True, his neighborhood wasn't all that attractive, but you could walk around at night without feeling like you'd be taking your life in your hands. The Long Island Railroad station and all the comings and goings helped. Maybe he should have put better locks on her door. Her building was always being broken into, as if the residents actually had something worth stealing. The cops seemed to think she'd let the person in, although they admitted given the condition of the locks and the door, it was hard to tell.

He picked up the Zippo, one of the few things he had left from his father. The old man had carried it wherever the hell he'd been during the war. The big one, a whole lot grander than his own war, to hear the old man tell it, and tell it he did, and often, whether you were interested or not. Ernie, of Ernie's Elbow

Rest, whose name was really Ted—but you know how expensive sign work is—Ernie collected the damn things, World War II era Zippos and such. Ernie had seen the lighter one of the times he'd tested himself, going into the Elbow for a soft drink. Wanted to buy it from him, got real excited when he'd mentioned the trunk and all the other crap in it, the uniforms with the name tags, the canteen, all that other junk he didn't want, but couldn't bring himself to part with. Apparently the value had something to do with it all having belonged to a known person. What did he call it? Provenance.

He looked at the lighter and for once, instead of conjuring up some incoherent reminiscence, he pictured a little girl's coat. And what's-her-face downstairs, Amy or Meg, one of those cute three-letter names, she could help, she has some little kids, she could tell him where to get the coat. At the Salvation Army? Maybe she'd watch his grandniece until he got the money for the stuff. Meg, no, Sue? Well, anyway she got her kids' things there, didn't she? They outgrow them so fast, she said, and they're so young, they really don't mind wearing someone else's clothes. When his little girl outgrew her coat, he'd give it to Meg's kids. That would be fair. His little girl. Shit, listen to me. Shit, probably can't be cursing like that either. She'll learn it on her own on the street anyway, hell, in this very building just walking up and down those damn stairs every day. Or in the elevator, if they ever get around to fixing it. Thank goodness we're not on the top floor. So much to think about. Well, if they let him keep her, anyway. It would be for the weekend, for sure, they said they wouldn't be back until Monday morning and even then they'd have all the other emergencies they'd have to deal with. And he couldn't give her back to the CPS without a coat. Hat. Mittens. A scarf, boots, socks, everything. And a decent meal, he thought, as he scraped the last of the canned beans onto the cigarettes. She'd eaten almost as much as he'd eaten himself. Poor little girl. When had she had her last meal, anyway?

He went to the bedroom door with a vague feeling he should check on her. What did you check for, though? The band of light between the door and the jamb flowed from the tiny hallway into the room and over his bed. His niece's daughter lay smack in the center. She'd rolled the blanket up like a rug and arranged it as a barrier around her sides and feet. What is she trying to keep out, he wondered. Or who? Then he thought, it's freezing in here. He went back to the living area, picked the afghan up off the couch, and returned to slip through the partially open door, cautiously, quietly, through a space that just admitted his slender frame, careful not to wake her, although with the time she'd had, and the late hour, surely she'd be sound asleep. Hadn't he seen Meg's little ones snooze peacefully in their stroller while ambulances screamed by? As he cleared the narrow opening, he barely glanced down at the floor, knowing full well the obstacle course of discarded items that lay between him and the bed. Later, he'd say that he'd never believed people who'd claimed their hair really did stand on end, and he now wished to apologize to them all, for he experienced it himself then, as he saw what she'd put behind the door—a stack of books topped by an empty bottle, the bottle that had contained what had so far been his last drink.

If he'd been bigger, he'd have had to push the door open at least a bit, and the books and the bottle would have fallen and woken her. Well, if she wanted to keep him out it didn't work. Good idea, though, for a five-year-old. Might give her enough time to hide. The open closet door caught his eye. It was where he kept the bottle. He knew he'd shut the closet this morning after he'd decided which of his three shirts to wear. She had to have opened it. Plus, it was the only place to run to in here, she wouldn't have been able to open the window to the fire escape, too heavy. He pictured his niece's apartment. Their fire escape opened off the living room window, and it had done neither his niece in the kitchen nor his grandniece in the bedroom any good.

He stood by the bed, watching her scrawny chest rise and fall. I guess this is what I'm checking for, that she's breathing. For the first time he thought, maybe that's why I ended up a medic in 'Nam, so that all these years later, if my niece's kid ended up in my care, I'd know how to do CPR if she stopped breathing.

Sure. His niece was always the one to connect the unlikeliest things. Lucky for you, she'd say, that you had that experience. No, he thought, if I'd been lucky I'd have had a high number in the draft lottery and learned CPR at the Y, which I'd never need because my niece would have married some decent guy and not gotten her head bashed in.

He folded the afghan in half and eased it down onto the sleeping child. Pajamas. She can't keep sleeping in her clothes. His mother had made that afghan for him when he was the kid's age. She should have it, wherever she ends up, have a connection to her great-grandmother.

He slipped back out. Seeing the bottle reminded him that in AA, it was acceptable to keep certain symbols of your former failings, your weaknesses. The cap off your last bottle of beer that you could trot out when it was your turn to share, there for all to see, a reminder of your sobriety. Who knew for sure if it was really the cap of the actual last beer, but you learned not to question things like that. The whiskey bottle was another story. What hypocrites they were to criticize him for having saved it and the hash pipe. Whose business was it if he wanted to torture himself with them? His fault for having mentioned it. If he'd really wanted to torture himself, he wouldn't have rinsed the bottle out. The smell, how much more dangerous that was, how easy a yearning to fulfill, what with the Elbow across the street and all. And when the Elbow closed, there was the all-night convenience store next to the entrance of his own building that he had to walk right past on the way up to his apartment. Sure, the choice of beverages was limited, but when you couldn't sleep, when the DT's were lying in ambush, just how picky would you be?

And those guys in NA, taking his inventory for him. How his drugs of preference were so bad compared with some of theirs. Illegal is illegal, right? High is high, right? Well, no, not according to them. Some of them took the stuff for a good reason, not just to get high. So if some do-gooder judge made them show up at NA with all the real losers like him instead of facing jail time,

well, they'd put up with it. Those were the guys who'd do ninety meetings in ninety days, get themselves off the hook, and be
gone. Until they got caught the next time.

He lay on the couch, in his clothes, too, but with no blanket. The lights were still on. It wouldn't be the first time, he told
himself, but, damn, it's a lot easier to sleep this way if you're in
the bag. You didn't notice the lights, the lumps, the cold. He
got up, flicked off the lights, put on his winter jacket. Outside
the Elbow, people still milled. The interior neon again escaped
into the night before a giant silhouette blocked it momentarily.
Same big guy leaving already? Or another Goliath like him? Like
his niece's boyfriend, the gorilla downstairs? Only, as far as he
could tell, this guy looked well-proportioned. Not like the gorilla. Not, come to think of it, like those guys who were in NA
because they were busted for using. What? They had the same
over-developed upper body, the same skinny legs, the same bad
skin, the same bad attitude. What had the leader called it? Road
rage? That made no sense.

He settled back on the couch, then bolted upright. Where
was that card the officer had flipped at him? The one who'd made
the crack about playing with bottles. She wasn't playing with
the bottles, you horse's backside, he muttered. A big man would
have had to push the door open, would have knocked those bottles down, just the way the cops had. Not road rage, 'roid rage.
Steroids, had to be. The guys at NA had bragged about how easy
they were to get where they worked out, if you knew how to ask.
The little girl saw or heard what happened and protected herself
the best she could, waiting it out until her great uncle came by.
It would only have been a couple more days until his next visit,
he'd made sure since his sister died, just after her granddaughter was born, that his visits would be the one thing she and his
niece could count on. The old boyfriend might have come back,
if he'd known the girl had seen something, but if she'd been hiding, if he'd been in a blind rage then about the new boyfriend or
whatever set him off, he might not have seen or thought about

her. Later, he could have just gone about his business, trying to avoid suspicion, still living in the building, still bodybuilding at the gym. The cops knew that he was around, they'd talked to him, and they'd moved on. But the little girl couldn't have known whether he'd come back or not. There was no phone, just a building full of indifferent, unfriendly people. He'd seen them first-hand. Who would she trust?

Call anytime if you think of something, the cop had said. He picked up the phone, dialed. The phone rang and rang. He was relieved when the ringing stopped and he heard a voice unmistakably dredged up from the depths of sleep. Officer? I thought of something, he began.

*

Copyright © Lynne Lederman

Lynne Lederman, Ph.D., has a doctorate degree in molecular biology and virology from the Cornell University Graduate School of Medical Sciences. She is a widely published freelance medical, science, and health writer, and is also an award-winning printmaker. She is hard at work on a mystery series featuring scientist and amateur detective Nanette Newman.

HE'S THE ONE
BY CYNTHIA BENJAMIN

Henry Stern noticed the sepia-tinted stain on his office ceiling as soon as he opened the door. The wincing morning light always highlighted every imperfection in the room. Now, it scudded across the blob of color that seemed to spread, amoeba-like, before his eyes. It looked like blood.

"Just my luck," Henry said to no one in particular. Then he picked up the phone.

~

Teddy Dunlop, the building handyman, repeatedly tapped the ceiling with the metal cane he had been using since his knee replacement surgery three months earlier.

"I like finding new ways to use this damn sucker," he said, gingerly climbing down the ladder. Henry extended his hand to Teddy, but the handyman waved him away. Out of habit, Henry rubbed the port wine stain on his right cheek instead. Was it his imagination or did the morning sun snaking through the broken Venetian blinds deepen the discoloration? Henry awkwardly stuffed his hand into his jeans pocket and turned his head slightly to the left so his good cheek was visible. "Putting your best face forward," his Aunt Ida had called it. The thought of her made him shudder.

"Any leaks in the office upstairs?"

"Nope. None that I know of. Doesn't mean it isn't happening somewhere above you, though. Damn leaks can be tricky."

"But the ceiling won't come crashing down, right?"

"Now that'd be a hell of a way for a writer to go."

"So there's nothing to worry about."

"Hell, I wouldn't go that far."

~

Henry was writing in his black notebook, when the girl with the silver-blonde hair sat next to him in the crowded coffee shop near Union Square. For three years, Henry had eaten the same lunch sitting in the same seat at the far end of the counter. That way, his bad cheek faced the wall, while his clear, clean-shaven one faced the seat next to him.

He had just finished the first page of an article about the best hotels in Shanghai when the silver-blonde girl tapped him on the shoulder, and pointed to something on the counter near Henry's right hand.

"The pepper. Please."

She was the most beautiful girl Henry had ever seen. The sight of such beauty so close at hand left him breathless. Her eyes were a deeper shade of gold than her hair; her features were small and perfectly shaped. Her skin was flawless. The effect was so overpowering that Henry broke his own rule, and turned his head around to get a better look at her. Doing so exposed his flawed right cheek. The girl didn't flinch at the sight of the thickened purple skin that pulled his mouth up when he tried to smile. Instead she smiled in return and—did he imagine it?—her fingertips skimmed his own as she picked up the pepper shaker.

"I've noticed you in here before. I always wonder about people I see outside the office," she said.

"Me too. I call them the random people."

"What a great way of putting it. I kind of like imagining what they do. Professionally, I mean. Like I just looked at you, and right away I said to myself, 'he's a writer.' That's right, isn't it?"

Henry nodded.

"What do you write?"

"Travel articles, mostly."

"How exciting. I love to travel. Not that I get much chance. But still, I love thinking about it. You know? So, where are you going next?"

"Back to my office, actually. That's where I do most of my research. With the Internet, you can travel all over the world without ever leaving your home base."

"What about your frequent flyer miles?"

It took Henry a minute to realize she wasn't joking.

⌒

Later, Henry and Elyse would refer to their meeting at the Union Square coffee shop as their first date. After lunch, they walked to the Farmer's Market in the nearby park. As they strolled among the stalls, they talked about nothing of consequence to either of them. It was the most ordinary conversation of Henry Stern's life. What made it extraordinary was that it took place at all. Forty-five minutes after meeting this beautiful woman, Henry was still talking to her. He knew what his Aunt Ida would have said. "It's a mitzvah, Henry, that such a girl would go for a man like you. A mitzvah."

Henry looked shyly at Elyse, who was chattering on about the cost of the organic food sold at the market.

"Jeez, can you imagine that? Seven dollars for a loaf of whole-wheat bread. I mean, come on. What does organic mean anyway?"

What indeed? On his right side, a rollerblading messenger had fallen asleep in the warm spring sunshine, listening to his iPod nestled in his lap. The earphones straddled his shoulder, so Henry could hear snatches of the hip-hop songs. Normally, such an intrusion into his solitary world would have infuriated him. Today, he welcomed its normalcy. As he listened, the music floated above his head and was burned away by the sun.

⌒

Without saying a word, Henry and Elyse started walking back to his office building near Union Square. As he turned into the lobby of number twenty-five, he realized she was still beside him.

"Shouldn't you go back to work?

"I am, silly. My office is in this building too. Fifth floor. Usually I go to lunch with my friend Vera."

"What happened today?"

"She called in sick, so I was on my own. I was going to do some shopping, but I ended up at the coffee shop instead. And I met you. Weird how these things work out. Guess it was just meant to be, huh?" She smiled her perfect smile.

"I guess so."

Henry pressed the elevator button, and stood aside so Elyse could get in first. He noticed the other passengers look at her appreciatively. When he got off at his floor, the twelfth, he checked out his right cheek in the narrow mirror that bordered the elevator door. Was it his imagination, or did the port wine stain seem smaller and paler?

~

On Friday night, Henry invited Elyse to his small, one-bedroom apartment for the first time. It was in Patchin Place, a cul-de-sac, just steps away from the nail salons and take-out restaurants that defined the nearby stretch of bustling Sixth Avenue. All of that seemed a world away as Henry closed the iron gates behind them. As always, he felt as if he were stepping back in time. And, in that moment, he was.

Henry carefully watched Elyse, trying to gauge her reaction to his secret world. She stared in amazement at the ten identical, brick row houses framing the horseshoe-shaped courtyard. Henry pointed to a nineteenth-century gas streetlight standing in the far corner.

"There are only two left in New York City, but that's the only one that lights, even if it's now electric." He shrugged. "I wrote an article about it for a travel magazine."

Slowly, they climbed the narrow stairs to his top floor apartment. Standing on the fire escape outside his bedroom window, Henry slipped his arm around Elyse's narrow shoulders and pulled her toward him. In the distance, the clock in the tower of the nearby library tolled the hour. Neither spoke.

Later, Henry and Elyse lay side by side in his narrow bed, staring at the ceiling. He stared at her body, looking for the slightest imperfection. There wasn't any. Elyse slipped her hand into his as he raised it to his wine-stained skin.

"Don't do that."

"What?"

"Touch your birthmark that way. I don't mind it at all. And please don't think it has anything to do with what happened tonight."

Henry sat up and turned away from her, but she grabbed his arm and, this time, held on.

"Don't be angry at me, Henry. It's not your fault. I just can't, that's all."

"Did it ever happen before?"

"All the time. No matter how much I want to, like tonight, I can't. My body shuts down."

"Why?"

"Men scare me. Haven't you ever been scared? Like when you want something so much you can hardly breathe."

"And you can't bring yourself to reach for it because your hands and feet won't move."

"Yeah, that's it. I knew you'd understand. We're a lot alike, you and me."

Elyse obediently rolled into him, and rested her perfect heart-shaped face on his chest. It was like holding a doll.

"What did you mean 'all the time'"?

Her voice sounded so small and far away that Henry had to strain to hear her answer.

"Five years ago I was raped. And, ever since, I can't. I just can't. No matter who I'm with, I see his eyes and smell his breath and feel his hands." Elyse tightened her tiny bird hands around Henry's wrists. The strength of her grip surprised him.

"You don't have to tell me about it." Henry said.

"But I want to," she whispered. "I've never told anyone all the things he did to me. But if we're going to be together you should know." Her bird hands tightened again. This time they had the strength of claws.

Henry kissed the top of her head. "I love you."

Elyse sighed and settled her head on Henry's right shoulder before beginning her story.

⁓

Elyse and Henry's life together easily settled into a routine that suited them both. Every morning, they left Henry's small Patchin Place apartment and walked up lower Fifth Avenue to Union Square. On the way, Elyse would play her favorite game, a variation of the what-if fantasy that Henry dimly remembered from his childhood.

"What if we win the lottery and could buy any apartment on this block?" she would say. "Which one would it be?"

Henry, still enchanted by the sound of her voice, the slight breathiness she brought to every word, would point aimlessly at any apartment building. He didn't care, as long as she kept talking to him. She would still be chattering as they entered the coffee shop, where they first met, to buy their morning coffee and pastry. The cashier knew them. Even Eddy, the counterman, blessed their union by setting aside two Danish: cheese for Elyse and apricot for Henry.

If it was warm enough, they took their breakfast to Union Square and sat side-by-side on a bench. Henry noticed the way other men looked at Elyse as she placed her hand lightly on his. Once, she brushed away a crumb from his mouth, tracing the outline of his lips with her forefinger. He had never known such joy.

One morning, they were entering the lobby of their office building, hand-in-hand, when Elyse made a choking sound. Her hand, resting easily in Henry's, grew cold, her fingers rigid. Her right arm, quivering slightly, pointed in the direction of a balding, middle-aged man slowly making his way to the first elevator, his head bent. At nine o'clock in the morning, he already exhaled weariness. Elyse was muttering something, but Henry couldn't understand what she said.

"Honey, what's wrong? Tell me."

"He's the one."

~

His name was Stanley Morris, and he was a paralegal for a small law firm on the sixth floor. For a week, Henry researched Stanley's life as carefully as he researched his travel articles. He found his address on the upper West Side, the names of his wife and eight-year-old daughter, and the year he received his undergraduate degree. Every day, Henry followed Stanley when he left the office building for lunch. His routine was as dull as Henry's had been before he met Elyse. Stanley always ordered the lunch special at a faded Chinese restaurant near Union Square. He ate hunched over the table, staring dully at a yellow legal pad. Henry noted that it was always blank.

One night after work, Henry trailed Stanley to the subway and followed him home to a rundown walk-up on West Ninety-Sixth Street. It pleased Henry to realize Stanley had achieved as little in life as he had. Not that it mattered. In another week he would be dead.

~

Henry had decided to kill Stanley Morris the first time he saw him in the lobby of their office building. As he held Elyse in his arms, and felt her body slump against his, he stared at Stanley's hands. He had expected them to be strong and thick, peasant hands capable of inflicting wounds that would never heal. But the sight of Stanley's small, carefully manicured fingers revolted him. The hands he showed to the world were pearly pink and white, polished, and soft to the touch. Stanley had used those hands to torture Elyse, long after she begged him to stop. Henry imagined what it would feel like to grab one of those soft fingers and bend it back until it snapped at the joint. Yes, he would kill Stanley Morris. There was no other way to obliterate those hands forever.

~

Every morning, Henry and Elyse sat at a window table in the Union Square coffee shop, eagerly awaiting their first sight of the man they would murder. When Stanley came into view, his back slightly bent, his hands shoved deep into the pockets of his creased raincoat, they pressed each other's hands with a ferocity that surprised them both.

Tuesday night at Henry's apartment, they reviewed their plan one last time.

"After tomorrow, it's important that we don't change our routines. I'll go to my office Friday morning at the same time."

Elyse fingered the ribbon of a white cotton nightgown that ended in a row of pink pearl buttons under her chin. "That's what I wanted to talk to you about. Please don't get angry, but I told Mr. Alonzo I'd be taking a week's vacation, starting this Friday."

Henry's body tightened. He willed his voice to sound normal. "What'd you do that for?"

"See, Vera asked me to switch vacation times with her. That was maybe a month ago, before we found out about…well, you know. And I figured it would look suspicious if I asked her to change things around now."

"It's not as if you'll be a suspect."

"I know. I know. I just thought." She looked up at him shyly. "There's a special reason I'm taking my vacation now."

"Why? Where are you going?"

"Lake Placid. I made reservations at a beautiful hotel right on the lake."

"You should have told me. I could have gotten you a special deal on the room."

"No, no, I wanted to do this on my own. It's a gift… from me to you. We've never been together in that way, and I want Friday night to be really special." She turned up her head and kissed him on his right cheek.

"I love you," she whispered.

Henry sighed deeply. He heard the hated voices one last time. "Hey, look at Henry tomato face. What's that on your cheek, tomato face? Did a bird crash into you? Wash hard enough, maybe it'll rub off." Finally, he floated past them, higher and higher.

"Henry, you're hurting me. Don't squeeze my shoulder so hard."

Henry loosened his grip. The voices were gone now.

"You'll see. Everything will be all right once he's gone," Elyse said, before falling asleep in the crook of Henry's arm.

~

They chose Wednesday, because it was the only night of the week that Stanley brought his car to work. It was an old Toyota, shabby and beige, like its owner. He parked in the building's small underground garage, but the video security camera hadn't worked in over a year.

In the morning, before leaving for work, Henry and Elyse rehearsed their parts, like anxious children performing in a school play for the first time.

"You'll come up to him just as he's about to open the car door."

"Suppose he has one of those automatic things. What do I do then?"

Henry willed himself not to feel irritated when Elyse used "things" to identify an everyday object she should have recognized.

"We discussed this before, remember? Stanley doesn't open his car door that way. It's an older model, so he always uses a key."

Elyse nodded, as if hearing the words for the first time. "Okay, he's taking out his key. And I look right at him and say…"

~

"Stanley, do you remember me?"

Stanley Morris looked at the small, young woman who stood in front of him. Probably one of Anna's babysitters, the girl who used to come over on Friday nights, when she was just starting to walk…what, seven years ago now? Or maybe she was the waitress from the bar? Hard to say. His head bobbed up and down, as it so often did when he was trying to be pleasant. He licked his dry lips, about to answer her, still unsure what the right answer was. He started to smile, when a noise startled him. It came from behind; he was certain of that. And it was an angry sound, like the growl of a dog. Yes, definitely angry, Stanley thought, as he started to turn his head. But how could a stray dog get in here? How very strange. It was the last thought of Stanley Morris' uneventful life.

⁓

Henry slammed the metal cane against Stanley's skull. The first blow knocked him unconscious, although his legs were still twitching, like a pitiful water beetle after a gargantuan shoe strikes its body, cracking the carapace into tiny fragments.

"Hit him again," Elyse said in a hoarse whisper. "Now, now," she cried, her small voice rising in a moan. "He remembered me. I could see it in his eyes."

Henry didn't need her urgent whispers of encouragement. When he withdrew the metal tip from Stanley's forehead, it was covered with blood and brain matter. Only then did Henry stop. In less than a minute, it was over.

Henry dropped the cane on the garage floor, removed his Latex gloves, and stuffed them in his briefcase along with the plastic trench coat he'd worn over his jeans and tweed jacket.

"Thank you," was all Elyse said. Then, she ran up the stairs. Henry rubbed his right cheek, as he looked down at Stanley Morris lying on the garage floor. He briefly wondered why she didn't say "I love you" as well.

⁓

The ride to the Westport train station was the perfect segue between Henry's old life and his future with Elyse. He had bought an engagement ring weeks before, and he liked slipping his hand into his jacket pocket to caress the small, black-velvet box.

He started reading the morning papers he bought at Penn Station, and was pleased to see that Stanley's death was already relegated to a one-paragraph article well past page ten. What was so momentous to him and Elyse was of little concern to the average reader. All in all, it had gone well. Although he had an alibi carefully worked out, no one even questioned him. He was, as always, irrelevant to the main action. This time his invisibility delighted him.

The only thing that disturbed Henry was the possibility of implicating the building handyman, but he wasn't even a suspect. Henry was relieved to read that Teddy had been at his physical therapist's office when Stanley was murdered. He told the police that someone must have taken his cane from the locker in his basement office. The last time he'd used it had been more than a month before.

Henry leaned back in his seat and went to sleep. His last thought was the look on Elyse's face after the cane hit Stanley's skull. He could only describe it as joyful.

~

She was waiting for him, as promised, in the lobby of the hotel. Henry noticed the way the other guests looked at him when she ran into his arms. "Yes, she's mine," he wanted to shout at them. "Imagine that, can you? This beautiful woman loves me." But words weren't necessary; the look on her face said it all.

"I made reservations at a restaurant that overlooks the lake. It's a little expensive, but I didn't think you'd mind."

Henry looked down at Elyse as he touched the black-velvet jewelry box in his coat pocket. "It sounds perfect," he said.

That night, they both had more to drink than usual. "In a way, it's our anniversary," Henry said, as he refilled Elyse's wine glass.

"I've never felt truly safe before, not as long as he was in the world. But now I do. And you gave that feeling back to me."

They lifted their glasses in a toast. "To us," Henry said.

"Forever and ever." Elyse reached across the table and laced her fingers through Henry's. As he lifted their joined hands, he felt her fingers tighten in his. Then her eyes widened. Henry had seen that look of terror only once before.

"What is it?"

Elyse nodded in the direction of a middle-aged man sitting at the bar. What first struck Henry was the care the man had taken with his appearance: the sharp part in his freshly clipped, pomaded hair; the perfect, rosy shine of his skin. His hands were immaculate, just like Stanley's.

Henry tried to keep his voice even. "Elyse. Honey. What's wrong?"

She bent her face close to Henry's, that beautiful, perfect face with its penumbra of silver-blonde hair. Her dry lips brushed his right cheek. They were one at last.

"That man. He's sitting at the table near the bar. Do you see the one I mean?

"Yes. What about him?"

"He's the one."

*

Cynthia Benjamin is a Manhattan-based writer. She has written television scripts for both primetime and daytime television. She also developed an original daytime soap opera for CBS. In addition, she is the author of twelve children's books. Her mystery short story, "The Actress," was featured in *Ellery Queen Mystery Magazine's* "Department of First Stories" in December, 2010.

A Vampire in Brooklyn
by Leigh Neely

Metallica's "All Nightmare Long" echoed throughout my room as I buttoned my blouse. The song's lyrics were about hunting prey at night, which was what I did as a homicide detective in Brooklyn.

I turned down the volume with a sigh, knowing my roommate, who preferred classical music, would complain soon. I've always found heavy metal music relaxing, probably because I became a vampire in the 1970s when music was an integral part of my life. It soothed me.

I glanced in the mirror and smiled. I looked good for 30-year-old woman who had been killed by a psychopath in 1971. He swore he fell in love with me, and kept me alive for three weeks, torturing my body with his hands and my soul with his words. Before he left me, he made me vampire.

He became vampire after his first killing spree in London's East End. The Whitechapel murders and Jack the Ripper had been a puzzle for years, the subject of countless books, and one of the most popular subjects on the Internet. I'd carried the truth inside for too many years. Jack was Dr. Francis Tumblety, a quack who became the first internationally-known serial killer.

I'd chased him since I became a detective in 1983: the year humans learned vampires really did exist. When a vampire scientist discovered vampire blood could fight blood-borne diseases like AIDS and leukemia, it almost made being vampire legitimate. Vampires donate blood for healing, and humans donate blood for our sustenance.

I grabbed my iPad off its stand and stuffed it into its case. "All Nightmare Long" had been my theme song since my partner and I began working our current case. As two of the top detectives in Brooklyn, we were on a task force for one of the biggest serial murder cases in New York City history.

Nine young women had been snatched from their beds, but only four bodies had been found. Somewhere in Brooklyn, a maniac was killing and mutilating young women and we couldn't find him. My gut said I already knew him.

Jack had a real love of using a scalpel on women. All the young women's bodies we had recovered were missing the essential elements that made them women, their uteruses. I knew Jack had a collection from his victims. He'd kept them in small jars he could pack in cases. He was still a bad, bad boy.

I felt his presence at all the crime scenes. Our supernatural connection existed because he was my Maker. It frustrated the hell out of me. I had no doubt he'd laughed at me for years, because I always arrived after he was gone.

I'd investigated his murders in Los Angeles, Seattle, Portland, Nome, Dallas, and Atlanta. Always too late.

I'd hang around until I heard of another crime spree in another city, then get a job there. Finally, I stopped chasing and came to New York. I knew he would come here eventually. He loved big cities. This time, I'd be patient and wait for him.

I dropped my purse on the table by the door, and reached in the closet to put my hand on the electronic lock that opened my weapons case. I strapped on my gun. Raising my trouser leg, I also fastened a thin wooden stake to my calf with a Velcro strap. It was so much a part of me that I often forgot it was there until I undressed.

When you investigate homicides by supernatural monsters, you must be prepared to kill them. My partner, Joe Burke, had his wood sheathed in a holster on his thigh. We've both used them, though it wasn't an easy thing.

Maybe tonight, I thought, as I did every night when I left for work.

My apartment was really a luxurious bedroom suite in the beautiful condo of Elsbeth Williams. Her generosity allowed me to live in one of the most coveted places in New York City, a group of elegant condos designed especially for vampires in an abandoned subway tunnel under City Hall. When I reached the foyer, Elsbeth stepped out of the library.

A wealthy vampire for centuries, she was a ravishing twenty-year-old woman, both calculating and extremely intelligent.

"Well, if it isn't my favorite homicide detective, Alice Landers," she said with a smile. "I need to talk to you."

I hurried to the door. "Can't right now. I'm already late."

"Wait a sec," she followed me. "I'm having a dinner party tomorrow night. Can you come?"

"I'm not in a party mood these days," I said as I opened the door.

"It's actually a business dinner. I want to talk to you about an offer," she said. "I'm opening a new resort near Barrow, Alaska, and I want you to be head of security."

I gave her a confused look, and she laughed.

"You haven't said anything about needing a job change, but I think it's time you did something besides keeping a running tally of Jack's bodies." She patted my arm. "Think about it."

"Sure," I said, knowing I'd stay a cop until Jack died.

I hurried to the elevator and pressed the button several times so it would come faster. My partner was probably parked beside a hydrant with his 'NYPD on duty' sign on the dash.

He'd just have to wait, though. I still needed to stop at Distinct Blends for my cup of Go Juice. This special blend of whole blood and plasma, with a squirt of Vitamin B-12 and a dash of iron sprinkles, gave me a little added boost and helped me avoid attacking unsuspecting humans. I still missed caffeine—and a good hunt for a frightened human—but discipline kept me on Go Juice.

Dr. Nancy Morrigan created her blood cafés when the retail spaces in the subway tunnels opened. A former vascular surgeon, Nancy lost her medical license when a procedure went wrong for the son of a Long Island billionaire who'd donated an entire hospital wing.

She came back with a vengeance, though, starting Distinct Blends. Although human donors are readily available and blood banks sell their products over the Internet, I prefer drinking blood sold closer to home, with the reassurance that everything served at Distinct Blends is safe: free of disease and viruses.

These days, Nancy used her wealth and medical skills to help the poor and homeless in a warehouse clinic near the Brooklyn Bridge. I had volunteered there, looking for clues about Jack. Nancy, who understood something about being victimized, had become a friend and an ally in my hunt.

By the time I emerged from the tunnel, Burke was angry. I laughed off his grumbling, because Joe Burke was strong, very fit, a great human partner. He'd left the FBI to be a cop. Every case was personal to him, and the Feebies hadn't liked that attitude. I listened to his griping with only half an ear while I drank breakfast. After a brief meeting with the task force, we took our leads from the tip line and headed out.

As we emerged from the house where two teenagers had thought it would be fun to call the tip line, Burke's anger exploded again.

"I'm damn sick and tired of this," he said.

"I know," I said, "but it's all we've got, and we have to check out every lead."

My phone rang and interrupted us. I was surprised to see it was Nancy.

"A young girl came into the clinic about an hour ago," she said. "Her name is Shelby Rawlings. She doesn't know where she's been for more than a month. She's had surgery, a poorly done hysterectomy."

Grabbing my iPad, I quickly opened the file on the serial killer case.

"She was reported missing four weeks ago. We're on our way." I gave Burke the signal for siren and lights.

Nancy sighed. "I knew I'd heard that name. I called an ambulance and sent her to NYC Medical Center. Head over there. I'll tell them you're coming."

I called headquarters, and the captain told us to come back in after we interviewed Shelby Rawlings. I held on as we sped through the back streets, jerking in and out between yellow cabs. My nostrils flared as we walked through the automatic doors of the hospital. I couldn't stop the little thrill that ran through me whenever I was near a lot of human blood. I shook my head to clear my thoughts, and followed Burke to the information desk. Shelby, we were told, was in surgery, so we went back to talk to the ER doctor who treated her.

I paused for a moment before stepping into the emergency room. I smelled fresh blood all around me. Like a good vampire, I smeared Vick's VapoRub under my nose before going through the door. It helped diminish the odor of fresh blood, just like it did for dead bodies. The receptionist checked our badges, and told us where to find Dr. Peter Abrams.

He was stitching the head of a sobbing three-year-old. When he finished, he joined us.

I clicked on my recorder, so we'd have notes for our files. I hated taking handwritten notes.

"She's anemic and malnourished. You don't see that often these days, unless the girl is anorexic," he said, dropping a chart on the counter. "She's also bleeding internally from what looks like a botched hysterectomy. Come on." We walked toward a treatment room. "Our new advertising campaign says patients are seen faster here, which means I gotta keep my ass moving."

He took another chart from the holder on the wall, and glanced at it before he continued. "The patient's uterus was removed by laparoscopic surgery. Whoever did it made tiny incisions in her belly, clipping the uterus free and pulling it out through her vagina without any guides. In the process, a blood vessel was snipped. That's what they're trying to fix upstairs now, but there's infection, too," he said as he laid his hand on the door to another treatment room. "If I had to guess, I'd say it was someone learning how to do the surgery. She's in bad shape."

We headed upstairs after we were told Shelby was in recovery. One of the nurses paged the surgeon for us, and he met us outside ICU.

"She's lost a lot of blood, and she's very weak. Apparently, she's received nothing but artificial nourishment for a long time."

"Did she say anything to you?" I asked quietly.

"She fought the anesthesiologist before we finally got her sedated," the doctor said.

Exhaustion was evident in the lines on his face. He'd probably been in surgery all day.

"When can we talk to her?" Burke said. He was fidgeting and nervous, ready to go out and look for the person who'd done this to Shelby.

The doctor gave us both a disapproving glare.

"It's important, doctor. Did she say anything about where she'd been held, or talk about what happened?"

He rubbed his face and was quiet for a moment.

"She kept talking about getting away, and 'no more needles.' You know, she was really afraid of the medical equipment and the room. As usual, she was pretty heavily sedated before she even got to the OR, but the minute they brought her in, she started fighting us. She sure doesn't like being in a hospital."

As he walked away, my stomach clenched with sickening rage. I understood why Shelby was afraid. Women were nothing more than lab rats to Jack. He loved terrorizing them, and he did it well. I shivered, remembering the awful things he had done to me.

To my knowledge, I was the only person who'd survived at the hands of Jack the Ripper. Until now. After all these years, was Jack getting sloppy?

Burke and I waited, but Shelby showed no sign of waking up. We checked in with the office, and Captain Campbell told us her parents were being brought to the hospital. While officers canvassed the area near Nancy's clinic, Burke and I talked with Shelby's distraught parents. They'd been searching for her ever since she didn't come home from work.

The night was fading, and my frustration was building. I knew Jack was out there, perhaps already with another victim. But he had broken his pattern and let this one get away. He could also be on his way to another city by now.

Burke dropped me off at the entrance to my tunnel around four a.m., and I grabbed another cup from Distinct Blends to take home with me, hoping it would help me relax. When that didn't help, I decided I need some air. The weather was clear and crisp; it was a good night for a quick flight before dawn. I finished my drink and dressed in black from head to toe.

Sometimes, I need to be vampire.

When I emerged from the tunnel again, the streets were quiet. I walked down Park Row to a shadowy area where I slipped out of sight and rose on a gust of power.

I swept up and away, reveling in the beauty of flight. The stars were bright, and I watched an airliner fly overhead, and laughed at the silly humans who would never experience this.

Though I often longed to see the sun, I loved New York City at night—bright lights, big city.

Without conscious thought, I flew straight to the area where Shelby showed up at the clinic.

I glanced down. The Brooklyn Bridge was lit up like an amusement-park ride. When John Roebling dreamed of this vast span in the 1830s, I was sure he never imagined anyone viewing it from this angle.

By the time the bridge was complete in 1883, Roebling was dead and his son, Washington, was crippled by Caisson's disease or 'the bends.' Washington actually finished the bridge by watching construction from his Brooklyn apartment, relaying messages to his crew through his wife, Emily.

I abruptly stopped and hovered near the end of the bridge. As weak as she'd been, Shelby couldn't have walked far. Was Jack in this neighborhood?

I dropped lower as I flew, and a light tingle in my blood answered my question. Jack was nearby. His blood was calling to mine. Looking down at the buildings along the river below me, I saw a hundred places he could be.

I came down lightly in the shadows under the Manhattan Bridge. My blood sang. Jack was somewhere between here and the Brooklyn Bridge. Above my head, a subway train rumbled on its way to Manhattan. I rose up again and hovered just above the buildings. Depending on my blood sense to guide me, I moved slowly along Front Street to Prospect Street, where I landed in a bushy area beside the bridge.

I saw the footpath that led to Prospect, and suddenly, full-blown desire heated my blood. I knew Jack was very close. I crossed the street, rounded a corner, and walked alongside the anchorage, a part of the Brooklyn Bridge that Roebling had intended to be a place enjoyed by the public.

There was no one around me in the predawn chill. I approached the iron sculpture of the three Roeblings silhouetted in iron. It was the only art at Anchorage Plaza. It was closed after terrorists attacked the World Trade Center. I couldn't imagine this sad, lonely place as it once had been—the scene of community concerts and art shows.

My blood was practically bubbling as I moved around the building to the front. Looking up, I saw two sets of long, narrow windows sealed from the inside, making this a perfect place for a vampire's lair. I slowly approached the first set of double metal doors. There was no budging them, although it was obvious the rusted locks had been moved and relocked.

Like all ancient vampires, Jack could move inanimate objects, so he could go wherever he wished. Since he made me vampire nearly four decades ago, I'd grown stronger, too. I knew I was ready to face him.

I braced to make a run at the door, and then remembered my last encounter with Jack. I hit speed dial for Burke and heard his sleepy rumble on the other end.

"I think I've found Jack's hidey hole," I said.

He was immediately awake. "Don't do anything stupid. Wait until I get there with backup."

"I'm at Anchorage Plaza at the foot of the Brooklyn Bridge."

"Wait for me," he shouted as I closed the cell phone.

I took a running leap and hit the door with both feet. It fell with a horrendous noise. Yanking out my gun, I slowly looked inside. There was nothing but blackness and a faint clinical smell. *Damn you, Jack,* I thought bitterly, *you've got another lab set up, just like when you took me.*

While Metallica's lyrics, "hunt you down without mercy," raced through my mind, I stood just inside the door and listened, but heard nothing. I took a deep breath and stepped into the darkness.

The smell of the river and stale garbage mingled with the musty, old air inside the huge structure. At one point, Roebling thought this could be a great vault for the national treasury, and he was right. The high ceilings and stone walls were massive.

Moving silently under the huge arches, I saw a faint light in a back corner, and headed toward it. As I got nearer, I realized the buzzing in my head was someone humming, and immediately recognized the tune as "Brigg Fair," Jack's favorite old English folk song. That tune had haunted me for years.

Jack turned as I approached. Of course he knew it was me. Our blood connection was a stronger signal than the door bursting open.

"Hello, Alice. I've missed you," he said as he adjusted an IV line in a young girl's arm.

"Hello, Jack. It's time for you to visit your friendly neighborhood prison," I said, with more bravado than I felt. "I'm here to rescue your hostage, and make you pay for what you've done."

He turned to me. My body immediately responded. He was perfectly sculpted in tight black jeans and a molded T-shirt. His vibrant eyes danced with laughter. If I gave in to my body, I'd ravish him.

But that was the problem with Jack. He looked like he was made for loving women. Instead, he hated them passionately.

He sighed. "I knew there was a chance you'd find me if I let that last one live." With a rueful chuckle, he added, "Maybe I wanted you to find me. What do you think?"

"This is the end, Jack."

He cocked his head at the gun in my hand. "Alice," he said reasonably. "Why don't you put down that nasty, useless gun and help me? I think this young woman's about to die, and I'm not finished with her yet. I've been trying some new methods, but I haven't quite got the hang of them."

"It's not like you to try something new," I said, hoping to distract him.

He frowned. "I know, and it's not nearly as satisfactory as my traditional route."

The young woman on the gurney groaned, and he smiled. There was lust in his eyes, and his fangs flashed as blood gushed from between her legs.

The desire that coursed through my body was suddenly replaced with cold fury. I was horrified that he expected me to help him do to this innocent creature what he had done to me. I put my gun on the floor.

"That's a good girl," he said quietly, and turned to take the girl's pulse. "I think if we push the IV, we can recharge her so I can finish my project."

Shelves lined one long wall, filled with little jars, each one holding a woman's uterus. Jack's preservation method was still the same. I knew the cards taped on the front of each one: the woman's name, age, status in life, homemaker, career woman, prostitute, and the year he took her womanhood. Mine had to be among them.

While Jack studied his watch, I pulled up my trouser leg, and slipped the long, narrow stake out of its small holster. I rose and pivoted in one, fluid motion. I brought the stake up, and put all my weight and forty years of fury behind it.

Jack turned, a wicked sneer on his lips. Without stopping my forward motion, I pushed the stake in just under his heart and shoved with all my might.

Jack's face was the picture of surprise.

He looked down at my hands on the stake, back up to my face, and smiled a horrible, sad smile.

"Murder is borne of love, and love attains the greatest intensity in murder," he said, blood dripping down his chin. "Octave Mirbeau said that, Alice, and it's true. I love you, too."

I gave the stake one last shove and backed away.

Jack began to laugh, but quickly stopped as more blood bubbled up in his mouth. He dropped to his knees, and fell face forward. While I watched, Dr. Francis Tumblety became a crusty, blackened corpse with my slender stake protruding from his back. Moments after that, he was a pile of ashes.

At long last, Jack the Ripper was dead.

"Goddamn it, Alice," Burke yelled behind me. "I told you to wait for me."

I turned to face him, feeling numb and dislocated. I pulled my badge off my belt and handed it to him and said, "I resign."

I nodded toward the young girl bleeding on the gurney behind me. "She's still alive. Get the EMTs." I walked toward the door, headed for the darkness outside. It was less than an hour till dawn and I needed to get home.

"Alice!" Burke's bellow fell flat against the stone walls. "Alice! Come back here!"

Some of the younger officers tried to stop me, but I shook them off like the silly, little flies they were. Once outside, I looked up into a clear, bright darkness that sparkled with stars and took off, leaving Jack behind me forever.

That night, I sat at Beth's lavish dinner table and listened to her plans for a posh vampire resort in Alaska, a place for vampires to play and pamper themselves with endless night.

I realized she was right—it was time for a change.

*

Leigh Neely's childhood dreams of living like famed reporter, Nelly Bly, led to a satisfying career as a writer and editor, and involved work in newspapers, magazines, and books. Among the notables she has interviewed are author Mary Higgins Clark, singer Michael W. Smith, and actor Grant Goodeve. Though she's focusing on fiction now, she still writes articles for publications and the Internet. Originally from Chattanooga, Tennessee, Leigh and her husband now live in New Jersey, and enjoy visits from their three children and four grandchildren.

REMEMBER YOU WILL DIE
BY SUSAN CHALFIN

The title of the Rubin Museum's latest exhibit was *Remember You Will Die*. As if I could forget. It's not the kind of thing that slips your mind when you have Stage Four liver cancer.

The exhibition compared Tibetan Buddhist and medieval Christian depictions of death. Both cultures, the brochure explained, used graphic images of death to remind us that life is fleeting and mortality inevitable. As I stood in the middle of the exhibit, I was surrounded by examples—sculptures of dancing skeletons, artifacts made of human bone, elaborately painted skulls. It was the perfect setting for my goodbye party.

The Rubin is a small jewel-box of a museum in lower Manhattan, its interior painted in vibrant shades of Chinese red and ocher and filled with Himalayan treasures. Rory O'Rourke, a Tibet expert I'd befriended after hearing him lecture at the museum, had helped me book the exhibit space. It cost a bundle to keep the place open after hours, but I wasn't sweating the expense. You can't take it with you, or so they tell me. I knew none of my invitees wanted to attend, but they had. It's hard to blow off a man who's about to be intimate with the Grim Reaper.

I watched my party guests examine the artworks. My first wife, Melissa, was studying a nineteenth-century Tibetan painting. It depicted yogis meditating in charnel grounds—fields where corpses were left to rot or be eaten by tigers and leopards. Rory, my guru on all things Tibetan, claimed that charnel ground meditation taught devotees to sever their attachment to life and accept mortality. "Yeah," I'd said, "anyone who thinks it's smart to meditate with feral felines will sure as shit sever their attachments." Rory told me I should be more receptive to other cultures. Live and let live. Or, in this case, die and let die.

I knew Melissa was puzzled by my deathbed conversion to Tibetan mysticism. Throughout our married life, she'd nagged me about my work schedule and urged me to be more spiritual. She got furious when I reminded her that my soulless talent management business paid for her yoga and meditation classes. She was too busy being ascetic to earn a living herself. Now that I finally shared her interests, it just made her more hostile. She didn't want me horning in on her territory.

A small crease formed between Melissa's brows as she moved on to the next painting, which portrayed the female lama Machig Ladrön. The sign explained that in the eleventh century, Ms. Ladrön—it *would* be a woman—had originated a new form of charnel ground meditation known as *Chod*. In *Chod* practice, adepts imagine that they are severing their limbs and offering them up to all sentient beings. This is intended to help them "cut through psychological and emotional hindrances and obscurations." As treatment goes, at least it was cheap. Unlike the fifteen years of Gestalt therapy I'd bought for Melissa, just so she could get self-actualized enough to hire her divorce lawyer, Perry the Piranha. I suppose I should be glad she hadn't asked Perry to bite off my limbs. The only part of me Melissa wanted to sever was my balls.

After Rory told me about charnel grounds, I'd done a little online research on them. One article argued that the modern equivalent of the charnel ground experience was "situations of extreme desperation," like the metaphorical charnel grounds of Hollywood, Madison Avenue, Wall Street and Washington, D.C. Funnily enough, those were the places where I'd amassed my fortune. "See babe," I wanted to tell Melissa, "I was a *bodhisattva* ahead of my time." Not that Melissa was a babe any more. She's my age, sixty-two, and her butt has grown considerably, despite all that yoga. Maybe she should try aerobics.

I realized I was having negative thoughts. I shook my head to clear them away. The point of this party was supposed to be forgiveness. I had to let go of my anger, and embrace empathy and acceptance. It was important that I remember that.

Norman, my thirty-year-old son with Melissa, was ogling a fourteenth-century Tibetan sculpture of a yogi riding bareback on a female zombie. Trust Normie to go for the cheap thrill. Though I can't really say Norm's hobbies—Ecstasy, knocking up Russian models, and torturing small animals—are inexpensive. Like Melissa always says, I shouldn't underestimate him. Melissa blames me for Norm's personality quirks. She thinks I was too parsimonious with quality time during his childhood. Melissa won't admit her heavy schedule of navel-gazing hadn't left her much face time with little Normie either.

I stopped myself again. Tonight's theme was absolution. I really had to stick with the program. I did a round of yogic breathing to calm myself. *Breathe out red, breathe in blue. Breathe out anger, breathe in peace.*

My second ex-wife, Lindsay, in her mid-forties and still icily hot, was scrutinizing a sculpture billed as "Lords of the Charnel Grounds." It depicted a skeleton couple dancing together, their skins unfurling around them like streamers. My Tibetologist buddy Rory stood next to Lindsay, pontificating about the artworks and trying to hit on her. Rory was a skinny, fiftyish guy in Tibetan robes, with a silver ponytail and sharp, handsome features. A tool, but a useful one. Rory liked to lecture women on the Tibetan concept of *Bardo*, the intermediate state between one life and the next. *Bardo*, he'd tell them, also refers to "transitional states," like sex or "poosy," as Rory liked to call it. Rory was welcome to try tantric sex with Ex Numero Dos. Lindsay too liked "poosy"—especially of the protégées she picked up at the shelter

she'd started, and I'd funded, for runaway girls. Lindsay's charity work was a triumph of efficiency. It got her into pubescent
pudenda and Park Avenue parties simultaneously.

Tiffany, my lovely twenty-two-year-old daughter with Lindsay,
stood at the other end of the room, as far away as possible from
her mother. She was texting up a storm on her iPhone, no doubt
lining up dates for the next few months. Tiff is more ecumeni-
cal in her tastes than her mom, though unlike her half-brother,
she keeps away from rodents. Tiffany was named for her mom's
favorite store. You'd think Lindsay wouldn't go for girly things
like jewelry, but no such luck.

My thoughts had strayed from my party theme again, I realized. Perhaps I should steer clear of family, always an over-
emotional topic. Maybe I'd get myself in a better mind-frame if
I concentrated on the colleagues and friends I'd invited. Like my
favorite client, Ted Hawks, a golden boy from the deep South.

A soft smile played over Ted's handsome mouth as he examined a ritual trumpet fashioned from a human shinbone. It was
used by Tibetan monks to remind them, yet again, of You Know
What. Ted was the first big client I hooked after I morphed from
entertainment lawyer to talent agent. I'd helped Ted transition
from modeling to acting, tripling his income and my fees. A beautiful friendship—until he decided he was too upscale for me and
moved to The Talent Atelier. When I bought up TTA a few years
later, I saw to it that Ted got fewer phone calls than a Trappist
monk. I'll say this for Teddy, he's mastered the art of the strate-
gic grovel. He was so stressed he managed to appear genuinely
contrite—the first competent acting job of his life. I like to help
my clients stretch themselves artistically.

A few feet away from Ted, my former partner, Steve Glass,
was earnestly examining a diagram of the six Buddhist realms
of reincarnation—the kingdoms of Gods, Demigods, Humans,
Animals, Hungry Ghosts and Hell. Realm-wise, Steve would fit
in well with the Hungry Ghosts. He had tried to steal five scripts,

eight clients and Erkka, our multi-talented Finnish receptionist, when he broke away from me. Too bad that hadn't worked
out for him.

Standing next to Steve was Liza Merck, another ex-employ-
ee. I'd congratulated myself on my professional attitude towards
Liza. Despite her good looks, I'd only hit on her once. Liza had
viewed my restraint as an insult, and chosen to follow Steve to
his new gig. I'd also invited some colleagues from my former law
firm. I'd forgiven them for spilling their guts to the state ethics
commission. Jealousy makes people act ugly sometimes.

I was getting negative again. I took a deep breath. It was time
for Rory to start the ceremony. The rite we had planned would
improve my mood. Rory clapped his hands together.

"Family, friends and colleagues of Leo Mack. Please take your
seats. It's time for us to commence our Ceremony of Celebration."
He pointed to the rows of folding chairs I'd had the museum set
up. Behind them was a long table, covered with bottles of champagne and boxes of fine chocolates. My guests obediently sat, and
Rory began his speech.

"As you can see from this wonderful exhibit, Tibetans believe a crucial task for the living is preparing for death. Tibetan
Buddhists believe that, after physical death, consciousness lin-
gers for forty-nine days, during which one hundred symbolic
deities—both peaceful and wrathful—appear to the departed.
If the deceased is able to recognize that these visions are illu-
sions, he or she will obtain nirvana. If not, the cycle of reincarnation continues.

"The Tibetans have developed a guide to this intermediate
state between death and rebirth, called the *Bardo Thodrol*. In the
West, we translate those words as 'The Book of the Dead.' A more
accurate rendition is 'The Great Liberation upon Hearing in the
Intermediate State.' Tibetans read the *Bardo Thodrol* to the deceased to guide them through their journey after death.

"A dear friend of mine called me last year to tell me his father was critically ill. He asked me to read to his father from the Book of the Dead. I told my friend that would be meaningless, unless his father had practiced Buddhism during his life. Instead, we should perform a ritual that would have real significance. I asked him what his dad most enjoyed, and he said 'Jerry Lewis movies.' So my friend and I sat by his father for five days and watched Jerry Lewis with him, and he went calmly and happily on his journey. I told this tale to another dear friend, Leo Mack. When Leo learned he had Stage Four cancer, he remembered my story. Leo is one of the few Westerners I know who faces death with open eyes and without flinching."

I bowed my head modestly at this tribute.

"Leo asked me to work with him to devise a dying ritual that would best celebrate his life. Leo and I decided to bring together all the people Leo is most fond of—his family, his friends and his colleagues. We put that together with Leo's new hobby, Tibetan art, and some of his old enthusiasms, champagne and chocolate, and that's how this party came to be. Leo's picked out special vintage champagnes to share with all of you. He has a special treat for the ladies, a lovely, vintage pink champagne. Dom Pérignon Rosé 1993. He hasn't neglected the boys either. You gentlemen are getting the remarkable Joseph Perrier Josephine 1990."

A few of the women rolled their eyes at the idea of separate but equal champagnes, but nobody protested. Cancer has its privileges. Besides, most of the women were hoping I'd remember the good times when I signed the final version of my will.

"I'm going to go around and pour for each and every one of you," Rory continued. "And then I'll ask you to take a bite of fine chocolate and a drink of champagne to toast Leo's life."

Rory got down from his podium and circulated among my guests, making sure that everybody took a small taste of champagne before the toast. Rory was my accomplice. There was a further sacrament hidden inside my ritual, or as Rory might put it, a jewel inside my lotus. The women's pink champagne, I'd informed

Rory, would be drugged with rohypnol—the date rape drug. The men's libation would be spiked with LSD. The males would be sent home, where they'd experience the finest trip money could buy. Once they'd departed, I would take the women on a journey to that most transcendent of states, tantric union.

"Even Tiffany—your daughter?" Rory had asked. I could tell the thought of incest gave him a *frisson*.

"What kind of perve do you think I am?" I'd rejoined. "But no reason *you* shouldn't be with her. Everyone in the Manhattan phone directory has." You see, I'd secured Rory's cooperation by a simple expedient, promising him a share of the spoils. Rory had proved invaluable, even convincing the museum to keep the guards on the first floor, far away from our party on Level Six. We'd planned to take our conquests to the fifth floor, where the museum had constructed two small chambers as shrines to the Peaceful and Wrathful Deities. Rory would bed down in the chapel of the Peaceful Deities, and I with the Wrathful ones.

"To Leo's life," Rory said. The assembled guests clicked glasses and drank up. Rory circulated again, making sure everyone drained their glass to the dregs. I'd worried that the perpetually-dieting women wouldn't drink their fair share. Finishing the drink was crucial to the ritual, Rory told them. "And now Leo will speak to you."

I went up to the podium.

"My dear wives and children, my friends and my colleagues," I began. "All of you have been with me on the long journey of my life. I want to thank you for coming on the voyage with me. I apologize if the trip hasn't always been a pleasant one. I'm not an easy man. I have high standards, and I grow disappointed when people don't meet them. I know I can be difficult, exacting, and critical."

The guests shook their heads, emitting a low hum of negation and reassurance. Rory came up to me and whispered in my ear. "They all drank. I made sure."

"I poured drinks for us as well," I whispered back, pointing to two champagne flutes. "Our very own Love Potion Number Nine. One hundred milligrams of Viagra a glass."

"I don't really need…" Rory demurred.

"Of course not," I whispered. "It's just to enhance your experience. And frankly, I do need it. I'm a sick man." I could see Rory was mortified at offending me. He picked up his glass and gulped it down.

"This is the end of my life," I told the crowd. "It's time for me to be honest. I know that at times—too many times—I've been a hard boss, an unavailable friend, an absentee husband and father." My guests were silent. They weren't sure how to play this. I could tell Melissa was dying to agree with me, but was restraining herself for the sake of Norman's inheritance. Melissa had actually liked me, once. We'd trembled as we'd undressed each other, grinned at our wedding album, rejoiced when she got pregnant with Norman, dreamed together of his bright future. We'd lived all the clichés in every corny flick I'd ever produced, and at the time they'd seemed fresh and real. That was why she hated me so vehemently.

My second marriage had been strictly a commercial arrangement, so there were fewer hard feelings when it imploded. "Just bidness," like Ted Hawks had said in his flowery Southern accent during his epic apology. I'd felt a small spurt of emotion at Tiffany's birth, but by then I'd seen the movie before. I knew it wouldn't have a happy ending.

"I ask your forgiveness," I said. My guests nodded. Nothing to forgive they murmured. My daughter Tiffany was looking a little pale. Rory had seen it, too. He was licking his chops imagining her incipient swoon.

"Honesty compels me to admit that your conduct hasn't been flawless either. My wives and children haven't been as loving as I wished. My friends and colleagues haven't been as loyal as I hoped. When I learned I had Stage Four cancer—a death sentence—I was consumed by rage and self-pity. All the injuries of a lifetime came back to me: your petty betrayals and frivolous slights, your deep shallowness and ingratitude. I was inspired to play a little game with you. I circulated a rumor that I was bankrupt as well as dying. Not one of you kept in touch. I lay wasting away in my hospital bed, my body choked with tumors, my veins pricked by a thousand needles and suffused with toxic chemicals. I heard nothing from any of you." I stared at Tiffany, whose pallor had increased. "Not even a text." I gave them a sardonic look. "Until I let it be known that the rumor was false. I was wealthier than ever before."

I could see the anger and consternation in the eyes of my guests. The murmur of their voices grew harsh, but not all were able to express their pique. Several of the ladies' complexions were beginning to resemble Tiffany's.

"My experiment only increased my wrath. My heart was filled with black rage against all of you, but then I began to reconsider. Rory had been teaching me about Tibetan art, and from Tibetan art we'd moved on to Tibetan Buddhism. The Buddha teaches that all sorrow comes from attachment. I realized that was the root of my problem. I was too attached. Attached to material things, to people, to power, to a vision of myself. And most of all, I was attached to my anger. In order to die in peace, I needed to let go."

Ted Hawks and Steve Glass exchanged little smirks. "The old man's lost his edge," I could hear them agree.

"Cancer was a great opportunity for me to learn and grow," I continued. "It was a chance to learn acceptance. To forgive you and to forgive myself. To release my attachment to anger, and try to achieve *nirvana*, right here on earth, in the few days remaining to me. I learned to meditate. I felt at one with the world, and with all of you, my family and friends. I followed the wonderful Buddhist practice of *metta bhavana*—loving-kindness meditation—which helped me to empathize with and understand you."

I paused. Ted and Steve were still smirking. So was Norman, and even Melissa.

"Yet despite all that," I continued, "I found my anger

returning. It was so hard for me to let it go. I struggled with my-self, and finally I resolved my conflict. My anger was merited. Why should I let it go? I was damned if I would. It looked like, sadly, cancer would not be my ticket to enlightenment. But it could be something even better, I realized. A golden Get Out of Jail Free card. I could do anything I wanted. At this stage, what did it matter?"

"Is he ever going to get to the fucking point?" I heard Tiffany murmur to her mother. I didn't resent it. Tiff was obviously feel-ing rather ill.

"You're quite right," I said. "I need to get to the point. Here it is. I've put aconite in your champagne. Wolfsbane, if you pre-fer the more poetic name. A lovely purple flower that grows, ap-propriately enough, in the Himalayas. It's a fast-acting poison. The effects manifest themselves somewhere between two min-utes and two hours after ingestion, depending on how much you ate for dinner."

Rory looked at me. He and I had dined together before the party, and he'd eaten greedily I didn't know where he put it in that thin frame of his. Unlike bulimic Tiffany, he wouldn't yet be feeling the effects. But his eyes told me that he guessed. He, too, had been poisoned. Only Rory had drunk the "Viagra" I'd supposedly prepared for the two of us. I gave him a small smile, confirming his conjecture. He hadn't really injured me, but his combination of sanctimonious mysticism and oily lechery grat-ed on me.

"It's not a pleasant death," I continued. "You'll freeze and burn and sweat. You'll experience vomiting, diarrhea, and stab-bing abdominal pain. Your pulse will slow and you may start to feel numb. You'll suffer convulsions, and if you're lucky, you'll go into a coma. Then you'll die."

I was being melodramatic, but what the hell; it was my big moment. Those guests who weren't already struggling with symp-toms started shouting and shrieking for help. Let them scream.

It didn't matter to me. If my money and my cancer didn't keep me out of jail, I was content to spend my last two months of life in prison, savoring happy memories of this party.

"Oh, and I'm afraid there isn't any antidote." This wasn't strictly true, but the dosage had been generous, and my speech was timed to take them beyond the window in which the remedy was effective. Chances of recovery were nil.

The guards had finally come running up from the first floor. I started laughing.

"After all," I said. "What can you do to get back at me? Kill me?"

*

Copyright © 2011 Susan Chalfin

Susan Chalfin has published articles on mystery gaming for *The Daily News* and essays on the darker side of parenting for *Big Apple Parent*. She lives in Manhattan with her husband (a bankruptcy lawyer and musical omnivore) and two daughters (a fifteen-year-old who writes fantasy novels about elves, and a twelve-year-old who pens myths about dryads). Susan is working on selling her first novel, *Preschool Is Murder*, a mystery that satirizes Manhattan preschools. For her day job, Susan is a securitization and derivatives attorney. She promises to stop wrecking the economy as soon as she gets a nice book deal.

The Cost of Cigarettes
by Nan Higginson

I stood silent, listening to my sister lie.

"Granny, we got no money for cigarettes," Jax insisted, poison twitching through her veins. She twitches a lot lately, eyes darting as if following a hummingbird, juiced up on God-only-knows what. She's good at getting away with every scam she runs, but one of these days she won't be so lucky. I try to stay prepared.

"Don't look so stupid, Granny. I told you 'bout that. They're taxing the crap out of us. Ten friggin' dollars for a pack of cigs? It's crazy!"

Gram rocked in her chair, round-shouldered, bleary-eyed, waiting to be called up to heaven. In the meantime, she was trapped in a worn project apartment in the Stapleton Houses on Staten Island's east shore. Her skin sags off her face so bad, you want to cry along with her even if she's laughing. When I help her into the bathtub, I see an old turtle with no shell. I've been praying for her a lot more lately. Don't want to see her go; do want her to rest in peace.

Jax snapped her gum and studied her false fingernails, done in a puke green that seemed to suit the occasion.

"Granny, focus! You gotta choose and you gotta choose now. Boner said he'd go in halves with you on the cigs, but not on the mac-and-cheese. So, what you want? Food or smokes? Which do you want?"

That's the only choice Jax gave. I avoided Gram's eyes.

Jax scares the crap out of me sometimes. She and me made

a pact last year: whenever she was doing something like gaming on a teacher or stealing earrings at the mall, I either backed her up or got the stuffing kicked out of me. My choice. Okay, so that makes me a capital-L LOSER who always does the stupidest thing. But I swear Jax is made of steel and barbed wire. Even when Jax makes Gram her victim, I keep my big mouth shut.

Jax hissed a warning. "What'll it be, Granny? I'm leavin' for the store. Macaroni and cheese or a split of cigarettes? Now or never." Jax checked her watch and grabbed her purse. "What's it gonna be, Granny? I don't got all day."

I shrugged into my raincoat as Jax headed for the door. Jax was bad enough, normally, but two weeks ago, she tongue-kissed some wannabe Bad Boy from the Berry Houses, south a ways in Dongan Hills. She's been stalking him ever since. Word's going around that Spitz plans to appear at a drugstore's opening party over on Victory Boulevard. Now Jax keeps saying he's her ticket out of the projects. Good luck with that.

"Old woman, we're leaving now." Jax gave Gram a stare that would kill. "What do you want us to bring back?"

Gram tsk'ed as she weighed her choices. "Look under the can of roach spray in the kitchen cabinet. They's a folded up ten there. Split it with Boner so's we'll both have some-a each." She sounded tired beyond measure. She stopped rubbing her forehead long enough to blow her nose with a crinkled tissue. "Glad you two don't smoke. It's a real killer."

Jax crouched down in front of the only cabinet door that still hung on both hinges. For a fraction of a moment, I hoped Jax would relax and tell Gram that our network of Native American relatives wouldn't leave us spinning in the wind. They still had tobacco that was not just for tribal ceremonials. Instead, Jax said, "Here's Grammy's ten!" and stood up, all smiles, tucking Gram's money into her purse.

Jax turned serious. "Granny! Listen up," She snapped her fingers. "We'll be back when we get back. There's a dinner's worth of leftovers in the 'fridge and a spare smoke's stuck behind the peanut butter jar in the pantry. Don't wait up."

I cringed when Jax slammed Gram's battered, paint-splattered steel door. I hated that door. The explosion of steel against steel rang inside my head like a dream shattered, trapping innocent people like Gram and me inside our own fears. A quick moment later I heard Gram's strip of deadbolts snicking into place, one after the other.

We headed for the garbage-littered elevator like freed prisoners. Once outside, in the dank, gray world, Jax fluffed her hair, tossed her platform shoes into her big slouch bag and strapped herself into her new four-inch heels. From there on, she unbuttoned yet another inch of cleavage, added another layer of mascara, hiked her skirt up until it was more like a ruffle than a skirt. And me? I kept my raincoat wrapped tight and stuck with Jax, despite all odds.

∼

I could hardly wait to catch the ferry ride across to magic Manhattan, where there's some real-life potential. Home is one step away from the ferry-tale ride of a lifetime. When I aimed myself toward the pearly gates of the ferry station, Jax grabbed my arm and growled. Brainless me.

We were headed to the new drugstore. Even though Jax calls Staten Island the Big Apple's Pits, she's got this guy Spitz in her cross-hairs, and he's staying on home territory to get all the news coverage he can get. They've been practically humping each other on his videos, but other than the promos, I wonder where this is all headed. To me Spitz is a Staten Island homeboy with not much talent, but he has a good drummer and bass guitarist, so he sounds better than he is. I wonder how Jax is going to take it when Wonder Boy either gets mega-hot or bombs out.

Jax tapped my elbow, her eyes narrowed into snake slits. "Hey, nerdling, you forget your chest pads?" She reached into her sack and brought out two wrapped maxi-pads. "Here. Give yourself a chance at getting kissed. Pop these babies into your bra like I told you. Shape up or I'll ditch you in the river."

I pulled my raincoat tighter and dropped the two maxi-pads into my left coat pocket.

I gotta admit, that new local drugstore's like a bit of heaven, or, should I say, a little *bite* of heaven? It's full of temptations— especially chocolate. Dark chocolate! I could hardly keep myself from running to the candy aisle and all that glitter. Jax headed for the cosmetics counter where her buddies, sophomore sluts we knew from school, were imagining a future full of hot sex.

I was in the candy aisle for about three minutes when the store exploded with lights and noise. All heads turned to the front as Spitz, the Boy du Jour, arrived complete with his posse and the Staten Island News crew. Girls gathered like lemmings, turning their heads and then their bodies toward him. Everyone moved toward the lights but me, Jax, and the oldsters, sitting in mis-matched plastic chairs, waiting for their prescriptions to be filled.

Jax hung back, smug with confidence, waiting for Spitz to plant his tongue in her mouth again and announce that she was his…all his.

"Hey, Jax! I need some money," I called. She waved me off, complete with middle finger topping. I knew my place. Lowly freshman, left to her own devices. The good news, now that the world was preening around Spitz, I had the candy aisle all to myself.

I decided I'd be smart for once and compare the calories and the carbs. Do the healthy thing for a change. Gram's diabetes really messed up her life. Not to mention the cigarettes turning her lungs into charcoal. And she was broke. The only joys left for her came from a pot of mac and cheese along with a couple cigarettes daily.

Okay, I have to admit it. I needed to remember the mac and cheese before we left, but I was too addicted to dark chocolate to stop and get it then. I swore I'd only indulge in the best choco-lates offered, and that kinda took priority.

Amazingly enough, packs upon packs of classic chocolates ended up in my right coat pocket. Tons of them, it seemed. New arrivals that needed scrutiny went into the left. I put the rejects back on the shelf as soon as I compared the labels and crunched the numbers. Since government researchers agree that dark candy is good for you, I figured the next thing I needed to do was convert our cupboards into climate-controlled, dark chocolate tins.

As if there wasn't enough noise already, a bunch of suits and cops, loaded with tasers and bullets busted in on the scene. Outside, sirens blared and strobe lights flickered. Spitz stayed calm, paying for a pack of cigarettes with a twenty. A guy in a suit near the cashier told everybody to stay right where they were. He flashed a badge and barked for quiet, as if he could be heard over the sirens from hell. A couple of girls near Spitz tried shouting back, but the big guy with the fat badge had heard it all before.

"Freeze! You have the right to remain silent. Do so! Everybody! Now!" The squad of armed-and-ready cops in blue flanked themselves against the doors, front and back. More suits appeared, fanned around, and sectioned off the store. I might have yelled, "What the hell?" a couple times.

Everybody but Spitz and my sister did as told. I started to yell to Jax to run, but the cop shouted, "Shut Up!"

"Hey, officer," Spitz said, with his right shoulder hunched and his chin tucked in, ready for some sort of fight. "Don't get all crazy on us now."

"I repeat for the idiots: You have the right to remain silent."

Spitz said, "We know all that crap. Just tell us what you want."

Out came the scratch pad and pen. "Your name? For the record."

"Spitz."

"That translate to Dudley Rankel on your driver's license?"

Spitz turned a little puke green, like Jax's nail polish. "Yeah."

I watched my sister for her reaction. She stood with her left arm cocked, like she was gonna jump into a slugging match, when the detective grabbed her right wrist.

Another suit tapped his notepad. "We need the name of the guy who got you to pimp out the twenty-dollar bills he's making. Counterfeiting. Federal offense." He turned a tough-guy eye to us all. This was starting to feel real, not like some Hollywood stunt. "If any of you'd like to save your American Idol here, you need to ID the counterfeiter for us. Trust me, this would be a good thing to do for Sparkey, here."

"That's *Spitz,* you moron," Jax shouted.

The girl standing next to Jax, tears running down her cheek, looked like she was going to collapse. She raised her hand, like we were in school and she was waiting for permission to speak. Jax responded with a fist, hitting the girl's nose. The cops caught the girl in mid-fall and had her sitting on the floor before I could shout, "Stop, Jax!"

The nearest cop smacked handcuffs on Jax, hands behind her back. Her wrists looked so small. The cuffs looked serious.

"Young lady, you just won yourself a trip to jail. You got anybody here you need to say good-bye to?"

Before Jax could say, "No," I said, "Yes! Me!"

The detective gave me a "come here" finger curl.

My brain froze. I wished I hadn't said anything. Jax was going to kill me for getting involved.

"You hot, kid?" the detective asked, nodding at my raincoat.

"What?" I choked. "Hot?" I garbled something and shook my head.

The detective started to pat me down, but got no further than my raincoat's side pockets. He reached inside and pulled out more candy bars than I remembered gathering. They lay in his big mitts, sparkling in all those overhead lights.

"I... I... I was, uh, just sorting...trying to choose..."

A lanky cop headed my way with his handcuffs aimed at my wrists.

"She didn't do squat!" Jax shouted. "I put the stuff in her pockets, gave her some change, she never touched any of the twenties."

A female cop came forward and finished the pat-down, pulling out a couple of new, crisp twenties that were stuck between my maxi pads. It felt like a bad dream. None of this could be happening. I wanted to go back to the candy aisle and its generous supply of dark chocolates.

Jax tried kicking the cop who held her by the handcuffs. He probably could bench press three or four times her weight, but she was demented enough to keep trying. The old detective who first ordered us to shut up cleared his throat. "Young lady, if you don't stop kicking, I'll stick you in a jail cell with the toughest psycho chicks I can find."

Jax looked at me for a moment. I mouthed the word "Please," and she looked away. One long breath later, she stood quietly looking at the floor.

The detective continued. "The more you cooperate," he said, looking at all the upturned faces around the room, "the sooner you'll be out of this mess."

Later on, Boner showed up at the jail, looking for us and his overdue half-pack of cigarettes. We were being held overnight, Jax and me, but the cops said if we cooperated we had a good shot of avoiding jail. The counterfeiters were the ones headed for the pen, so us idiots were likely to catch a break.

Before releasing us to Boner, they brought Jax and me into a room for questioning. They let Jax tell her story first. She took all the blame, told them I didn't know anything. Said she'd put her money into my raincoat, along with the two maxi-pads that never made it into my bra. She said I was too dumb to commit any crime unless by accident. She stared at me as she spoke. We both knew she was lying outright.

But I stood silent, listening to my sister lie.

*

Nan Higginson, Agatha Nominee for "Casino Gamble" (published in *Murder New York Style)*, started her writing career as a winner of the Phyllis Whitney Creative Writing Award. By day, for twenty-four years, Nan taught literary arts, journalism and social studies. At night she coached writers, edited their stories, and contributed stories to *Tuesday Tales,* anthologies published by the Middle Country Public Library. She also freelanced for *Newsday* among other publications. Throughout her adventures, Nan says the support and advice provided by the Sisters in Crime, particularly the Guppies and the New York/Tri-State chapter, have been invaluable.

A COUNTDOWN TO DEATH
BY DEIRDRE VERNE

It all started with the package.

I pulled the yellow slip out of my mail slot and peered through the four-inch box assigned to apartment 4D, Windsor Tower, Tudor City, NYC.

"Hey Luis, you got my package back there or at the front desk?" Luis set a stack of mail aside, rolled his chair over and peered back at me.

"I come around, Miss M. We talk."

"Sure thing." I wondered how much Luis suspected. Ordinarily a superb doorman, he'd been distracted of late. Luis' girlfriend was four months pregnant, and they'd been fighting the same amount of time. He had already packed on fifteen pounds of sympathy weight, straining the seams of his neatly pressed uniform. Unwittingly, I had become the in-house consultant for the doormen in my building. I'd never been able to help myself when it came to matters of a personal nature. I'm one of those individuals who feels perfectly at ease posing questions. This inevitably leads to conversation and soon I'm asked. "So, what do you think?"

"Is it Teresa?" I asked as we exchanged the package for the slip. "I'm surprised. The second trimester is usually the honeymoon phase."

"No, no. My Teresa, she's good." Luis waived politely to an elevator full of tenants exiting the lobby for the mad morning rush through the streets of Manhattan. "It's Mr. Rudkus. He's dead."

"Dead? That can't be." My disbelief bordered on defensive. "I was just at Mount Sinai hospital for a visit and he fully intended on coming home."

In fact, Mr. Rudkus was so concerned with public opinion, he specifically asked me to spread the news of his recovery. With hospital machines pumping and beeping, he was surprisingly purposeful as he squeezed my hand. "It's very important, dear. Make sure the neighbors, the building management and the shopkeepers know that I'll be home before New Year's. And, mail these holiday cards. I must keep up appearances, and we agreed when it got to this point, you'd be my voice. It's what you do best."

We had formed a purely platonic, May-December relationship about a year prior, although our initial meeting was less than random. To this day, I'm certain Mr. Rudkus sought me out. A night owl by nature, I had been toiling away the wee hours as a fact-checker for WPIX in *The Daily News* building on 42nd street, returning to Tudor City by 6 AM. This, it turns out, was the exact time Mr. Rudkus completed his daily chore of depositing one single bag down the garbage chute. We connected over his empty box of Mallomars. There are, of course, two camps. Those who freeze, and those who don't. We both froze, and this culinary commonality was the start of something wonderful, our regular breakfast routine. I absolutely adored our mornings together, as did he. If it wasn't for my reverse sleep pattern, I am sure we could have lingered well past lunch. How we veered from the virtues of cookies to death, I have no idea but the progression was seamless. It happened while I was replenishing his daily pill dispenser.

"I don't think I'll renew the yellow pills." He tossed the bottle in the garbage.

"I don't think you have a choice."

But I was wrong. He did have a choice, and after much discussion, Mr. Rudkus helped me understand his need to live each and every day with humility and grace. More than that, I wanted to help him maintain the quality of life he deserved.

"Well, he's not actually dead." Luis grabbed a ring off his belt and proceeded to sort through a hundred seemingly identical keys.

"He was sent to hospice. That's like dead. My uncle went to hospice and never came home." Like a magician shuffling a deck of cards, Luis plucked the winning key from the stack. "The building manager, he asked me to empty Mr. Rudkus' fridge today."

I clutched my package like a teddy bear and searched frantically around the lobby. A frigid winter breeze whooshed across the lobby as the front door swung shut. The brisk air stung my flushed face, revealing my discomfort. It's not like I didn't know Mr. Rudkus would end up in hospice care. Mentally, I had prepared for this day, but my emotions swelled like a two-year-old begging for attention.

"I have to sit, Luis. Can you join me?" Luis checked his watch, nodded, and we made our way over to the well-appointed seating area.

"Teresa, she loves this furniture. She comes in late at night and pretends like we're rich."

"She's not alone." I assured him. I felt the same way when I'd toured Tudor City searching for a rental within a short walk of *The Daily News* Building. The nine lobbies in the buildings that make up Tudor City, smack dab in midtown Manhattan, are a gothic throwback designed for the diehard anglophile. Stained-glass windows inset with faux family crests, soaring arches lined in burled wood, and stone floors as thick as bedrock are sure to impress even the most jaded New Yorker. Unfortunately at that moment, it felt downright crypt-like.

"Are you going to be okay Miss M? You and Mr. Rudkus, you two are the nice ones. Not everyone is so nice in this building."

"Like Mr. Johns in 5C? I can't stand to be on the same elevator as that man."

Luis chuckled softly. "The guys, we call him El Diablo."

"That's good. I may have to borrow that." I leaned in to Luis and lowered my voice.

"Luis, I try to be one of the good ones but I need to do something bad."

"Lemme guess. You want a little peak in Mr. Rudkus' apartment. Just to say goodbye."

"How did you know?"

Luis tapped his temple. "It's my job."

Luis waived to Fernando at the front desk and rattled off something convincing in Spanish. "I have to clean the fridge anyway, so why not have some company?" He handed me some plastic garbage bags as cover.

Entering Mr. Rudkus' apartment was like stepping into my favorite restaurant at an off-hour. Familiar, but lonely. It was all I could do not to look at our pair of coffee mugs on the kitchen counter.

"So, where do we start?" I placed my package on the hall credenza.

"I got the fridge. You say goodbye to Mr. Rudkus."

I wandered into the living room and ran my hand along the built-in bookshelves lined densely with books on the history of New York City. If it happened south of 42nd street and north of Gramercy Park post World War I, Mr. Rudkus was the man with the details. I counted seven copies of *The Jungle* by Upton Sinclair highlighting Mr. Rudkus' obsession with Manhattan's meat packing industry. "Tell me," I could hear him say, "where do we go for fresh meat now? Fairway? You call that fresh?"

I hesitated before opening the cabinet on the lower half of the bookcase, although I knew full well what I'd find. Rows of ledger books. The type a bookkeeper used before computers wiped out a generation of mid-level management. Green and white marbled fronts with a thick black band running down the side. The ledgers were neatly labeled and organized by year—two per year, one hundred books in total. I knelt down and pulled out the most recent.

"Wow, pretty cool." I said out loud.

"What's that Miss M?" Luis called to me from the kitchen.

"Mr. Rudkus wrote down every penny he spent each week." I flipped the pages back to the third week in October. "Here it is. We went for coffee that week, his treat—$5.50." I scooted into the kitchen to show Luis. There was a certain satisfaction finding documentation of our friendship, as if the ledgers made it official.

"Look at the notation. 'Time with a dear friend.' That's so sweet." I felt a stab of loss.

"Go to May." Luis said as he chucked some old mayo in the garbage. I licked my finger and tabbed backwards.

"There." Luis leaned over my shoulder and pointed with his elbow to a line item. "He gave my nephew Martin a $250 check at his graduation from Baruch. Good man, no?"

"Very good man. The notation says 'Worthy Investment.'" A prideful smile spread across Luis' face.

I ran my hand down the column of numbers and did some quick calculations. "Not only was he good, but generous. A $250 gift is a considerable sum on a fixed income."

"How much money has he got?"

"Now, that's a nosy question even for me, Luis." I shut the ledger firmly to punctuate the end of our snooping. "I can't tell anyway. The ledger just lists the expenses, and my guess is that he was on a tight budget. I don't think he spent more than $1000 in any one month. Interesting, huh?"

"I guess. If you like numbers." Luis frowned his disinterest and heaved the garbage toward the hall.

I replaced the ledger and closed the cabinet. Less two bags of old food, Luis and I left Mr. Rudkus' apartment the way we found it. Almost.

"Luis, my package. It's still inside." He handed me the key and headed for the garbage disposal. I slipped back in, grabbed my package, and ever so gently swiped the spare keys off the hall credenza. I tossed the master key back to Luis, and returned to my apartment feeling just a little guilty.

I set the package down on my coffee table, grabbed a Diet Coke, and headed straight back to Mr. Rudkus' apartment.

Mr. Rudkus' desk was positioned directly under a large casement window framing a sliver of the East River. The light was extraordinary for a city apartment, thanks to its position perched atop a granite cliff. If you could snare a Tudor City apartment just south of the United Nations, the view was golden. The current residents, I'm sure, had no memory of the turn of the century tenements, slums and slaughterhouses that originally lined First Avenue. I imagined Mr. Rudkus spending numerous hours filling out his ledgers in this very spot, back when Tudor City was truly the urban utopia it set out to be. The tree-lined sanctuary hovering over Second Avenue was home to well-groomed gardens, lively playgrounds and a host of cozy restaurants. I opened his day planner, the object of my curiosity, and perused his scheduled activities for December, 2010. True to form, he had honored his part of the agreement. The calendar was packed with plans. Drinks with friends, the movies, senior functions at the YWCA. The upcoming month of January told the same story.

As I had hoped, and as I had been promised, nothing in his planner indicated imminent death. The details of his life could trip up the casual observer and that's exactly how he wanted it. "Remember, tell them I'm coming home. That's your first job."

I was jolted out of my reverie by the buzz of the intercom. My Coke upended and fizzled its way down the side of the desk. Like a trained seal, I made a beeline for the door and pressed the buzzer. Not a smart move. Why not just announce myself to the caller? I was just about to release the button, when I overheard Luis' voice on the other end of the intercom.

"Silly me. I pressed the buzzer out of habit. Please take the keys and go on up. The fridge, it's clean." I heard feet clicking across stone and the thud of the elevator landing in the lobby. This time Luis' voice came through sounding an awful lot like an angry Ricky Ricardo. "Are you crazy Miss M? Mr. Rudkus' cousin, she's here with a real estate agent. You get out of there."

I released the button faster than a handle on a hot skillet. I had about three seconds to disappear. I grabbed my Diet Coke and fled for the door. I turned the lock just as the elevator was opening. Taking two giant steps sideways, I slid silently into my own apartment.

I had heard volumes about the Rudkus clan. Most stories included a revolving door of prep schools, followed by long summers abroad, financed by a family real estate business. "Flip, flip, flip. Never made sense to me." Mr. Rudkus' paltry ledgers supported his depression-era mentality, and, despite his apparent lack of funds, he was convinced his family was ready to pounce. In all fairness, I had been warned by Mr. Rudkus to expect an onslaught. "Oh, they'll come at the slightest hint of trouble."

I dashed for my kitchen, grabbed a juice glass, and propped it up against the wall. Nothing. I poured out the remnants of my mug and repeated the same routine. I caught some muffled sounds before trying a location further down the room. Balancing on the back of my couch about midway up the wall allowed for a few snippets of conversation.

"Cash deal in two weeks." That's all I could make out. A cash deal before the end of the year? A pipe dream given the economy, but who was I to argue? As Mr. Rudkus had predicted, the wheels were in motion, and his failing health was the starting gun. That was my cue.

I collapsed into the sofa and dialed Luis' cell.

"I can't talk, Miss M. You'll get me in trouble."

"Luis, something is wrong. Mr. Rudkus is not even dead, and his apartment is up for sale. I didn't even know Mr. Rudkus owned! In fact, now that I think about it, his ledgers had no expense for rent or maintenance. Don't you think that's strange?"

"Miss M., I told you. I'm not good with numbers."

"Fine Luis. Where's Martin these days?"

"Some fancy place on Wall Street with lots of names."

～

Luis was more than happy to unload me onto his nephew, Martin. I punched in the number and worked through the automated phone tree at Kravits, Klein and Couchman until I got to Ramos. Martin, the eager new recruit, picked up on the first ring.

"Commercial investments. Martin Ramos speaking. How may I help you?"

"Martin, this is Susan Miles—Mr. Rudkus' neighbor."

"Is this about an investment? I'd be happy to introduce you to our portfolio of financial products."

"Don't be ridiculous. I'm broke. But Mr. Rudkus needs a favor, and he said you're good with numbers."

"Sure thing, how about if I come by this weekend? I owe Mr. Rudkus a visit."

"No, it has to be now."

"Miss Miles." Martin whispered into the receiver, and I imagined him crouched low in his cubicle. "I've only been here two months. I can't just up and leave."

"You get a lunch break right?"

"Yeah, but I eat at my desk."

"Tell your boss you're coming uptown to meet a client for lunch. He'll be very impressed."

I filled Martin in on the events of the morning, putting considerable emphasis on the $250 graduation check he'd received from Mr. Rudkus no more than seven months ago. My pleading eventually wore him down, and we made plans to meet at my place at noon. That gave me about two hours to massage my conscience. I swore to Mr. Rudkus I wouldn't make my next move, but it was inevitable. I needed to see him one last time.

I bundled up like an Iditarod racer and headed west. Droplets of snow hung in the air as I weaved my way through a dozen Salvation Army Santas. I caught the 6-train up to Mount Sinai and headed straight for the nurses' station.

As luck would have it, I spotted a physician right off.

"Excuse me, Doctor. May I have word?"

"Pfizer rep? Sorry, but I've got a house full today." He jammed a chart in the door sleeve and reached for the antiseptic dispenser. His body language seemed impenetrable, but I had something up my sleeve. Tears. Real ones, too. They were surprisingly easy to conjure up given Mr. Rudkus' impending death. I threw in a snort for good measure, and was hustled immediately into the doctors' lounge.

"You are?"

"Susan Miles. I need to see Mr. Rudkus." I accepted the tissue and dabbed at my eyes.

"Mr. Rudkus. Quite an interesting fellow. He drove the kitchen crew crazy with his requests for higher quality meat." He smiled softly. "On the upside, his lungs cleaned up beautifully."

"That's the problem. It seems he's gone to hospice. Only family can visit, so I'll need a doctor's permission."

"Hospice. I'm so sorry, I didn't know." The doctor appeared genuinely baffled as he flipped through a stack of papers. "I don't see anything unusual in the chart. Unfortunately, at his age, recovery can be fleeting. I'm sure his family felt it was the right decision."

"Please, Doctor, eighty is the new sixty."

"That may be, but Mr. Rudkus is 102."

Words, my reliable friends, evaporated faster than the tears on my cheeks. Thousands upon thousands of words to choose from, dictionaries filled with innumerable variations, yet they ran off my tongue and dribbled down my chin leaving me without a proper response.

"Oh," was all I could muster.

The doctor mumbled on about the gruesome effects of aging, allowing me a second to regain some semblance of composure. Mr. Rudkus had lied. Or had he? It's not as though the movie theatre carded seniors. And frankly, I had no idea what 102 looked like. A number that high was usually reserved for fevers or heat waves. The question, the hard question, was whether he had lied about something else. In the end, I went with my gut. Life was the issue, not age, and regardless of what happened next, I felt as though I had delivered on at least part of my promise. I had announced his intended return with conviction. Tie a yellow ribbon, fellow Tudor City inhabitants, Mr. Rudkus will be coming home.

And home was where I needed to be, since it was too late to cancel Martin. I sprung for a cab and arrived just in time to meet Martin in the lobby. I rehashed the morning, leaving out my momentary lapse at the hospital.

"Let me get this straight. Mr. Rudkus is broke, but fears his relatives are after his nest egg." Decked out in his interview suit, Martin embodied the naivety of youth. Trusting and green.

"That's right."

"And as of two weeks ago, he thought he was coming home from the hospital."

"Right again."

"So when did he send you this package?"

"Package?"

Martin pushed the package across my coffee table. "I recognize the handwriting from my graduation check."

"Oh my gosh, the package." As it was getting increasingly difficult to remember my role in Mr. Rudkus' final affairs, I had forgotten the package. I tore at the brown wrapping, tossed the box aside and handed Martin the contents of the package. Another green-and-white speckled ledger. It took about twenty minutes for Mr. Rudkus' worthy investment to pay off.

"Holy shit. This ledger itemizes his income." Martin loosened his tie, whipped out a Blackberry, and worked his thumbs at break neck pace.

"Susan, the guy is worth millions. I don't know what the hell he was telling people, but Mr. Rudkus is rolling in it." He laughed with sheer delight as he ran through the numbers.

"Remember his obsession with meat? It's all here." Martin pulled out some yellowed papers and a tintype photo from the box. "He owned a slaughter house between First and Second Avenues, right below this building. He didn't sell when Tudor City was constructed. He traded his property for part ownership in the entire complex. That's him in the photo under the Rudkus Meat sign."

"Well, I'll be darned. That's why the ledgers didn't include a line for rent. Martin, you're a genius!" I reached out to give Martin a pat on the back, but he was shaking his head violently like a dog out of water.

"What's wrong?

"His family. Mr. Rudkus thought they were after his money."

"Well yeah, but the point seems moot. At his age, their inheritance is inevitable."

"Half the inheritance was inevitable. But *all* of the inheritance is a sure thing before January 1, 2011."

"You've lost me, Martin." I squinted as if I was listening with my eyes. I had practiced this look for Mr. Rudkus, hoping it would come in handy. Feigning confusion when you know the answer is harder than you think.

"During the Bush administration, Congress raised the estate-tax exemptions on inheritances. That law's due to expire. The new law doesn't come into effect until January 1, 2011. If Mr. Rudkus dies within the next few days, his estate will not be taxed. Not a penny of it." Martin handed me the ledger. "Susan, don't you see? He sent you the ledger as proof of his family's guilt. By forcing him into hospice, his relatives are withdrawing medical attention in an attempt to hasten his death. The motive is in their timing."

"Martin, he's been in hospice care for a few days already. What if it's too late?"

"I'm dialing the police now."

And he did. Of course, Martin's frantic call to the police came too late. That's exactly how Mr. Rudkus wanted it.

Martin left me curled up on my couch with a pile of soggy tissues.

"Can I get you anything else before I leave, Susan?"

I pointed to the stack of 78's Mr. Rudkus had given me before going to the hospital.

"Put on 'The Entertainer' by Scott Joplin." The 1920s ragtime theme from The Sting seemed fitting as I recalled the morning Mr. Rudkus presented his elaborate scheme to choreograph his own death.

～

"Mr. Rudkus, explain it to me one more time." I held my coffee cup for a refill.

"It's simple. My money, all of it, is going to charity. My family will contest the will and insist I was not of sound mind. By framing them for my murder, any attempts to dissolve the document will only increase their guilt."

"Where do I come in?"

"You must alert the players in my life that my intent was to live. The police will investigate, and their conclusion must be airtight. The authorities must believe in my desire to live."

"But you don't want to live."

"My time has come. If my medications are halted, my days will be numbered."

"If I help, isn't it assisted suicide?"

"Technically. But it's my choice, and your participation in an otherwise illegal activity will be masked by layers of diversion. I've edited the ledgers to tell a story. I've maintained the social calendar of a debutante. The graduation check was planned to garner Martin's participation. The package is important. Remember to reveal the package at the right moment."

"Do you have to do it now? Can't it wait?"

"No Susan, it can't wait."

I rose from the table to wash our mugs. Really just an excuse to hide my tears. I was thinking how lonely I'd be each morning when I heard my own thoughts echoed.

"Susan, I'm going to miss this, too."

✴

Copyright © 2011 Deirdre Verne

Deirdre Verne is the Curriculum Chair of Marketing at Westchester Community College where she has been teaching for the past ten years. In addition, she is a freelance writer and has contributed to business publications, college textbooks and *Murder New York Style*. Prior to joining the faculty, Deirdre worked in new product development and marketing for Time, Inc. representing magazine titles such as *Fortune, Money* and *Parenting*. She holds a B.A. in Economics from Georgetown University and a MBA from Hofstra University. She resides in Edgemont, NY with her husband and two children.

A Poet's Justice
by Eileen Dunbaugh

Senida leaned over the old lady's knobby shoulders, surrounding the fragile limbs as carefully as if they were bone china. Together, they sifted through the pictures in the box, Senida helping her to hold each one as she tried to recall who it was and where it had been taken.

"Peter," she prompted. "Astoria Park."

They had a guest today, but with her first expressions of delight in seeing her great-niece over, Maddie's eyes and hands had wandered back to her picture box.

"You must do this for hours," the niece said.

Senida nodded without resentment, knowing that life, tentative as the fluttering of a butterfly, could not keep hold of her employer for much longer.

The relative, who'd given her name as Ellen, picked up Maddie's tea service and headed for the kitchen. Senida started to get up too, but Ellen urged her to sit.

"I used to be requisitioned to wash up here all the time when I was a kid," she said. "Aunt Maddie would tie these giant aprons around me and my sister, and leave us to it. The cracks in the sink are deeper now, but everything else is still pretty much the same."

The tension in Senida's chest eased a little, but then the phone rang, and she picked up to a familiar sharp voice.

"For me?" Ellen said, coming back into the room and taking the handset from her. "Jean?"

She lowered her voice.

"You can't imagine how strange it is to be here. Remember how all these places in Maddie's neighborhood seemed so full of mystery when we were kids coming in from the suburbs? When I drove up today, all I could see from La Guardia all the way to Ditmars and down into Maddie's neighborhood by the Hell Gate was one row of brick two-stories after another, each with its same tiny patch of garden and plaster Virgin. As similar as Monopoly houses, and lined up just like them."

Senida had kept very still, trying to catch what was said, but an amplification device had been installed on the phone for Maddie's benefit, and it projected the voice on the other end so startlingly that Ellen jerked back from the receiver.

"Will you come down to earth, Ellen! They could be robbing Maddie blind. How *is* Maddie anyway?"

The back of their visitor's neck reddened like mercury rising.

"Maddie's fine," she said. "Look, I can't talk now. I'll call you back later."

When the phone was back in its cradle, a guilty glance from Ellen found its way to where Senida perched behind Maddie.

"The sunflowers are still here—well, not the same ones, of course," came her raised voice a moment later. "My sister and I used to play tag around their giant stalks. We'd be feeling all confined in these silly starched dresses girls used to wear.

"Sorry, I'm blabbering away," she said when Senida appeared in the kitchen doorway. "Is there a towel?" She held up a dripping plate.

Senida opened the door to the basement and pulled a cloth from the rod on the back of it. She was about to close it again when Ellen latched onto her arm, and leaned forward to peer down the stairs.

"Oh my God, I just remembered. Aunt Maddie had a tenant down there once, who owned a player piano. We thought it was the most amazing thing, like ghost hands were flying over the keys."

"Yes, well, it's there still," Senida said, "along with so many other things, almost you cannot move."

Her dish suddenly deposited on the counter, Ellen started for the steep stairs.

"*Na, na,*" Senida said, pointing to her heels.

Not that a wobbly heel would have stopped the old lady. Senida had been told that before she arrived, Maddie had climbed that flight of stairs alone, hauling laundry. It was only after she slipped on a patch of ice that her lawyer, Antonelli, had taken over.

"And not one single family member came!" Antonelli's wife had whispered to Senida on the way back from the hospital with Maddie.

Senida had expected Antonelli to feel contempt for Ellen, coming so many months later. But he hadn't. She'd stood with him while Ellen parked her rental car and, introductions and greetings exchanged, he launched right in to a cheerful account of how he'd used Maddie's power of attorney, pointing to a step that had been repaired, and to Senida herself, whom he'd hired to be on hand for Maddie's return.

Senida, meanwhile, had gone for the car's trunk to get Ellen's bag. Antonelli had booked a hotel room near the airport for Ellen, but it suddenly occurred to Senida, as they stood there in the kitchen cleaning up, to offer the woman the tiny bedroom next to Maddie's where she'd been sleeping.

"Then where would you sleep?" Ellen said. "From what I understand, that little apartment upstairs is shut up and in pretty bad shape."

Senida pointed to the basement door. "A what-do-you-call-it—pull out? Down there."

Ellen's gaze wandered to the mullioned window over the sink for a moment, and then, before Senida could stop her, she was on her way down the stairs. "No need for you to give up your bed," she shouted up from below. "This will be fine for me if you've got some clean sheets."

While Senida unfolded and made up the sofa bed, Ellen tried everything she could think of to get that old piano—fond memory of her childhood—going again. But then, as if she'd suddenly recalled her sister's sharp reprimand, she headed upstairs and settled herself at the desk in the living room, where the chits she needed to check Antonelli's accounting were kept.

Her gushing enthusiasm was all gone, Senida saw, when she peeked into the living room a few minutes later. And her intentness had raised an alarm in Maddie. Senida could see wounded pride in the old woman's eyes.

Finally Maddie's words came, hard fought, the muscles in her face almost too weak to form them.

"I shhhould be doing that."

She made an ineffective attempt to point at Ellen, her arm bobbing like a compass needle.

Senida could feel Maddie's hurt radiating across the room. Unable to bear it, she came in and hugged Maddie, and suggested, in her jolliest voice, that they listen to show tunes on the cabinet stereo.

She longed to point out to Ellen that she could have waited until Maddie went to bed, and to let her know, too, that she was working unpaid overtime. It was Sunday, when Antonelli normally sent a volunteer over from the church so that she could relax and telephone her mother back home.

Once Maddie was absorbed in the music, Senida did slip back to her room to make her call. But when she heard the stack of records finish and Ellen's voice, full of instructiveness, replace the music, she quickly told her mother she'd call her back.

From the entrance to the living room, Senida observed Maddie's fingers tapping on the arms of her chair. Ellen eyed the tapping fingers as if she thought her great-aunt might be hearing phantom music. The rasp of exasperation entered her voice as she said: "I think there will be enough money for you and Senida to stay on here if we can refinance the house, Aunt Maddie."

"I dh-hon't *want* to sssell…"

"This is so you can *keep* the house!"

Maddie shrugged, then nodded at Ellen and looked up at Senida. "Ssooo beautiful," she said.

Ellen scowled as she turned toward Senida. "I don't know what she finds so beautiful. Her eyes must be going if it's me. My sister's the beautiful one. Aunt Maddie always said so."

Senida's cheeks went hot for Maddie. But this was an interesting piece of information: a grudge as ancient as Cain's. A resentment of that sister, Jean, that had never been overcome, and that could perhaps work to Senida's advantage.

As Ellen stood up and closed the desk's writing flap, a photograph slipped through the space where the desk hinged, and floated to the floor.

There was Maddie in a cloche hat, like a movie star from the 1920s. "That's me," she said, putting her hand out for the photo. "I dhon't know whh-when…"

Brightening, Ellen reached into her handbag and fished for something. Her hand reappeared with a disposable camera, still in its cardboard, probably bought at the airport.

"Time for a *new* picture," she said.

Senida hurried to escape, but her foot caught on Maddie's box of pictures, which she'd carelessly left on the floor. Suddenly, she knew how to lead Ellen back down—what was the expression?—the lane of memories. She picked up the box, and when Ellen had finished taking Maddie's picture, she handed it to her.

Ellen was reluctant at first. She drew a footstool up beside Maddie's chair and began to flip distractedly through the top dozen photos, failing to identify a single face. Senida felt her lips tip into the ghost of a superior smile as she stepped forward to help.

"How do you know all these names?" Ellen said.

"Maddie tells me." She placed a hand gently on one of the knobby shoulders. Maddie still had her lucid times, even if clouds were beginning to pass across the bright spaces.

"And you *memorized* them? Like baseball cards!" Ellen laughed.

Senida struggled to bite back a sharp retort. She was a poet, and someday, maybe the whole world would know it. In the evenings, when Maddie nodded off to sleep, she sometimes wrote poems about these men and women in the yellowing pictures. She'd composed all sorts of poetry since childhood, keeping her *Krajina* epics—the last one a story of the war—in notebooks that had probably been destroyed by her family after she left for America. She'd sung them to groups of students back in that time before her life changed. But to Ellen, she was nothing more than the woman who helped her aunt to the toilet, washed her soiled clothes, and made sure she ate the little bits of food her stomach would tolerate.

A picture that Ellen recognized finally came to the top of the stack and she beat both Senida and Maddie to it, snapping out the name.

"I had ssseven brothers and sssisters," Senida heard Maddie say once she had backed away.

"I *know* that, Aunt Maddie. My grandmother was one of your sisters. Look, here's Mark's son." She shuffled through the pictures with purpose now, so absorbed, after a while, that she didn't notice Senida studying her from the doorway.

"I went to sleep last night smelling lily of the valley on the sheets," Ellen said next morning as she stretched her back and lit the stove for coffee. "That brought me back. I'd forgotten how Aunt Maddie always used to smell of it."

She looked younger and more at ease in the jeans and T-shirt she'd put on today, Senida thought. Forty-something. Just about her age. The ring finger bare. Just like her own.

Senida knew all about the kind of memory a long-forgotten smell can trigger. Who would know that better than she, who had left so much behind in a country torn by war? Her memories now were like the fading scent that clings to a completely empty bottle of perfume.

After breakfast there was another phone call, and she heard Ellen say: "Oh, Jean, I should have come sooner. One of us should have. Do you remember those presents Maddie used to bring us, all wrapped up with beautiful bows? It's like we owe her, and now she floats in and out, I can't be sure we're communicating."

She had no opportunity to indulge her regrets, however. For at that moment, Antonelli appeared at the door.

While Maddie sat in front of a morning show, and Antonelli and Maddie's niece settled down to their business, Senida put on the wide-brimmed sun hat she wore to work in the garden, and positioned herself just beneath the open window where they sat.

As always when she worked outside, greetings were directed her way, partly because she herself was liked, partly because Maddie, at the age of 101, was of interest to everyone.

When Maddie was a girl, there were still a lot of Irish families in the area near Astoria Park. But most of them were at least two generations gone now, to suburbs on Long Island or elsewhere. Senida knew this from Antonelli, who'd lived here since childhood himself, his grandparents part of a wave of Italian immigrants who came in the twenties, a tidal wave of Greeks close behind.

Maddie occupied the bottom-most layer of the rock here, as Senida saw it—each group laying down its own distinct sediment, living side by side with but never really blending into the rest. She, on the other hand, was at the very top, where the dust of a foreign culture had yet to be pressed into those hyphenated-Americans she read about. If it weren't for the war, no one in this place would even have heard of places like Bosnia. But here she was, along with so many others. Victims. Escapees.

She bent over for a moment and breathed deeply. She wouldn't let herself go to that dark place this morning. She needed to hear what Ellen and Antonelli were saying.

She missed Ellen's question when a delivery truck rumbled by, but she heard Antonelli answer, "Yes, she knows a lot of the neighbors. She helps them can tomatoes, make wine. She's made herself liked."

"I'm sure she's very nice," Ellen said. "I mean, she *seems* nice. But there's something…"

Antonelli was wearing a blue T-shirt over his soft paunch this morning. Gone was the pinstripe in which he'd greeted their guest and quickly excused himself the day before.

"How much do you know about her?"

Senida could imagine Antonelli's wispy brows rising beneath hair gone to gray.

"I get the feeling that she's, well, trying too hard. What about her references? I assume she had some."

Antonelli sighed as if he had known this moment would come. "No references. One of our parishioners met her at a hostel. You have to understand. Your aunt's money isn't going to last long..." His voice went too low to hear, then rose again. "I had to make a decision and I thought we should try to conserve her money, hire someone who wouldn't expect much..."

Senida let the words float through her, as if she were nothing but air. Of course she wouldn't expect much. She wasn't *able* to expect much after what had happened. Her own brother was unwilling to put a roof over her head afterwards, saying she was nothing but an enemy soldier's leavings.

"I know," Antonelli continued. "We should have checked her out. We should be making Social Security payments. But these women at the hostel are mostly running from abuse. References, work records, those things create a risk for them of being found. But of course, this is your decision now."

There was silence for a beat. Then, just at the wrong moment, a woman who was walking her dog shouted out a hearty hello. By the time she was gone, Senida had missed whatever their visitor said on discovering that she was working off the books.

Senida slipped back inside, but stayed out of their way while the subject was business. Finally, the conversation segued into observations on Astoria and how it had changed, the perfect chance to inject some casual questions. But before she could decide whether to throw her line in, Antonelli fished with a question of his own. "You must have a lot waiting for you back in Dallas," he said. "I was dazzled by all the letters that come after your name."

"It's always busy, that's for sure," Ellen said. But instead of taking the bait, she sent a question Senida's direction.

"You have family here?" she asked.

"No, I came by myself. From Liskovac. A very insignificant place. You would not know it." She was trying to think of how to evade the inevitable question of why she'd come—and how—when a sound from Maddie saved her. Senida'd given her a yardstick with which to poke the ancient television on and off, and now she tapped it against the leg of the nearby end table. She'd become bored with television and wanted to get up.

Antonelli took it as his signal to leave.

Senida stepped out to the curb with him to seek some reassurance. But there was nothing reassuring in what she saw when she glanced back through the screen door. Their visitor was using her absence to dart across the hall to her aunt's bedroom. She tried to hurry Antonelli away, but he was suddenly garrulous—his words tumbling forth, Senida thought, out of sheer relief at being finished dealing with Ellen.

When she finally made it back inside, Maddie's niece was in the dining room, the silver drawer open. She tried to cover her intentions by leaning against the drawer and gathering her papers from the table, but Senida was no fool. That visit to the bedroom had probably been to check Maddie's jewelry boxes.

In her race to inventory the house, Ellen had left Maddie dangerously alone, pushing weakly up from her chair. Half-standing, she had managed to pick up her yardstick, and was waving it at Ellen.

As soon as Senida saw it all, she flew to Maddie's side. Lips pressed into a hard line, she eased the old woman back into her chair and cajoled her until she agreed to remain seated.

No words were needed. With Ellen's lapse, Senida had gained the upper hand. She might be only the hired help, but she would not have left Maddie at risk of falling and breaking a limb.

Ellen blushed and retreated to the basement to retrieve her things.

Senida was adjusting her enormous sun hat with its corsage of silk flowers on Maddie's head when Ellen came back into the room. The look on her face said she regretted suspecting Senida of stealing from her aunt, especially when Maddie began to giggle like a girl playing dress-up. But Ellen would need to convince that sister of hers. Maybe that was why she did it, Senida thought. Senida didn't see it coming because she had moved to crouch behind Maddie.

Suddenly Ellen's throwaway camera clicked and flashed, and their guest said, "Oh, that will make a beautiful shot."

Senida's hand went to her mouth.

"What is it?" Ellen said. But then she must have remembered what Antonelli had told her about hostel women being on the run.

Senida didn't have a man after her—unless you could count a man's ghost—but she had good reasons for not wanting Ellen to have that picture.

Maddie beamed at them both.

Ellen didn't move, except to let her eyes scan the room. On the wall behind Maddie was a framed letter written to Maddie's grandfather in America during the potato famine in Ireland. To Maddie, Senida knew, it represented what family was all about: recognizing one's own; knowing the difference between one's own and others.

But it wouldn't end well for Maddie if she was left to the care of her own family.

Ellen came out of her reverie—resolved, apparently, to interfere no further. She leaned over and kissed Maddie goodbye. As she did so, a tear slid down her cheek.

"Don't worry," she said. "This picture isn't going anywhere but into an old box of snapshots just like Maddie's. Someday, when I'm old like Maddie, maybe I'll bring it out and look at it. But otherwise, no one will see it."

She came over and put an arm around Senida's resisting shoulder, and then she was gone.

Only the other sister, Jean, came at the end.

Ellen must have been too busy with her own affairs to attend the funeral. Or perhaps it was simply that Jean wanted to marshal the sorting out of Maddie's belongings alone. She made piles to be shipped to herself back home, others for Goodwill.

After she'd packed her own meager possessions, Senida attempted to help Jean, rescuing Maddie's dirty, but cherished, ormolu vase from the pile for Goodwill and putting it with the things Jean should keep.

"Put it back," Jean directed her husband. Adding, when she thought Senida was out of earshot, "It's not her place to tell us what to do with Maddie's things!"

The words stung.

When Senida reached Maddie's door, prepared to pass through it for the last time, her hand went to the hook that held her giant sun hat. There the diamonds were, in the center of the hat's corsage. But you had to look to see them, unless the light caught them just so. It was Maddie herself who'd suggested pinning them to the hat when they were looking for ways to attach the silk flowers to it in decoration.

"Take a little something for yourself at the end this time," the other women at the hostel had urged Senida.

Senida had huffed her rejection of any such suggestion. Who did they think she was?

It wasn't until Maddie insisted that her most valuable jewels be pinned to the hat that Senida started to imagine she would one day walk out with them—for it seemed to her then that Maddie meant them as a sort of legacy for her. After all, she was the one truly bereaved by Maddie's death.

But Ellen and her camera had spoiled that fantasy. The camera's flash might have sparked the diamonds to life, lit them up in the photo so that Ellen might one day notice.

She was about to unpin the brooch from the hat and hand it to Jean when inspiration struck.

She raised her voice. "This old hat?" she said, catching the eyes of Jean and her husband. "Maddie was very fond of it. I'm sure she would like you to keep it."

Then Senida stepped out into the bright October day, leaving the hat on its hook by the door.

She had given Jean a chance. If she tossed the jewels out, unaware they were there, Senida would at least have—how did you say it, a poet's justice?

Just like in Liskovac, when she'd left it to that soldier's vanity whether to believe the girl he'd taken by force had really crawled back to ask for more. Undressed, his nakedness like a brag, he'd been as easy to slay as a newborn lamb.

*

Copyright © 2011 Eileen Dunbaugh

Eileen Dunbaugh's first work of fiction appeared in the Mystery Writers of America anthology *The Prosecution Rests*, edited by Linda Fairstein, in 2009. "A Poet's Justice" grew out of some real family memories and the many years she lived in Queens, the most ethnically diverse county in the United States of America.

THAT SUMMER
BY JOAN TUOHY

"Nana, what's this box?"

"I don't know, honey. What've you got?" Grace Ann, my nine-year-old granddaughter, was helping me sort through a box of papers and photographs among my mother's things. She was sitting cross-legged on the floor, a position I could no longer manage, and separating papers from photographs. "Is it heavy?" Listing a little, Gracie managed to move the unwieldy box to the coffee table and lifted off the cover.

"Oh, look," she giggled. "Who's this old-fashioned-looking man?"

We were sitting in the living room of my ninth-floor apartment in Fort Lee, New Jersey. It was an older building with windows wide open to the afternoon breeze. By great good fortune, nothing had yet been built between those windows and Manhattan, so, in addition to the warm spring air, there was also a splendid view of the New York skyline and the George Washington Bridge.

It was the right setting for this chore. My mother had been living in Manhattan when she died, and I imagined she was hovering out there somewhere while her great-granddaughter and I tackled this box.

The picture in my hand was of my uncle, George Prestato, my Aunt Tess's husband, who, at the time of the photograph, was about forty years old. He was tall and thin and very elegant. I have only the one picture of him. He's wearing a bowler hat and a topcoat. His face is straight toward the camera, and he's smiling, just as I remember him. The picture looked as if it had once been torn in half but had been repaired. I wondered why.

"Nana, are you OK? You look like you've seen a ghost." I smiled as I reached out and patted her hand.

"Yes, baby, I'm fine. Just memories from a long time ago."

"Who is he? What happened to him?"

What happened to him? The real question was whether or not I was willing to take the story to my grave. And I was sure her parents weren't ready to have her hear the story of the family murder. I hadn't told *them* everything. But maybe it was time someone besides me knew the truth, and I could certainly tell her the beginning.

~

When you make the turn off Broadway, 211th Street is in the heart of Inwood, on the narrow, northernmost tip of Manhattan. The small street is only one block long—the subway station, a few blocks away, an easy walk. There is no grass anywhere, only gray cement and building doors right at the sidewalk; 514 is across from the schoolyard, but in the summer, it was empty and quiet. In the summer of 1944, the whole block and the schoolyard, in fact all of upper Manhattan and the Bronx, was my country idyll.

My father, who had enlisted in the navy in the fall of 1943, was stationed somewhere in England. I lived with my mother in Elmhurst, Queens, and in early 1944, my mother got a job doing war work in Manhattan. Most children who had no one to care for them were sent away to summer camp, or at least to family and friends in the country. I got 211th Street and Aunt Tess and Uncle George. But mostly I got Uncle George. My aunt worked in an office, and my uncle didn't work at all. He had a bad heart, but had declared himself ready and able to take care of a nine-year-old for the summer. For as long as I could remember, my aunt always seemed angry, so I wasn't sure how it would work. But it turned out I only saw her in the evenings, because I went home on the weekends. The rest of the time I spent with Uncle George.

"Here," I said, handing Grace some more pictures, "look at these." Uncle had found other girls my age in the neighborhood to be my summer friends. He was an amateur photographer and had taken pictures of us wherever we went. Barbara, Judy, and Agnes came with us on day trips to Van Cortland Park and for swimming in Croton Park and Orchard Beach. There were pictures from Dyckman House, and the *Santa Scala,* and eeling in the Hudson River.

Looking through the pictures, I realized there were none of Mrs. Gormley. Rita Gormley lived in the same apartment building as my aunt and uncle, but on the second floor. One time, when the elevator stopped to let someone off, I saw a little flag with a blue star on it hanging from her apartment door. We had one at my house, too, for my father. When I asked about it, Uncle knocked on her door so I could meet her.

She could only have been in her early twenties, and, with her red hair and porcelain skin, she reminded me of my Irish aunts. Holding my hand, she drew me into her living room, eager to hear about my adventures. I fell in love with her on the spot. She explained that the blue star was for her husband, who was in the army, fighting in Europe. After that she would sometimes go with us on our explorations. I was sure she was there when Uncle took some of his pictures.

Nobody told me when Mrs. Gormley's husband was killed in France. She simply stopped going places with us, and one day I noticed that the flag with the little blue star had been replaced with one that had a gold star. When I asked why, Uncle finally told me. She only went out with us one time after that, when we went to the Edgar Allan Poe cottage in the Bronx. Poe had been widowed, and Mrs. Gormley talked about being widowed and how sad she felt. That's why it really stuck in my memory. She now seemed such a sad and unhappy creature, and Uncle worked hard at trying to get her to smile. I didn't tell Grace about Mrs. Gormley, but I knew.

~

"Here," Aunt Tess said one afternoon, tossing the envelope on the table, "I picked up the pictures you had developed at the drugstore."

"Oh, let me see, let me see!" I grabbed for the thick package that would tell the story of our latest travels. My uncle beat me to it.

"Me first, kiddo," he said. "Me first. How did you get them?" he asked. "I still have the ticket."

"Oh, they know me," she said. "I stopped in to get some things, and Mr. Rozzano asked if I wanted to take them. There are a lot, and they were pretty expensive." She seemed put out.

Uncle walked to the other room with the pictures and I quickly followed—but not before I noticed the steady glare with which my aunt watched him. Despite my jumping up and down and my uncle's lapse into Italian—"*Aspetta, aspetta!,*" I had to suffer while the contents were removed one by one. He first looked through the whole group, without showing them to me, and seemed relieved. As he handed each photo to me, I ran back to my aunt in the kitchen to show her. At last, we had seen them all. Maybe not all—there were no pictures of Mrs. Gormley at the Poe cottage for me to share with my aunt.

Uncle's heart was so bad that he had to sleep sitting up in a chair or on the couch in the living room. I slept with my aunt in the big bed in the bedroom. Sometime during that night, I became aware of their voices. They weren't exactly loud, but my aunt sounded really angry, my uncle placating. I remember hearing her say "Rita Gormley" and "you promised." Not really awake when she came to bed, I could still sense her stiffness and her anger as she lay next to me.

The summer continued as it had begun for my uncle and me. We still had our excursions, usually with my friends, but not with Mrs. Gormley. He was a great cook, and we sometimes spent our day making ravioli, which was set out to dry on clean sheets throughout the apartment, or a red sauce with clams, or maybe a *caponata*. Uncle would often leave the apartment to take his handiwork to "a neighbor." I didn't need to ask who the neighbor was, and I didn't need to be told that I shouldn't say anything about it.

Their apartment was on the fifth floor, and the day the elevator broke, Uncle George only made it up the steps to the landing between the second and third floor. His breathing was so bad, he was prepared to sit there until the elevator was fixed. I rang the super's bell to tell him what had happened, and then sat with Uncle to keep him company. We were together when we heard a door bang and then footsteps hurrying down the flight behind us.

"Go, look downstairs and see if you can see anything. Maybe someone fell or is in trouble." My uncle, always so concerned about others, now had me as his legs. I slowly walked the hall on the second floor and came back to the stairs to call up to him.

"Mrs. Gormley's door isn't closed."

"Ring the bell, see if she's there."

I rang the bell and waited. No answer.

"Mrs. Gormley? Mrs. Gormley?" Slowly, I pushed the door open. Prepared to run, I tiptoed to the back of the apartment. I could see only some clothes thrown on the bedroom floor, and there was a funny smell. I returned to my uncle to report.

He looked at me for what seemed like forever and slowly pulled himself up. Shuffling down the stairs to the second floor, he walked into Mrs. Gormley's apartment, and to the bedroom, with me close behind. He sniffed and looked closely at the pile of clothes. Suddenly he pushed me toward the door. "Get the super!" he whispered. "Tell him to call the police."

"What is it?" I asked. Suddenly scared, I began to back up to the door, and then, without waiting for an answer, turned and fled back to the super's apartment again.

This time, the super was cranky. "What?" he snapped.

"Please, oh, *please,* come, and my uncle said to call the police!" I was nearly shouting.

"What?" he said again. "Come where? Why the police?"

Shaking, I grabbed his hand and dragged him up the stairs. I waited just inside the door of the apartment as he joined Uncle in the bedroom. Still unsure of what was wrong, but certain that it was something awful, my eyes focused on the floor.

"Holy Mother of God!" exclaimed the super as he ran past me.

Shortly after, I understood what people mean when they say that 'all hell broke loose.' Mrs. Gormley was dead; she'd been stabbed with her big kitchen knife. And the elevator, under police pressure, had miraculously been fixed. Uncle and I had been sent back to our apartment, with a police officer in charge. Uncle was in the living room and I in the kitchen, and we each had to tell what we knew, what we'd heard, what we'd seen.

All the time I kept thinking: Who would want to kill Mrs. Gormley? Uncle seemed devastated. Wiping tears from his eyes, he kept saying "So sad, so sad. So unnecessary." He was holding rosary beads in his hand, and at some point it dawned on me that they weren't his but my aunt's. They were made of rolled rose petals; I had bought them for her at the *Santa Scala* shrine that summer. She always carried them with her. I wondered where he had gotten them, but that wasn't the question I asked.

"Uncle, what is it?"

"Ah, *carina*, I think your mama has to take you home now."

"Why, what did I do?"

He gently stroked my head. "You, my little one, did nothing. But another has done great evil. So unnecessary."

My aunt and my mother arrived at the apartment almost simultaneously. As my aunt walked through the door, Uncle George held out his hand with the rosary beads.

"Where did you get those?" She patted the pocket of her dress, thinking that her own beads were there. They weren't.

"You dropped them. In the apartment." That was all he'd said, but Aunt Tess was suddenly very pale and she looked frightened.

My mother and I did go back to Queens that day. She was able to take days off from work until school started, and we had adventures of our own. There were times when she seemed really sad, but she never said what it was about, and I never asked.

Uncle George died that September. His heart finally gave up, and Aunt Tess had him waked at the apartment. The casket was in the living room where he'd slept for so many years. When I went with my mother to pay our respects, I was terrified. I had never seen a dead body, and I didn't want to see Uncle George. In my nine-year-old eyes, Mrs. Gormley didn't count. When I saw what I thought were clothes, I hadn't known there was a body in them! As I knelt on the small *prie dieu* in front of the casket, my aunt slid down beside me, her voice a small murmur in my ear, asking if I would like to kiss Uncle. My mother's *no* shot out of her mouth faster than I could have imagined. Without another word, she grabbed my arm and led me, shaking, out of the apartment.

As we waited for the elevator, I became aware of a few men standing a little distance away. One of them smiled at me, and I realized that he had been the policeman that had questioned me the day Mrs. Gormley was killed. I had no clue why they were there, but before I could ask, I was whisked onto the elevator and we were on our way down.

At the second floor, the doors opened, and I gaped in surprise. There stood my uncle, just as he looked in my picture. Mrs. Gormley was beside him, holding his arm. He smiled and tipped his bowler hat. I smiled and waved. My mother peered around the open door and looked at me in surprise.

"Who are you waving at?" she asked.

I didn't answer. I just shrugged. By the time we got to the lobby, I had stopped trembling. In all the years that followed I never talked about that summer again.

~

At the bottom of the box Grace and I were so carefully emptying, I found two yellowed newspaper clippings. One told of the death by stabbing of the recently widowed Mrs. Rita Gormley of 514 West 211th Street in Manhattan, the other of the death of the recently widowed Mrs. George Prestato of the same address. Mrs. Prestato's death was believed to have occurred at her own hand by arsenic poisoning. I had never seen the papers before.

"Nana?" Grace Ann leaned into me as I carefully returned the papers and pictures in the box. "I think you should write your stories down so that we all know them."

I took a deep breath and gave her a non-committal smile. I knew that some stories were better left unwritten.

*

Joan Tuohy is a happily retired administrator/college professor from New Jersey. Asked to describe herself, she will usually say that she is an Irish, Italian Catholic from Queens figuring that pretty much explains everything. But perhaps not quite. She also holds a doctorate in the Foundations of Education, was a founding faculty member of her university's Women's Studies Program, and was awarded a travel Fulbright Scholarship in China. She has four children and seven perfect grandchildren. She is presently working on an historical mystery that grew out of her interest in the development of western New Jersey prior to the Civil War.

DEATH WILL TANK YOUR FISH
BY ELIZABETH ZELVIN

"Sure, I'll feed your fish," I said. "No problem."

"You gotta promise, Bruce," Neil said. "Those little fellas mean a lot to me."

The Monday night AA meeting in the High Episcopal church at the corner of Fifth Avenue and 90th Street had just ended. As we stood at the curb outside, the smoke and babble of recovering alcoholics bonding eddied around us.

"I know, man, I know."

Neil was probably the only alcoholic in town whose story about hitting bottom involved stumbling home in a blackout and crash-landing in a tankful of guppies. Apart from that, we'd heard it all before in the church basements of New York: the shattered glass, the brokenhearted children bawling, and the soon-to-be-ex-wife screeching as she kicked him out. How does an alcoholic make amends for a two-hundred guppy mistake? If you've flushed your dead, you can't apologize or visit their grave. All Neil could do was replace the tank and take very, very good care of it.

"It would break the kids' hearts if it happened again." Neil lit another cigarette from the stub of the last and ground the old one into the pavement with his heel. "And Angie would kill me."

Angie was his ex. We'd all played in the streets together, back when the yuppie Upper East Side was working-class Yorkville. Angie's mom had been a woman who never forgave or forgot, especially broken glass. I knew, from when I'd pitched a memorable curve ball right into her living room window. Angie had turned out just like her.

"So give me the key."

I held out my hand, and he forked it over, along with instructions—guppies, care and feeding of—and directions to his apartment that I didn't need. I knew where he lived, in his parents' old rent-controlled apartment, like me.

"I'll only be gone a couple of days," he said.

"I got it, dude," I said. "Food's on the foyer table. Sprinkle it across the top, check that the heater's on, say the Serenity Prayer, and it's a wrap."

Neil growled low in his throat. His Higher Power had not yet lifted his temper.

"It's not a joke, man! I don't want those little guys to end up floating on the top of the tank."

They didn't. When I walked into Neil's living room around noon on Tuesday, fish food in hand, I found him face down on the floor with the back of his head crumpled and bloody. The tank was shattered, because he'd fallen on it. The dead guppies were scattered, not only around him, but on his shirt and jeans. There were even a few in his hair.

"He was supposed to be out of town," I told the cops. "He gave me the key last night."

"Any witnesses, Mr. Kohler?"

Yeah, about five dozen smoke-filled sober drunks.

Should they remain anonymous? No. Neil was dead, and my best friend Jimmy wouldn't want to see me in the slammer. He'd been drinking coffee and schmoozing a few feet away when Neil handed me the key. I'd shown it to him before we said goodbye. He knew Neil from the old neighborhood, as well as AA.

"And this morning, Mr. Kohler?"

All I'd done was get up, flush the system with coffee, and walk the few blocks to Neil's.

"What kind of work do you do, Mr. Kohler?"

I was still temping, a recovery job that didn't interfere with my real life in those church basements. I hadn't called the temp agency this morning. Now, I was sorry I'd rolled over and gone back to sleep instead. No alibi. But they wouldn't find my fingerprints on anything but the fish food.

"I didn't do it," I told my friends Jimmy and Barbara in Starbucks a few hours later. My encounter with the cops had left me in grave need of a triple-espresso latte.

"Do the cops know that?" Jimmy asked.

"Did they search you for guppies?" Barbara asked.

"If it had happened this morning," I said, "his clothes would have been soaked. That tank held two hundred gallons. But his shirt was dry. Besides, if I'd killed him, I wouldn't have called them."

"So, who wanted Neil dead?" Barbara looked like a robin with a worm, bright-eyed and perky. It would be deerstalker hats for three again, for sure.

"I'd put Angie at the top of the list," I said.

"She never coshed anyone back in school," Jimmy said.

"She was a thrower," I said. A shoe, stiletto heel-first. An algebra textbook heavy enough to raise a classic goose egg. A live mouse.

"I could go talk to her." Barbara's eyes sparkled. She loves to hear about our dysfunctional childhoods, since she's a nice Jewish girl from Queens with the kind of parents we only saw on TV.

Jimmy and I looked at each other.

"Naaah," we said simultaneously.

"Why not?"

"She's not, um, psychologically oriented," Jimmy said.

"Probably paste you one in the mouth if you said, 'And how do you feel about that?'" I translated.

"Not as a counselor," Barbara said.

"Yeah, right," I said, because Jimmy was too nice to say it. We both knew Barbara could seldom resist playing shrink when she got the chance.

"Woman to woman."

"Forget it."

"One of you go see her."

"It had better be Jimmy," I said. "Angie and I have history."

In tenth grade, Angie had flirted with me, trying to make Neil jealous. So, Jimmy promised to attend the wake and snoop around some.

"What about Neil's AA sponsor?" Barbara said. "He'd know Neil's secrets if anyone would."

"Who was his sponsor?" I asked.

Jimmy knew, and Barbara persuaded him to tell. She said that death trumps anonymity.

I already knew Hank from the program. I found him the next day, at a meeting in the gym of a church, off Central Park West in the Seventies. When it ended, I suggested we go out for coffee.

"How's it going?" I asked when we were settled in the nearest Starbucks.

"Not bad at all." He took a sip of coffee. You could tell he was an old-timer, because he didn't order a latte. "I just made my twenty-five years."

"Awesome." It actually was. He'd been sober even longer than Jimmy. "I guess you've been qualifying at a lot of meetings."

"I share my experience, strength, and hope," he said. "All any of us have is today."

"Look at poor Neil," I said. "There but for the grace of God, huh? I found the body."

Hank seemed suitably shocked when I told him I felt scared I might be the prime suspect. I lied, but it got me what I wanted, three names from Neil's resentment list.

"I hate to break his anonymity," Hank said.

"Dead is dead," I said.

Pete, another kid from Yorkville, had gone into business with Neil before Neil got clean and sober. They'd opened a pizza place on Second Avenue. I remembered it well. The pizza wasn't bad, but the weed they sold out of the back room was outstanding. When Neil got into the program, he bowed out of both sides of the business. Pete couldn't make a go of it alone, progressed from booze and pot to crack, went a little psycho, and blamed Neil for wrecking his life.

Then, there was Ted, a guy Neil had sponsored for a while. He was also from the neighborhood, another son of a drunk with a long pedigree. When Ted relapsed, Neil decided he needed some tough love. So, he refused to sponsor Ted until he got clean and sober again. Ted had been slipping and sliding ever since. He, too, blamed Neil.

"Did you know Angie's sister?" Hank asked.

I did. Stella was a chubby kid with a headful of dark curls and a whiny voice, who tagged along with the gang because Angie had to babysit her. She had morphed into a major hottie at puberty.

"Neil had a fling with her," Hank said, "before he stopped drinking."

"Before or after he married Angie?"

"It started at the wedding. He felt very bad about it."

"Don't tell me," I said. "He made amends by confessing to Angie."

Hank plucked four sugar packets from the holder on the coffee shop table, flicked them against his palm a couple of times, tore the corners across, and poured the sugar into his third cup of coffee.

"I told him not to. He was so set on 'clearing the wreckage of his past' that he couldn't see he was only stirring up trouble."

It sounded like a motive to me, for both Angie and Stella. The sisters' relationship must have deteriorated after that little revelation.

∿

"I bet it wasn't planned," I told Jimmy and Barbara later. "Someone lost their temper."

"Someone angry enough to bash him on the head," Jimmy pointed out. "Then they freaked out and ran away when he went crashing into the fish tank."

"I would have stayed to save the fish," Barbara said.

"You wouldn't have killed him in the first place, petunia," Jimmy said.

"The point is the divorce wasn't about the guppies," I said. "He cheated on her with her sister."

"If he was paying child support," Barbara said, "you'd think Angie would want him alive, not dead."

"Maybe she didn't need his money," Jimmy said. "That funeral cost a bundle, and she paid for it. I heard she went back to school and became an accountant."

"Angie arranged the funeral?" I asked. "They've been divorced for years."

"The kids are his kids," Jimmy pointed out. "And Neil didn't have any family left."

I remembered Neil's parents. His dad had been a hard drinker with a short fuse and a heavy hand. His mom had been one of the downtrodden fade-into-the-wallpaper moms, rather than a yell-out-the-window mom like mine.

I knew where to find Ted. When he wasn't out on a slip, he was a regular at a big afternoon meeting on West 90th Street near Amsterdam. He told me he was back on track, working on ninety days.

"I feel bad about Neil," he said. "I had a resentment. I didn't forgive him, and now it's too late."

"Yeah, well, they say it's never too late to make amends."

"Just for today, I'm giving myself the tough love poor Neil tried to give me."

Ted edged into my personal space, his head bobbing a couple of inches from my face.

I stepped back a pace.

"One day at a time," I said. "Gotta go now."

I was afraid he'd offer me a hug. Some days, I can't believe the company I keep to stay sober.

I caught up with Pete on East 37th Street off Lex, in the basement of a building—not a church—where they had meetings more-or-less around the clock. I found him by the communal coffee pot near the door. His hand shook, making the brown liquid in his Styrofoam cup look as if it had minnows beneath the surface instead of sludge. By the look of him, he needed a new slogan: Don't drink, go to meetings, and shampoo.

"Hey, man," he said, biting at the knuckles of the hand not holding the coffee.

"Pete. Haven't seen you for a while."

"Just got out of the cuckoo's nest." He tittered and winked at me.

He meant Bellevue or someplace else with a locked psych ward. I wondered if that gave him an alibi.

"You heard about Neil?"

"Oh, man, what a bummer." He winked the other eye.

Pete seemed more brain-fried than last time I'd talked to him. You never know when a relapse will be one relapse too many, and you can't make it all the way back.

"Saaay, don't I know you from somewhere else? Detox maybe?"

The guy'd sat next to me in kindergarten.

The cops talked to me a couple more times, but I was sure they never considered me much of a suspect. They never found the weapon. I couldn't have killed Neil right before I called 911, because of the evaporated water. They didn't find my fingerprints on anything but the box of fish food. And I didn't have the shadow of a motive. Eventually, they left me alone. The detective in charge, a grizzled black guy named Washington with world-weary eyes and a soft voice, gave me his card and told me to call if I thought of anything that might be relevant.

The next thing that happened was that Jimmy got a wedding invitation.

"Angie's getting married?" Barbara squealed. "Neil's ex-Angie? Oh, Jimmy, we've got to go!"

"Women!" I couldn't resist jerking Barbara's chain. "Next thing out of her mouth will be 'What'll I wear?'"

"What'll I—oh! Bruce, you are a dead man!"

"Who me?"

"Never mind that," she said. "It's a motive."

"What do you mean? They were long divorced."

"Were they?" Barbara bounced up and down the way she does when she gets excited. "Are you sure?"

"I remember the big Catholic wedding," Jimmy said. "Barbara's right. We've been assuming the quiet divorce. But maybe they never got one."

"Less hassle from her family," Barbara said.

"Why bother unless you plan to remarry?" I said.

"She's marrying in the church again," Jimmy added, waggling the invitation at us. "She needed to be a widow."

"And now she's prettying it up," Barbara said, "by inviting Neil's old friends."

"Not me," I pointed out.

"If you'd gone to the wake, she would have," Jimmy said.

Don't ask how Barbara talked me into crashing the wedding. I slipped in the door with her and Jimmy. I exasperated her by not dressing-to-blend in gray slacks and a navy blue blazer like Jimmy, but my olive-green cargo pants with the pockets, not just front and back but all down the legs, were the nicest pants I had. I hadn't been sober long enough to own a navy blazer. But I wore the white shirt and corduroy jacket I used when I temped and, under protest, a tie.

We found Pete at the food table, scoffing up shrimp puffs and baby *cannoli*. He didn't even look up. Ted, on the other hand, buttonholed me and Jimmy as soon as he spotted us.

It was not a sober wedding. Waiters circulated with trays of champagne. The insidiously cheerful hubbub of normal people getting tanked swirled around us.

"So where do the rest of us get a drink?" I asked.

"The sodas are on that table over there." Ted pointed out a white-clothed table bristling with bottles, the recovering folks' designated watering hole.

I had just snagged myself a ginger ale when Barbara joined us. Champagne fizzed merrily in the glass she clinked with mine.

"Cheers," she said.

"Church basements," I responded.

"Have you seen the sister?" Barbara asked. "She's one of the bridesmaids."

"Oh, is that what the Barbies with the matching orange dresses are?"

"Not orange. Pumpkin."

"What's with the giant bows on their butts?" I asked. I'd seen half a dozen girls wrapped like Halloween presents floating around. I hadn't spotted Stella yet.

"Hideous, aren't they? I think the idea is to make sure the bridesmaids don't outshine the bride. Oh, look, Stella has the right idea."

I followed the path of her pointing finger. The bouncing black curls had been gelled or moussed into soldierly spikes, with the big bow, ripped off the rump of her dress, perched on top of the hairdo.

"She looks like a cockatoo at a Tupperware party," Barbara said.

"The bride looks happy," Jimmy said. "Is that Hank she's talking to?"

"Looks like it," I said.

"That's the guy who was Neil's sponsor?" Barbara asked. "It looks like he's got a glass of champagne in his hand."

"Hank's been sober forever," Jimmy objected. "It must be ginger ale."

"No, look," Barbara said. "He just knocked it back, and now Angie's pouring him a refill."

She was right. I know a *Veuve Clicquot* bottle when I see one.

"She's making a statement," Barbara said. "Her own personal living-with-an-alcoholic hell is over. She's vowed never to worry about someone's drinking again."

"Wait till her kids hit their teens," I said.

"I can't believe Hank's drinking," Jimmy said. "I heard him qualify at a meeting two nights ago, and he was sober then."

"Or faking it," I said. "He's been getting a lot of mileage out of that twenty-five years. Maybe being a star went to his head."

"There are no stars in program," Barbara said. "Lying about his sobriety won't hurt anybody but him."

"Denial," Jimmy said. "If he's drinking again, he's not thinking straight."

"But when did it start?" Barbara asked.

I thought hard, trying to follow the faint thread of possibility beginning to shimmer in my mind.

"How about this? Hank picks up, but he manages to hide it at first. Neil finds out."

"How?" Barbara asked.

"Suppose Neil made one of those three-in-the-morning phone calls that your sponsor keeps telling you it's okay to make, and Hank was drunk enough that he couldn't cover it up."

"He should have admitted he's back to Day One," Jimmy said, "so he can't sponsor Neil any more."

"But instead," I said, "Hank lies. Neil knows he's lying."

"Anyone would freak out if his sponsor relapsed," Jimmy said. "So what do you do?"

"Suppose Neil confronted him," Barbara said. "Are we saying Hank killed him? To stop him from telling the world that he had relapsed?"

"Neil wouldn't break Hank's anonymity outright," Jimmy said. "He wouldn't gossip. But you know how it is. Neil raises his hand in a meeting and says he's having a rough time because his sponsor has picked up and refuses to get help. Anyone who knew who Neil's sponsor was would have known. I would have known."

"He got off on being an old-timer," I said. "Maybe he thought he could pull himself together and stop drinking again without anyone having to know."

"Denial," Jimmy said. "No way."

"He didn't mean to kill Neil," Barbara said. "But you know what booze does to judgment and impulse control."

"Neil tried tough love," I said, "and Hank lost it and beaned him."

"And then did a Chappaquiddick," Barbara said. "Except nobody knew he'd been there at all."

"The cops have never even heard of Hank," I said. "But they

may have found his fingerprints in Neil's apartment."

"So, do we tell them?"

"Let an active alcoholic get away with murder?" Jimmy said. "To call that enabling would be an understatement."

"We can give the police his name," Barbara said, "but suppose his fingerprints aren't on record anywhere. If he's never committed a crime or worked for the government, they're probably not. Jimmy?"

"I can't break his anonymity about what I've heard him share at meetings. But hypothetically, no."

"So, suppose they have these unknown fingerprints from Neil's apartment. The only thing they can do to compare them to Hank's is to get Hank's fingerprints. But don't they need some sort of reason to ask for them? I mean something more concrete than us telling them he was Neil's sponsor, and we think he might have a motive."

"I know a way around that," I told them. "Be right back."

I headed toward where I'd seen Hank and Angie talking. The bride had moved on. But Hank was still standing by the same table, hanging onto his glass like grim death. As I approached, he caught my eye. He whipped the glass behind his back. Averting his eyes from me, he drifted away. He left the glass sitting on the table. That was fine with me. I pulled out a red bandanna and wrapped it loosely around the glass. It would give Detective Washington something to go on, once he checked these fingerprints with the ones in Neil's apartment. I said a quick Serenity Prayer, raised the glass to my nose, and sniffed cautiously. Yep. It was champagne all right. I discovered that I didn't even want to sample it before I stowed away the glass.

I knew the pockets in those cargo pants would come in handy.

∗

Elizabeth Zelvin is a New York City psychotherapist who has directed alcohol treatment programs. Her mystery series featuring recovering alcoholic Bruce Kohler includes *Death Will Get You Sober* and *Death Will Help You Leave Him*, as well as four short stories. Two of these, including one that appeared in *Murder New York Style*, were nominated for the Agatha Award for Best Short Story. Liz's stories have appeared in *Ellery Queen's Mystery Magazine* and various anthologies and ezines. Liz's website is www.elizabethzelvin.com. She blogs on Poe's Deadly Daughters. Next: a novel about Columbus and a CD of Liz's songs.

North on Clinton
by K.J.A. Wishnia

Lots of people think they know Long Island, but most of them don't know from shinola about the place. All they know is the Gold Coast and the Hamptons, but nothing about the endless miles of strip malls in between. They don't know about towns like Roosevelt, the subprime foreclosure capital of Nassau County, or Wyandanch, where the public schools are full of ratty old textbooks telling you that JFK's still the president, or Brentwood, where a murder vic can lie out in the street all night before the detectives decide to drop by and get to work.

You've probably heard of that other Brentwood, out in some fancy part of L.A. where all the rich and famous live, like O.J. Simpson and that nutty Lewinsky babe. Not the Brentwood I know.

Today, we're taking Jamaica Avenue all the way across Queens to darkest Hempstead, south of the LIRR tracks, where the potholes are as big as missile silos and the dope dealers own half the corners from here to Freeport. So, we've got to keep a close eye on the goods as we unload a shipment of TV tables at a warehouse surrounded by security cameras and razor wire, where they're going to sit until they're ready to move into their new home—a five star hotel with state-of-the-art meeting rooms and banquet facilities next to the Nassau Coliseum in Uniondale. Don't ask me what the fuck there is to see in Uniondale that's gonna make people want to stay at a five star hotel. But we're more than happy to fill the order. Three hundred TV tables is a big order these days. That's six hundred matching Formica shelves plus twelve hundred brass, screw-in legs with heavy casters. We deliver them disassembled. Let those bowtie-wearing pricks put them together on their own time.

Besides, do you know how goddamn boring it is to have to make *six hundred* copies of the same piece? Usually, we just slap that stuff together with particle board, contact cement, and maybe a millimeter of Formica, but people will pay real money for the designer logos on some of our customized pieces.

One time, we were putting in some countertops—cobalt blue with sparkling highlights—in a place up near Little Neck, when all of a sudden, Tony stops spreading the drop cloth and goes, "Holy shit. That's not a reproduction. That's a real Lautrec."

He's staring at a six-foot-high framed picture of a scrawny dancing girl kicking her skirts up. It looks like a crayon drawing to me.

"A what?"

"Toulouse Lautrec. A French artist. That poster's gotta be at least a hundred years old."

I nod and purse my lips like I'm impressed. Tony knows about that kind of stuff. The other guys in the crew are Isaiah, a bass player from Trinidad, and Julio, who's gonna go back to Ecuador as soon as he saves up enough of those off-the-books *dolares* to build his dream house way up in the Andes.

The company van's from the Crustaceous Era, so it doesn't even have a working radio, never mind an iPod docking port or something so we could hear music from *this* decade. So, all we've got for a soundtrack is a whiny tape player spitting out '80s crap like "Wake Me Up Before You Go-Go" and "Do You Really Want to Hurt Me," and I'm about to throw the thing out the freaking window when Richie finally turns it down.

"Culture Club, for Chrissakes? *Culture Club*?"

"Yeah mon, I was wondering what your breaking point was," says Isaiah, laughing and shaking his dreads at us.

"Yeah? Well, you found it."

We're heading north on Clinton, and as we cross Meadow,

the dividing line between Hempstead and Garden City, it's like that scene in the *Wizard of Oz* when everything changes from black-and-white to Technicolor. Suddenly, the houses get way nicer and shoot up in value. Garden City is one of those places that pays extra for its own police force, a bunch of glorified rent-a-cops who've got nothing better to do than cruise the pothole-free streets and lay traps for anyone who doesn't wipe their feet first and gets caught tracking in dirt from the other zip codes. They didn't even let Jews in till the early 1960s, for chrissakes.

I hate working for these country club stiffs. I mean, a regular Joe either wants the job done or he doesn't. But rich people—they'll hire you for a job so big you've gotta take on three extra guys and clear the schedule for four straight weeks. Then, the morning you're supposed to load in they change their mind and go with something else, and you've gotta lay off the three guys you promised a month's work to, and run around like an idiot trying to get back some of the jobs you turned away to make room for the big one that just vaporized. And the ten percent non-returnable deposit? Doesn't mean a thing to them. It's just pocket change. Thirty or forty grand is just pocket change to these people.

Isaiah's looking at the map and clucking his tongue at street names like Francis Lewis Boulevard and William Floyd Parkway.

He says, "Mon, those two guys signed the Declaration of Independence, and all they get is a couple of streets named after them."

"I guess those citizenship classes are good for something," says Richie.

"Yeah, he can read a map now," I say.

But Isaiah just shakes his head and says, "I wonder what they'd think if they could see what you've done to their land, burying the Indian trails under layers of Babylon's garbage."

"And don't forget that Whitman guy from South Huntington," I say.

"Walt Whitman didn't sign no Declaration. He was a rhymin' man."

"You're kidding. You mean the Walt Whitman Mall is named after *a rapper*?"

Tony chokes back a laugh so hard he almost inhales his sandwich.

"Wasn't he some kind of fruitcake or something?" says Richie.

"He was a transcendental poet," Tony explains through a mouthful of grilled cheese.

"Same thing."

Clinton Road finally changes to Glen Cove Road and after a while we're passing the real deal, mansions with long curved driveways and separate drive-up service entrances in the back.

We pass the security hut, and the guard buzzes us through the aluminum gates leading to one of those modern castles, where the property taxes alone can run you upwards of three hundred grand.

The lawn hasn't just been mowed, it's been manicured, hot-combed, and shampooed till it gleams like the Blue Diamond grass at Yankee Stadium. There's a satellite dish on the roof that looks like it could pull in TV shows from the moons of Saturn, and a Dumpster full of torn-up carpet and freshly split molding that still smells of raw lumber. I wonder if today's installation is gonna be one of those change-of-life things where the owners gut the traditional wood-stained interior and remodel everything in 21st century steel and glass, or if they're the kind of people who do renovations every season because nothing ever satisfies them, which can really spell trouble for us.

The lady who answers the door is a skinny blonde with a tight mouth and a pair of designer breasts, size 38C, if I'm any judge.

"Why didn't you call?" she says sharply.

"We did," says Richie. "We left a message with Mr. Edgehill."

"Well, my husband didn't give me the message," she says, glaring at us like it's *our* fault. Then, Julio walks in and her eyes widen. You'd think he was sporting MS-13 colors and a couple of prison tats from the way she looks at him.

"You can't just show up at a person's home whenever you feel like it," she says. "But as long as you're here, you might as well get to work."

Oh, brother. Something tells me this is gonna be a long day, because she's clearly the type who keeps hovering around you all day until Happy Hour comes around and she can finally knock back a couple of stiff belts and get the fuck off our case.

We unload the van and troop into the foyer with our gear. The place is so huge I take in the high ceiling, arched windows, and tapestries for a full minute before I notice the grand piano in the living room, right in front of my eyes between a couple of potted palms.

Of course, Tony's got to go and piss on it.

"Man, there's something creepy about a million-dollar home with no books in it," he mutters as we go down the hall to the bedroom wing.

"Maybe they're all stored on that gizmo," I say, nodding toward the ginormous flat screen TV in the middle of the entertainment center. "Looks like it's got enough disk space to back up every TV show ever made."

We're installing a walk-in closet complete with standing units, outfitted with pull-out compartments, drawers, retractable hooks, and all kinds of space-saving devices that they don't really need, because the master bedroom is roughly the size of a two-family house. Even the bathroom has a hot tub on a raised platform that's big enough for six people.

But we're here to do a job, and our priorities are as follows: Don't damage the pieces and keep the walls and rugs clean. But we can't help noticing certain things, like the private office with the framed M.B.A. on the wall, the half-finished cup of cold coffee on the credenza next to a pile of unpaid bills, and the cigarette butts overflowing from the ashtray that tells anyone with half a brain that the guy who's paying for all this is burning up the fast lane at some big Wall Street investment firm, where the only honorable way to leave the place is feet first after having a heart attack at your desk from overwork. Plus, there are so many papers scattered all over the place, it looks like someone's being murdered in slow motion here.

Or else drowning in red ink. We move some of the woman's clothes aside and a piece of paper falls to the floor. It's a bill for one of her jackets, a black-and-white checkered number that costs—*Jesus.* Eight-and-a-half grand.

Richie tries to warn me exactly one millisecond before a smooth white hand swoops in and snatches the paper out of my hand.

"Do you always go through other people's pockets when you're on a job?" she asks.

"I wasn't—"

"And you'd better get back to work—that is, if you ever want to work in this town again."

I can feel my face heating up even though I haven't done anything wrong.

Richie comes to my rescue. "Ma'am, the contract states that this closet should have been cleared out before we got here."

She flicks her head at him.

"All right, then. Clear it out. You can lay the clothes on the bed in the guest bedroom. And be careful not to wrinkle anything. I just had everything dry-cleaned."

And she marches out of the room like a four star general who's got more important things to do than dress down a couple of buck privates.

Great. Now she's got us clearing the crap out of her closet, too.

We're trying to sink the screws for the fifteen-foot brass closet pole, but the closet space is a modern addition and the wall's got no studs in that location, just a half-inch of sheetrock that couldn't support a straw hat on a six-penny nail, so we've got to build a floor-to-ceiling column to anchor everything.

I go out to the van and set up the sawhorses, so I can cut the lumber down to size, when the woman calls out from the patio, "Oh, *boy.*"

Boy? Is she serious with that shit? Then, I see she's talking to Julio.

"I need you, uh, *por favor...un momento.*"

Julio nods, and she leads him through the bushes to the other side of the house. I catch Richie's eye and he gives me the Bay Ridge salute, fisting his own arm while the both of us are chuckling at the old-school porn scenario of the hired help sticking it to the lady of the house.

At least we can plug in a radio out here so we can catch the game.

I switch on the air pump and wait for the pressure to build so I can spray a thin web of gummy red contact cement on the lumber and the underside of the mica. I do the sides first and file down the edges till they're flush with the one-by-three so I can lay the finished sheet on top. The spidery threads of red cement bond immediately.

I can see Julio's busy hauling trash bags to the Dumpster and tossing out boxes of shredded paper.

A newsbreak cuts in on the radio: a third-grade teacher found a loaded .25-caliber semiautomatic pistol in a student's desk at North Elementary School in Brentwood. Richie says the whole town should just be fenced off and everybody inside should be rounded up, tagged, and sent back to El Salvador or wherever the hell they came from, when all of a sudden the woman appears in the sliding doorway.

"Aren't you done with that yet?" she says in a voice that would crack glass. She stands there a moment, staring at us as if she's surprised that we're still here, then she turns and disappears inside the house.

I go back to what I'm doing, filing away the flash so there's no lip, then I put on some pink rubber kitchen gloves and start scrubbing off the excess contact cement with a rag and some lacquer thinner. I asked the boss for some heavy black industrial gloves and a breathing mask, but the cheap dickwad wouldn't spring for them. At least I'm doing this out in the open where the fumes can't concentrate, because whenever I work with the chemicals for more than a couple hours I wake up the next morning with the taste of that crap coming up the back of my throat.

Out of the corner of my eye, I spot Julio dragging a heavy sack through the bushes and tossing it on the trash heap just as the Dumpster boys show up to cart it all away. It must have been pretty heavy 'cause he looks bushed.

"You look like a fairy wearing those things," says Richie, needling me about the pink gloves.

I tell him, "Yeah, well maybe the women *you* go out with like guys with rough hands, but the women *I* go out with like guys with smooth hands, you know?"

"Oh, you need them to get laid. Why didn't you say so?" He's always busting my balls about the pink gloves, but what can I say? I don't want my fingers to end up looking like someone gave me a manicure with a rusty cheese grater.

We keep hitting snags because, like I said, the closet space is made of cardboard, so it's pretty hard to hang any weight-bearing hardware, and everything's got to be just so. Meanwhile Julio keeps disappearing with the Soft Scrub and rags. What the hell is he up to?

I go down the hall, and find him wiping the floor around the tub and toilet bowl with a damp rag.

"And when you're done with that, you can empty the trash," says the woman, drying her feet with an embroidered towel.

She stops short when she sees me.

"You're supposed to use the *other* bathroom," she says. Her eyes flit to the trashcan. There's a pile of bloody chick rags ripening in the garbage, ranging from pale red on top to dark smoky red beneath.

Well, *that* explains a lot.

I head back to the master bedroom.

It's past 5:30 when the boss calls to check on us, and asks if we want to put in the overtime and stay on site until we get the job done, or pack everything up and have to drive all the way back out here tomorrow and set up all over again. It's unanimous: we'll stay and get it done tonight.

The lady actually surprises us with a couple of pizzas and

soda. But it's Domino's, for God's sake. We've got more Italians per square mile on Long Island than anyplace else in the country, and she sends out for freaking Domino's. But hey, we appreciate the gesture. We finish our dinner break just as the sun is going down, and the Yankees finish off the Orioles with a broken-bat dribbler up the middle. Jeter snags it and throws to first to end the game.

By 9 p.m., Julio's washing up in the sink, turning the water a rusty brown, and that hot tub is starting to look mighty good to us, but we keep working.

It takes us another hour to finish the job, pack up the tools and vacuum up the sawdust from the holes we drilled in the particle board, and the lady's husband still isn't home yet. Hasn't even tried to call, as far as I can tell.

She inspects her new closet and thanks us for all our hard work.

"Thanks again for dinner," says Isaiah.

She smiles, and her face relaxes for the first time since we got here.

There's something in that smile—maybe it's something about the presence of all these strange men in her bedroom, that thing that's unavoidable whenever men in work boots are around high class women like her. I think that's a bit of it. And maybe some of it's—what, embarrassment? That we can read the signs that her marriage is on the rocks? Or that we're such lousy stand-ins for the guy who's supposed to be here? Or maybe she's just glad to finally get rid of us.

Because any idiot can see that the poor schmuck is working himself to death to pay for the place, and he isn't even here to enjoy it.

Christ, you couldn't pay me to live like they do. A dollar isn't worth that kind of aggravation. You know?

We go out for beers after, and Julio starts off with a double shot of Andean rum to steady his nerves, then he buys the first two rounds.

"Thought you were saving up," I say.

"Oh, the lady, she give me a tip for doing some extra work for her," he says, flashing a pair of twenties.

"Really?" says Richie. "'Cause it looked like you did a *lot* more than forty bucks worth of work, bro."

"Yeah, she sure stiffed you," I say.

But that's the rich for you. They think they can get away with anything.

*

k.j.a. Wishnia's first novel, *23 Shades of Black*, was nominated for the Edgar and the Anthony Awards. His other novels include *Soft Money*, a Library Journal Best Mystery of the Year, and *Red House*, a Washington Post Book World "Rave" Book of the Year. His short stories have appeared in Ellery Queen's Mystery Magazine, Alfred Hitchcock's Mystery Magazine, Murder in Vegas, Queens Noir, and elsewhere. His protagonists are usually much nicer (and a lot smarter) than the guy in this story. His latest novel, *The Fifth Servant*, is a Jewish-themed historical set in Prague in the late 16th century. He'd like to thank his students at Suffolk Community College, especially Nick Bo, Shaun Hantzschel, Sara Jabbar, Grace Osso and Patrick Sullivan, for their comments on an early draft of this story. www.kennethwishnia.com

Murder New York Style

Print ISBN 978-1-60318-032-0
Ebook ISBN 978-1-60318-033-7

Watch out for mayhem around every corner in *Murder New York Style!* Explore Manhattan, The Bronx, Brooklyn, Queens, Staten Island, Westchester, and the Outer Reaches. The twenty-one stories in this anthology are classic New York. Imagine bargain shopping in Chinatown, working in the Metropolitan Museum of Art, belly dancing in a Turkish nightclub, or teaching a course at a diverse New York College. These are some of the circumstances and locations that find murder and mayhem around every corner in Murder New York Style. Several stories are set in the New York of days gone by. Among those, one takes place during a 1913 labor strike, and another explores the effects of the House Un-American Activities Committee on the New York cultural community. One Brooklyn story solves a mystery involving an eighty year old murder and the ghost of a Hessian soldier from the Revolutionary War.

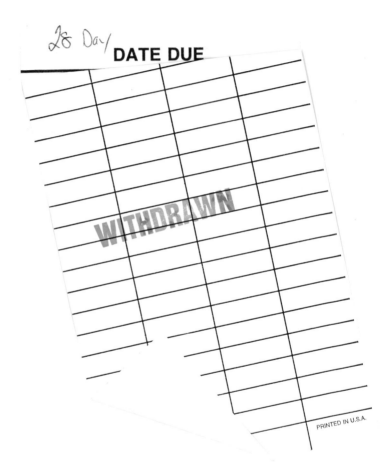

28 Day

DATE DUE

WITHDRAWN

PRINTED IN U.S.A.

CPSIA information can be obtained at www.ICGtesting.com
Printed in the USA
BVOW030159151111

276105BV00006B/7/P

9 781603 184236